The Heart's Journey

Other books by the author

A Time to Love, book one in the Quilts of Lancaster County series
A Time to Heal, book two in the Quilts of Lancaster County series
A Time for Peace, book three in the Quilts of Lancaster County series

Her Restless Heart, book one in the Stitches in Time series

The Heart's Journey

Stitches in Time Series

Barbara Cameron

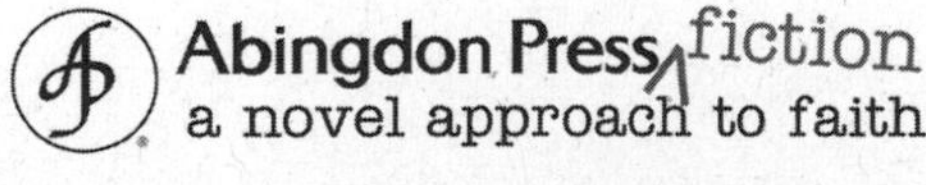

Nashville, Tennessee

The Heart's Journey

ISBN: 978-1-4267-1433-7

Published by Abingdon Press, P.O. Box 801, Nashville, TN 37202

www.abingdonpress.com

Cataloging-in-Publication data has been requested with the Library of Congress

Printed in the United States of America

1 2 3 4 5 6 7 8 9 10 / 17 16 15 14 13 12

For domestic abuse counselors everywhere

Acknowledgments

Growing up, I loved books so much my family knew they could always find me up in my bunk bed, reading in my own sort of indoor tree house. I read everything—from Robert Louis Stevenson's poems to real-life murder mysteries in *Life*. (Dad was alarmed when he found me reading those!)

So I love connecting with readers who make books necessary—and thus, my job! My dear editor, Ramona Richards, also loves books and helps me make mine better. I want to thank her for her dedication and, most especially, for squeezing out a little more time for me to polish a book when I need it. Thank you, Ramona!

Christian fiction readers are so wonderful! I want to thank them for buying my books. They write me and let me know that they've enjoyed my stories and the blogs I write about the Amish.

Judy Rehm is always a source of comfort and advice on all things and she was especially invaluable on this book. I don't know what I would do without your listening ear and your comments on the manuscript.

I visited Pinecraft, a charming little neighborhood of Sarasota, Florida, a number of times at the invitation of Sherry Gore. Sherry lives in Pinecraft year-round and talked a lot about how many Amish and Mennonites visited Pinecraft in the winter, eager to escape the northern cold.

I got the idea to have my characters take a trip there, and Sherry and her friend, Katie Troyer, answered my questions. Sherry also gave me permission to use recipes from her cookbook, *Taste of Pinecraft: Glimpses of Sarasota, Florida's Amish Culture and Kitchens.* Katie also features her wonderful photos on her blog. I especially love her photos of children. These two talented women are the unofficial ambassadors of Pinecraft who are letting others know about this delightful little winter hideaway for the Amish and Mennonites.

I save thanks to God for last only because it is a way for me to remember that He makes it **all** possible: books, special people to help me write them, and all those who read them. I am blessed.

1

She should be the happiest young woman in Paradise.

But Naomi dreaded being asked about her upcoming wedding. She feared she'd scream if one more person asked her about it.

Marriage in her Amish community was more traditional than an *Englisch* marriage, to be sure. But she'd never thought she'd have to change so much to please the man she would soon marry.

Sighing, she set her quilting aside, got up, and walked over to look out the front window. Business had been brisk that morning at Stitches in Time, the shop where she worked with her grandmother and two cousins.

Stitches in time . . . and place: she and her two cousins were working together as they had played and studied together all their lives. Their wise grandmother had bought this place and they'd all fixed it up, and now they created items for sale. Naomi quilted, Mary Katherine was a master weaver, Anna knitted, and their grandmother, Leah, created little Amish dolls and other crafts. They were two generations of Amish women who were bound by strong threads to each other as well as to their creativity and their community.

Here in this shop crowded with colorful quilts and hand-knitted items, with fabrics galore and every single thing you could ever need to quilt or knit or sew . . . well, she should feel like she was in heaven—working on a quilt and helping customers at this very successful shop, with family members who loved her.

Instead, she felt more and more false, covering up how she felt, wearing a mask each day.

"Looking for someone?" her grandmother asked, smiling as she looked up from tallying the day's receipts. "Is John coming to pick you up after work?"

Everyone thought it was a sign of his attachment, his devotion to her, that he came for her nearly every day after work. In fact, it was a way of keeping track of her, of making certain that she didn't make other plans.

She'd become so cynical. It was enough to make her sigh but she noticed her grandmother was still watching her.

"*Ya*," she said, pasting a smile on her face.

She walked back to sit and stitch on her quilt. Its bright, cheerful pattern of watermelon slices with little black ants marching across it should have propped up her sagging mood. Anna had already said it would be perfect for the summer window display with some props to make it look like it could be used for a picnic.

Off she'd gone to plan what she'd knit for the display, then badgered Mary Katherine and her grandmother for what they'd make.

Naomi glanced over at Mary Katherine when she heard quiet humming. "What are you making?"

"Some fabric for big floor pillows," she said, looking up. "You don't think this looks or feels too . . . rough or nubby, do you?"

"I think it looks really sturdy for a kid's room or for outdoor use. The pillows'll fly out of the shop."

Nodding, Mary Katherine went back to weaving and humming, weaving and humming.

That was what a woman who was happily married and had recently celebrated her first anniversary looked like, Naomi thought. Happy, content. Dreamy. She and Jacob were a good match. They'd been friends since they were scholars in the same school, and when he'd thought he'd lose her to Daniel, a charming Amish Mennonite man from exotic-sounding Florida, well, Jacob had woken up and shown her he was the *mann* for her.

And soon, Naomi would be marrying John. Two cousins married in two years.

Anna was still looking for the right man and enjoying flirting with several young men. The three of them were cousins who looked much alike with their oval faces and brown eyes. Well, Mary Katherine was taller and her hair was more auburn but they looked more like sisters than cousins.

However, Naomi mused, their personalities were so different. She'd often wished she was as outgoing and assertive as Anna or as creative as Mary Katherine, who'd even been invited to speak about her weaving skill at the local college of arts and design.

A shadow fell over her as her grandmother carried some bolts of fabric to the storage room. She heard her talking with Anna and then her cousin emerged, following Leah as she walked back to the cash register. Leah handed her a slip of paper and then opened the cash register and withdrew some money. Anna slipped out the shop door.

Then Leah went to stand at the shop window and she stood there for so long, staring out with an unreadable expression, that Naomi got up and walked over to her.

"Is anything wrong?"

"No, I just sent Anna for pizza for lunch. My treat."

"And you're watching to make sure she gets there?" Naomi asked, smiling indulgently.

"No," Leah said, shaking her head and laughing. "Although Anna has been known to dilly-dally."

Turning, Leah sighed. "I'm just feeling a little restless, maybe a little moody, that's all. I have to confess, I'm not usually pessimistic, but I'm not looking forward to another winter here in Lancaster."

"That's a ways off, Grandmother."

"I know. Just ignore me. Like I said, I'm a little restless and moody. This probably started it." She held up a postcard of a scene in Florida. "Daniel's mother is trying to get me to come down to Pinecraft for a visit."

"Well, maybe you should this time. It'd do you some good. All you do is work here and at home."

For the first time she noticed that her grandmother—just in her fifties—looked tired. Older.

Anna bustled in, carrying a pizza box that smelled of pepperoni. "Come on, everybody, let's eat it before it gets cold."

"Or before you eat it all," Mary Katherine teased as she got up from her loom. "I'm starved. I'm so hungry all the time lately." She stopped as she realized the three women were staring at her. "What?"

"All the time?" Leah asked, a hopeful note in her voice.

"I've been working a lot lately. It's not easy juggling a job here and being a farm wife, you know. Sometimes I forget to eat."

Anna shoved the pizza box at Naomi, who fumbled to catch it and winced as one of her wrists complained.

Walking over to Mary Katherine, Anna counted on the fingers of one hand. "You could be . . ." she trailed off meaningfully.

"Could be what?"

Anna patted her cheek. "Think about it," she said. "You're a bright girl."

Mary Katherine followed her into the back room. "Oh, honestly, you all want me to have a *boppli* so badly that you started making comments a month after I was married."

"It can happen that fast," Naomi told her.

"Yes, and we know it can happen even before marriage, no matter what community people live in."

Mary Katherine goggled at Anna's words. "You're not suggesting Jacob and I anticipated our vows, are you?"

"No, dear, although some of those looks the two of you exchanged when you thought no one was looking were quite sizzling." Anna waved her hand as if she were overheated. "I wondered if flames would erupt."

She took the pizza from Naomi and sailed toward the kitchen.

"Well, she's certainly not moping around today," Naomi remarked.

"She never is, especially this particular month," Leah noted, jerking her head toward the calendar. "I don't want to see her depressed but there's such a thing as covering up your feelings that can be harmful. I'm hoping she's not doing that."

Frowning, she walked toward the back room. Naomi followed and helped get out plates and soft drinks.

She and Anna knew all about covering up their feelings, Naomi thought as she nibbled on her own piece of pizza and found it tasteless.

"Is something wrong with your pizza?" Mary Katherine asked.

"I'm just not very hungry today." She pushed the box closer to her cousin, who took a third piece.

They chatted about the weather—it was the time of year between the too-brief Pennsylvania spring and the always-long summer that drew customers. They'd be returning after they enjoyed a big Amish lunch.

Mercifully, her wedding plans weren't a topic of conversation today. She managed to force down a few bites of pizza, then covered what was left on her plate with her crumpled paper napkin. She rose and walked to the sink to wash her plate and place it in the drying rack.

"Done already?" Leah asked.

"I'm full. I'm going to get back to the quilt. I promised it to a customer by next week."

She sat by herself and sewed on the wedding ring quilt and tried not to think of how one day she and other women would gather around the big quilting frame and stitch hers.

Someone knocked on the window and she jumped. She looked up and saw John staring at her through the glass. But instead of gesturing for her to open the door, which they'd locked so they could eat lunch, he waved carelessly and walked on.

"Who was that?" Leah asked as she walked over to sit in a chair next to Naomi.

"John."

Surprised, Leah stared at her. "He didn't want to come in?"

Naomi shook her head. "He was just making sure I was here."

"Where else would you be this time of day?" Leah pulled her chair up to the quilting frame and threaded a needle.

"He likes to make sure I'm where I said I'd be." Her voice sounded flat.

Leah's hands, which had been busily threading her needle, stilled. Her eyes searched Naomi's face. "There's something wrong, isn't there? It's not my imagination."

Naomi started to say it was nothing, but her grandmother placed her hand over hers.

"Tell me," she said quietly. "Tell me."

That's all it took. The floodgates opened.

"John's turned into—into someone I don't know," she said, reaching into her pocket for a tissue. "He tells me what to do and where to be and checks on me all the time. Just like now."

She dabbed at her cheeks. "I want to be obedient and learn to be a good *fraa*," she said. "But he—he scared me the other night."

"How?" Leah asked, her voice almost a whisper. "How did he scare you?"

Naomi couldn't look her in the eye.

"Tell me, how did he scare you?"

"I went to walk away from him and he grabbed my wrist and hurt me."

Leah reached over and unerringly chose the very wrist John had grabbed. Naomi winced. Her grandmother didn't release it but pushed the sleeve of Naomi's dress back, exposing a bruise.

"I thought you were favoring it," she said, frowning. She looked up at Naomi.

"It only hurts a little," she said, wiping at her cheeks again with her tissue.

"It only hurts a little there, but a lot in your heart." Leah's eyes were damp and filled with sympathy.

"He said he was sorry."

Leah pulled down the sleeve. "And how many other times has he said he's sorry?"

Sobs rose up in her chest. "Too—too many," she admitted.

There was a knock on the door. Naomi jumped.

"You go wash your face," Leah said. "Then let's go in the back room and talk."

"We don't have time. We have to work."

Leah stood. "We'll make time."

True to her word, after Leah opened the door and took care of the customer, she got Anna and Mary Katherine to run the shop while she and Naomi talked.

"You have to break it off with him."

"Maybe counseling—"

"Counseling is a good idea. For you."

"Me? I'm not the problem."

"But how you responded to John's treatment of you worries me. I want you to think about it. Really think about it." She hesitated, then forged ahead. "I know that some people who act like John can be helped, but I wouldn't count on it. And it's a terrible way to start out in a marriage. I don't want to be harsh or seem unforgiving. But it's too big a risk to take."

Naomi nodded. "I know."

"Next time it could be a bigger injury."

"I know. Don't you think I know?" she burst out. "That's why I kept it to myself."

"Which is what he counted on, so he could exert more control."

Leah got up and paced. "It's so important to make a good match. There's no divorce. You'd be with him until one of you dies."

Naomi shuddered and got up to take some aspirin for the headache that was pounding behind her eyes. She turned to her grandmother. "I don't think I love him anymore."

"Yes, you do," Leah disagreed gently. "Otherwise, you would have spoken up by now."

The door opened and Anna poked her head inside. "Everything okay? We heard Naomi raise her voice."

She glanced at her cousin and saw the tears. "What's wrong?"

Naomi started to say it was nothing but then realized that holding everything in was how all of it had started. "I'm breaking up with John."

She watched one emotion after another chase across Anna's face. "I thought something was wrong, but I could never get you to talk."

"I didn't want to burden anyone."

"You thought I wouldn't understand, didn't you?" Anna asked her. "Happy, carefree Anna hasn't got the depth to understand, right?"

Shocked, Naomi stared at her. "No, I didn't think that at all. But you've had enough sadness."

"You have no idea what I've experienced," Anna said. "Maybe I haven't wanted to face it myself."

With that, she spun on her heel and went out, shutting the door firmly behind her.

"I need to go after her."

Naomi stood but Leah put her hand on her arm, stopping her.

"Let me. I think I know what's wrong. And I've let her get away with it for too long."

Leah hurried after her and Naomi followed, watching helplessly as her grandmother opened the front door of the shop, stepped out, and slipped and fell.

2

Naomi rushed out the door and found her grandmother sitting on the concrete in front of the shop.

Mary Katherine was right behind her. "What happened?"

"Are you all right?" Naomi asked her grandmother as she knelt before her.

"*Ya*," Leah said quickly. "It was just a little fall. Stupid of me. I wasn't watching where I stepped."

But her face looked pasty white and perspiration dotted her forehead. She reached out her hands. "Help me up. Please."

Naomi and Mary Katherine looked at each other. "Maybe we shouldn't move you."

"I'm fine. The only thing that hurts is my ankle. I probably twisted it a little."

They each took one of her arms and lifted her, but when Leah stood she winced and cried out. "Oh, my ankle! I must have sprained it."

"You could have broken it," Mary Katherine told her.

Slipping their arms around her waist, they guided her slowly back into the shop and set her carefully into a chair. Mary Katherine pulled another chair over and gently lifted Leah's foot and placed it on the seat cushion.

Naomi hurried to the shop telephone.

"Who are you calling?" Leah wanted to know.

"911."

"Don't you dare!" she said. "You put that phone down now!"

Shocked at the vehemence in her voice, Naomi did so and nearly said, "Yes, ma'am!"

"You call Nick. Ask him to come take me to the doctor."

Naomi looked at Mary Katherine, who nodded. Resigned, she made the call.

A few minutes later, he was striding into the shop. He was a handsome *Englisch* man, tall and dark-haired, with piercing green eyes. Although those eyes lit often with laughter as he drove them around, Naomi felt uncomfortable with the way he always seemed to be observing her—studying her.

He was a favorite of Leah's and she often found him visiting her grandmother, clearly enjoying her company as well as the baked goods and coffee she'd fix for him in her kitchen. Naomi often heard him asking questions about the Amish faith in a way that didn't seem like prying or idle curiosity. The two of them seemed to enjoy discussing a passage or a person from the Bible.

Leah looked up from supervising the application of ice on her ankle. "Well, that was quick."

"I happened to be in town. Aren't you the one who's often said there's no such thing as coincidence?"

She nodded, looking serious. "*Ya*. Well, shall we go? Naomi's already called the doctor and he insisted we go to the hospital and get an X-ray."

"Could have just let me call for an ambulance," Naomi muttered.

"No need to pay for something like that when our Nick is around."

He winked at Naomi. "Let's get you in the car, Leah."

Before she could say anything, he scooped her up in his arms and carried her to the shop door. Naomi hurried to open it.

"Now there's no need—" Leah began.

"For you to fuss," Nick finished for her. "Gets you up and out faster than helping you and hurting your ankle more."

He gave her one of his intense looks. "Did you hit your head when you fell? Truth, now!"

"I'd say if I did," she said with some tartness. Then her face softened. "Just like you to ask such a thing."

Naomi felt a stab of guilt. She and Mary Katherine had asked their grandmother if she was hurt anywhere besides her ankle, but neither of them had thought to ask that particular question.

He paused at the door. "You coming?"

She nodded. She'd already put her and Leah's purses on the counter, along with their sweaters.

"Don't worry about a thing," Mary Katherine told her grandmother as she bent to give her a kiss on the cheek. "Anna and I will take care of the shop and make the deposit."

"If Anna comes back." Leah frowned.

"She'll be back. She just needs to walk it off," Naomi assured her. But she couldn't help scanning the sidewalks as Nick carried Leah to the car.

"How'd it happen?" he asked when he settled Leah in the backseat and made sure she fastened her seat belt.

"Just a silly accident," she said, looking up and down the street.

Nick turned back to start the car, and as he did, Naomi saw him glance in the rearview mirror at Leah. "Looking for someone?"

Leah sighed. "Anna. She left the shop a little while ago."

"Do you want her to go with us?"

Naomi looked over her shoulder, then met Nick's gaze. "I don't think we should look for her," she said in a low voice. "Grandmother looks like she's in a lot of pain."

"I heard that," Leah spoke up from the backseat. "I'm hurt, not deaf."

Turning in her seat, Naomi nodded. "Sorry. But I don't think we should wait. You're hurting."

"Don't need to tell me what I know," Leah said tartly.

Naomi touched Nick's hand. "Wait just a minute, okay?"

She scrambled out of the car and heard Leah protesting, "Now where is she going? She was the one in a big hurry to get to the hospital."

Mary Katherine glanced up, surprised, when Naomi ran into the shop. "What—?"

Snatching up the ice bag that lay on the chair Leah had vacated and grabbing a set of kitchen towels that lay on a nearby display table, Naomi turned and ran back out of the shop. She opened the back door of Nick's car and after quickly wrapping the ice bag in a towel, placed it gently on her grandmother's injured ankle.

She climbed back into the front seat and shut the door. "Okay," she said to Nick. "We're ready."

His mouth quirked into a grin. "Yes, ma'am."

Naomi surreptitiously studied him as he drove. He was so different from John. Nick was easygoing and pleasant. Well, maybe not pleasant. Not that he was unpleasant. But pleasant sounded dull—and he wasn't dull. He had a whole bundle of stories that he'd pull out and entertain them with if prompted.

While Nick was easygoing, he didn't have that same charm that John possessed, which had been one of the reasons she'd fallen in love with him . . . and which now worried her. It hadn't taken long for her to realize that instead of being charmed, she'd started to feel manipulated.

On the seat, she felt a hand on hers—and realized that Nick was patting it. "Stop worrying. She's going to be okay. We'll be there soon."

He'd mistaken her silence—and no doubt, her frown—for anxiety. She nodded, not knowing what to say. He wasn't a person in whom she should be confiding her growing doubt about her engagement.

She knew he wasn't married. Her grandmother had mentioned that once in passing. He never talked about a girlfriend, and she wondered about that because he talked so easily about other areas of his life: his travels, the books he'd read, all sorts of things. Lately he'd taken up running, and it was a change from the relatively sedentary driving he did for the Amish and tourists each day.

The hospital came into view. He pulled up at the emergency room entrance. While Naomi went to get a wheelchair, he helped Leah out.

When Naomi returned, he helped Leah into the chair. But when Naomi started to reach into her purse for money, he held his hands up. "No charge," he said. "Listen, I'll go park the van and sit with you while Leah's seen."

"You don't have to do that."

"It's my pleasure," he said. "Besides, I don't have any other jobs this afternoon so I might as well wait for you. I'm sure they'll send Leah home after they X-ray her ankle and wrap it or cast it or whatever."

A car horn honked. A driver was motioning for him to move his vehicle so he could pull closer and let someone out.

"Let me help you with her chair."

"No, go, go!" she said, waving her hands. "Those people could have an emergency."

She pushed the wheelchair toward the magic doors—she always called them that because they were the kind that opened on some mysterious signal. She always thought a person didn't need such, but today she was grateful she didn't have to try to open the doors and maneuver the chair inside at the same time.

The waiting room was filled. Naomi sighed. They were in for a long wait. She sat filling out paperwork, thankful that she'd remembered the ice pack, as her grandmother sat there, her face etched with pain.

Finally finished with the paperwork, Naomi carried it over to the clerk.

"I need your driver's license and one other form of identification," the woman said, not looking up.

Naomi stood there, waiting, and the clerk looked up, frowning, until she saw who was standing before her.

"Here's my grandmother's identification. No driver's license," she said with a slight smile.

She handed it over and watched as the clerk photocopied it before handing it back.

When she returned to her grandmother, Nick was sitting there, saying something that made her smile.

It was an unusual friendship, she thought, watching them as the clerk looked over her grandmother's paperwork—an *Englisch* driver and an older Amish woman.

When it came time for Leah to be seen, she refused Naomi's offer to accompany her. So Naomi moved to take a seat beside Nick.

But it was empty. She shrugged. Maybe he'd decided to leave after all. It wasn't as if she and her grandmother hadn't insisted. Vaguely disappointed, she took a seat and waited.

Nick appeared before her a few minutes later, holding a cup of coffee for each of them.

She blinked and took the cup from him. "I thought you'd gone."

"I told you that I'm not leaving until we can take Leah home."

Naomi bit her lip and glanced at the door where Leah had disappeared with a nurse.

"She'll be okay," he told her quietly. "She didn't seem to have any injuries other than the ankle. But even if she had, she's a strong woman."

She found herself lapsing into thought again. Leah was strong, like Nick said.

A lot stronger than she was. Her grandmother wouldn't be acting weak like she was right now, staying with someone she knew wasn't right for her. Leah wouldn't have fallen for someone like that in the first place. She was too smart. Too confident. Even when she'd lost her husband and the years passed, she never let anyone know she was lonely—even when it was easy to see the loneliness, the sadness in her eyes when she thought no one was watching. She'd never fallen in love with someone who charmed her.

And Leah would surely never let anyone pressure her into thinking she needed to have another *mann* to be a complete woman.

No one had pressured Naomi into becoming engaged. But so many of her friends from school had already married and had children by now. They'd given up their jobs while they took care of their young children and appeared so content they—

"Look who's here," Nick muttered, interrupting her thoughts.

Naomi glanced up and saw John striding toward her.

"When did you call him?"

"I didn't," she muttered. "He just . . . finds me."

Nick stood, but John barely acknowledged him.

"What's taking so long?" John asked, taking off his hat and impatiently tapping it against his knee.

Not, *Is she okay*? *Are you okay*? Naomi noted, then chided herself for being critical. After all, she was sitting here wishing they'd hurry up.

But that was because she was nervous having someone she loved behind a closed door. She needed to *see* that her grandmother was okay.

Just at that moment, a nurse stuck her head out the door and gestured to Naomi. She got up and hurried over.

"The doctor wants to talk to you." She looked up, over Naomi's shoulder. "You'll have to wait here."

Naomi glanced at John and saw that he was frowning at the woman. "But—"

"Sorry, sir," the nurse said briskly, already turning away. "Miss, come with me."

Leah was sitting on a gurney, listening intently to the young doctor pointing out something on her X-ray.

"How do you do," he said, holding out his hand and pumping Naomi's enthusiastically. "I was just explaining to Mrs. —"

"Leah," she inserted.

"Leah," he said, returning his attention to the X-ray. "I was just pointing out to Leah here that it doesn't look like anything's broken, but she's got a nasty sprain."

He looked at Naomi. "I have a question for you. I understand you're Leah's granddaughter. Tell me, how is she about listening to what a doctor asks her to do? How is she about bed rest?"

Naomi's mouth quirked. "Well, I don't remember her ever being hurt like this. And she's never sick. But she can't sit still for two minutes."

Leah sniffed. The doctor laughed.

"I suspected so. My mother doesn't sit still, either. I don't think any of them do."

"Well, I'm a grandmother, but thank you, young man," Leah told him.

The doctor raised his eyebrows, then turned to the X-ray. "I think it's a bad sprain. I don't see any fracture." He handed her a printout. "Follow these directions and call your own doctor for a follow-up appointment."

Naomi helped her into the wheelchair and wheeled her to the checkout window.

"This is ridiculous," Leah muttered as she read the sheet in her hands. "I can't stay off my feet this long. I have a shop to run, a house to take care of."

"We can take care of everything," Naomi told her. "Let's just get you home."

"Nick! You stayed!" Leah exclaimed.

He walked toward them. "I told you I would. I'll go get the van and pick the two of you up at the door."

"I can take them home," John told them.

"Hello, John," Leah said quietly. "I didn't know you were here."

"Mary Katherine told me where she was when I went by the shop."

"Do you have your buggy outside?" Nick asked him.

"No, a friend dropped me off. I can call a driver."

"One's already here," Leah said quietly but firmly. "Nick stayed to take us home, so I'd like him to do so."

She turned to Naomi. "Let's go. I can't wait to get my ankle up."

"When will I see you?" John asked, putting his hand on Naomi's arm as she began pushing the wheelchair toward the door.

She stiffened and glanced down at his hand, then into his eyes. "I'm sorry, I'll have to take care of Grandmother tonight so it'll have to be another time."

"But—" He sighed and dropped his hand. "Of course."

"If you need a ride home, I can drop you off on the way," Nick told him as they started walking toward the exit.

"*Danki*," John said.

But Naomi noticed he didn't look very happy about it. Nick pulled the van up to the ER entrance and they piled in—Naomi and Leah in the back, John riding shotgun with Nick.

Leah allowed herself to be persuaded to turn sideways on the backseat and rest her ankle on Naomi's lap. A nurse had filled a plastic bag with ice, wrapped it in a towel, and sent it with them for the ride. Naomi held it in place as they rode.

"How's the pain?"

"I'll live," Leah said, managing a smile.

But Naomi saw the pain in her eyes and squeezed her hand to comfort her.

When she glanced up, she saw Nick give her a brief glance in the rearview mirror. Just as she met his gaze, John looked back at her and saw her looking at Nick, and something in his eyes flashed, an expression she recognized: anger.

Nothing was said, but it didn't have to be. Naomi was sure the look lasted only a moment. It felt like minutes. She let out a breath she hadn't realized she'd been holding when he turned back in his seat.

She felt her hand being squeezed and realized that her grandmother was sending her a silent message.

Nick slowed the car, flicked on the turn signal, and pulled into the parking lot of a drugstore. After he stopped the car, he turned in his seat. "Give me the prescription and I'll run in and get it filled."

"There's no need," Leah told him.

He held out his hand. "Trust me, you're going to need it later. These things always feel worse in the middle of the night. I ran track in college and had my share of injuries. Now hand it over."

With a sigh, Leah pulled the prescription from her purse and handed it to him with a twenty.

He got out, ran through a drizzle that had begun to fall, and disappeared into the drugstore.

Naomi watched John stare in the direction Nick had gone. It was so quiet in the car you could hear a pin drop.

"An ice bag," Leah said suddenly. "And some Epsom salts to soak my ankle tomorrow."

She winced as she moved her foot from Naomi's lap and rested it on the floorboard of the car. Reaching into her purse, she withdrew another twenty and pressed it into Naomi's hand.

"Will you go get that for me?"

John turned in the front seat. "I can go."

"No, *danki*, young man," Leah told him. "Naomi knows what I need." She made a shooing motion with her hands at Naomi.

Then she turned to John and smiled a smile that didn't reach her eyes. "Besides, you and I haven't had much opportunity to talk and get to know each other, have we, young man?"

Naomi glanced back as she got out of the van. John gave her a beseeching look. Biting back a smile, she closed the van door and started toward the drugstore entrance.

"She looks depressed."

"I know."

"What are we going to do?"

Naomi motioned with her hand for Mary Katherine and Anna to move back so she could close the door to the cozy little back room of the shop.

"She's been that way ever since she got the postcard this morning," Naomi said as she filled the teakettle and set it on the stove to boil.

"Postcard?" Anna asked as she dug into the cookie jar.

"From Florida," Mary Katherine told her, taking the cookie jar away. "Save some of these for other people."

"But you're not eating them," Anna protested.

"Some of us have self-restraint."

Anna made a face at Mary Katherine as she got out mugs and set them on the table.

"She won't stay home and when she's here all she does is stare out the window. We have to do something." She sighed. "She wouldn't have had her accident if she hadn't been rushing after me that day. All this because I needed to get away for a few minutes and calm down." She sighed again.

The door opened and Leah maneuvered herself inside with her crutches. "What's going on in here? You girls having a private chat?"

Before they could answer, she stepped over to the table. Anna jumped up to hold out her chair.

"I must say, the three of you are looking a little guilty." She peered at them over her reading glasses.

"We're worried about you," Naomi said when no one else spoke up. "We're afraid you're depressed."

"I know," Leah said, looking at the rain sluicing down the nearby window. "I'm not being very grateful, am I? My fall could have been worse. And people have been so kind coming by to see if I'm okay."

"But the weather is depressing," Mary Katherine said, taking the chair next to Leah's so she could hold her hand. "You need a little pick-me-up."

"A pick-me-up? Like what?"

"Maybe a little time away."

Leah reached into her pocket, pulled out a brightly colored postcard, and tossed it on the table. "You saw this when it came in the mail today, didn't you? I thought of visiting Ida in Florida. But it's no use now."

Naomi sat down on the other side of her grandmother. "Why do you say that?"

"I can't get on a bus like this," Leah said, gesturing at her foot.

She sat silent for a moment and then took a deep breath and attempted a smile. "I'll be fine. Really." She stirred her tea and took a sip.

Troubled, Naomi took her cup of tea into the shop and set it on the table beside her chair. She'd gotten a little behind on a quilt commission because she'd been taking care of her grandmother for the past week.

The Trip around the World quilt required a lot of attention to detail—not that every quilt she made didn't—but it was perfect for taking her mind off thinking about John.

Her grandmother hobbled up on her crutches, shaking her head and frowning when Naomi started to put aside the quilt to help her.

Settled into her chair, Leah leaned forward to study the quilt on its frame. "Beautiful work."

"Thank you."

"Is this a commission?"

Naomi nodded. "It's due in a few weeks."

Leah smiled slightly. "You'll get it finished. You always do."

That was back then—the time she called Before John. It was harder now. John would get so upset when she didn't spend time with him. But she couldn't say that to her grandmother.

Naomi thought the shop was so quiet you could have heard a pin drop if she'd dropped one. But it was a nice break. When Leah didn't speak, Naomi left her to her thoughts.

When Naomi looked up a few minutes later, she found Leah staring out the window at the gray day. The little Amish doll she'd been stuffing lay in her lap.

"You sighed again."

Leah glanced at her. "Sorry."

"*I'm* sorry. It must be hard to have to sit when you want to rush around."

"*Ya*," Leah whispered and it seemed her shoulders slumped a little more.

Naomi set her work down. "Grandmother, Mary Katherine and Anna and I are worried about you."

Someone rapped on the window glass, startling them. John stared in, unsmiling, and nodded when Naomi waved. Then he walked on.

Leah stared after his retreating back. "Why didn't he come in and say hello?"

Naomi picked up her needle. "I told you before. He just wanted to make sure I was here," she muttered. "It was check-in time."

"I see," Leah said quietly. "Naomi, I think we need to—"

The shop door opened and the bell overhead jangled.

"Well, look who's here!"

Naomi's hands froze on the quilt.

"Nick! What a nice surprise!"

He walked over and withdrew a bunch of flowers from behind his back. "I thought these might cheer you up."

How perceptive of him, Naomi thought, watching them. He'd known how Leah would feel having to stay off her feet whether it was at home or at the shop.

John hadn't bothered to come by to see how Leah was doing—only to check that Naomi was where she was supposed to be. He'd called the shop but never asked about Leah, only sounded very disappointed when Naomi would say she couldn't make plans with him.

She shook her head as if to clear her thoughts. It wasn't fair to compare the two men. They came from different worlds, different backgrounds. Different views on women.

So, then, why shouldn't John have been more thoughtful, more considerate of Leah, Naomi's grandmother and a member of his Amish community?

But Nick was in a business relationship with them—he was a paid driver and made money from the arrangement.

Just as that thought came to her, she quickly discarded it as being less than gracious. It wasn't like her to be judgmental.

"Naomi?"

She blinked. "Sorry, you said something?"

"Would you put these in a vase for me? There's one in the back room, in the cupboard at the rear of the room."

Nodding, Naomi took the flowers and carried them into the back room. The deep pink rosebuds immediately scented up the room with a rich perfume as she located the vase, filled it with water, and arranged the flowers in it.

She carried the vase back out to the shop and set it on the table near her grandmother.

Leah sighed as she looked at them, but it was a sigh of satisfaction, not of sadness.

"They're lovely," she told Nick. "You shouldn't have."

"Yes, I should have," he said with a grin. "I remember what it was like to hurt my ankle and how bored I got."

"Did somebody bring you flowers?" Naomi couldn't resist asking as she sat down and picked up her needle again.

"Why yes, it was a woman," he said, grinning. "It was Betsy Norris and she was fourteen like me, a cheerleader who'd seen me hurt it at a basketball game."

She lifted her gaze and studied him. He stared back, humor lighting his green eyes, and she couldn't look away.

Leah stood and Naomi popped up. "What do you need? I'll get it for you."

"You can't, *liebschen*," Leah told her, her lips quirking into a smile. She hobbled away on her crutches in the direction of the ladies' room.

Her face felt warm as she sat again and picked up her needle. Nick took a seat on the opposite side of the quilt frame and stretched out his long khaki-clad legs.

He'd been their driver for years, but she felt a little self-conscious as he watched her work.

"What's the pattern?"

"Trip around the World," she told him.

"Interesting quilt for you to make," he remarked.

"Oh?"

"Well, the Amish don't travel far from home, do they?"

"We also make Wedding Ring quilts and we don't wear wedding rings," she said dryly. "Besides, we're mostly making quilts for *Englischers* here, not for our own homes."

"Touché," he said.

"Hmm?"

"You're right." He glanced behind him, then leaned forward. "Leah seems a little . . . down."

"You can say depressed," she told him quietly. "Mary Katherine and Anna and I were talking about her earlier. We've never seen her like this."

"It's hard when you're an active person and suddenly you have to sit still."

"Talking about me?" Leah asked behind them.

They jumped. Grinning and shaking his head, Nick got up and helped Leah maneuver herself back into her chair and then set her crutches within reach.

"I didn't know you could sneak up on a person when you're on crutches," Naomi said, pressing a hand to her thumping heart.

"It's a new talent of mine." Leah gazed at the quilt, seeming lost in thought.

"Grandmother?"

"Hmm?" Leah looked up at her and her expression cleared.

She pulled the postcard she'd received earlier that day from her pocket and studied it, then looked up. "I've decided I'm going to Florida—to Pinecraft—for a vacation."

3

Naomi stared at her grandmother. "You're what?"

"I'm going to go visit Ida in Pinecraft. I just can't stand another minute of this weather and sitting around doing nothing."

"But you won't be able to do anything there!" Naomi felt a little panicked. She didn't remember her grandmother ever being so impulsive before. It was unnerving.

"I can sit on the warm sand and watch the ocean," she said, staring at the image of the Atlantic Ocean on the card.

"But—" Naomi glanced at Nick, waiting for him to say something.

"It sounds like a great idea," he said.

Naomi glared at him, then turned back to her grandmother. "How are you going to get there?"

"There's a chartered bus going there day after tomorrow."

"You're going to try to get onto a chartered bus with these? How will you manage the steps? The seats?" She held up one of her grandmother's crutches for emphasis.

"I'm not saying it'll be easy," Leah said. "But I'm just tired enough of the weather and this foot to try it. If I don't, well, I won't have any right to complain, will I?"

Leah picked up the doll she'd stopped working on earlier and calmly began stuffing it.

Naomi glanced across the shop at Mary Katherine and gestured for her to come over. Her cousin raised her brows but finished straightening a display of fabric and walked over.

"What is it?"

"Grandmother says she wants to go to Florida."

"Grandmother said she's *going* to go to Florida," Leah corrected Naomi.

She finished tucking the stuffing into the doll and began closing the open seam on the side with small, careful stitches.

"But what about the shop?" Mary Katherine asked her. "What will we do about the shop?"

"Take a deep breath," Leah advised.

Mary Katherine did as her grandmother had advised but she didn't appear any calmer.

"Don't make me think you can't run the shop while I'm away when I know otherwise. Who did it when I had the flu? The three of you."

Anna came out of the supply room with a bolt of fabric. She stopped. "What's going on?"

"Grandmother wants to go to Florida, to Pinecraft, to see a friend."

"But—" Anna began, only to be interrupted.

"No buts," Leah said, tying a knot and snipping the thread. She began dressing the doll in the tiny little Amish garments she'd sewn. "We'll sit down tomorrow and assign responsibilities."

"I'm going with you," Naomi announced.

"Oh?" Leah's eyebrows arched high above her wire-rimmed reading glasses. "Did I invite you?" she asked without rancor.

"Otherwise, all I'd do is worry that you'll hurt yourself again and there won't be anyone around to help."

"I won't be the only passenger on the bus," her grandmother pointed out.

"Doesn't matter. Family takes care of its own. If you're going to go to Florida, I'm going to go to make sure you're safe and to take care of you."

"What if I said no?" Leah asked, tilting her head and studying Naomi.

Naomi bit her lip. "You wouldn't do that, would you? I'd worry."

Leah laughed. "Oh my, now the guilt. We're Amish, not Jewish, *liebschen*. Stop with the guilt. Besides, you know that God's looking out for me."

"Well, He must have blinked the other day," Naomi muttered.

"Sometimes we don't understand why we get hurt. Or why we can't protect someone else."

"Huh?" Anna asked.

Naomi knew what her grandmother meant by her veiled remark. Leah had her own concerns about Naomi being hurt by John. They hadn't talked about it again since the day Leah had discovered the bruise on Naomi's arm. Naomi knew that it was because her grandmother wanted her to think about what she'd said.

She glanced at Mary Katherine and Anna but they were staring curiously at Leah and not focusing on her at all.

Nick had been quiet all this time. He must have moved because suddenly Naomi became aware that he was still there, patiently waiting and listening.

"I'll drive you," he told Leah.

She perked up. "You'll what?"

"I'll drive you. We can take the van and you can stretch out on the backseat and be more comfortable."

"You can't do that," Naomi interrupted. "Your business—"

"I have two drivers—one who's been asking for more hours lately."

"But the cost," Naomi, ever practical, said.

"We'll work it out," he said. "I've always wanted to see Florida. And I haven't taken a vacation in two years."

Vacation. That was a term she didn't hear often in the community. The only time some Amish left it was to attend a funeral, a wedding, or some family-related events. She'd heard some of the northern Amish enjoyed visiting Niagara Falls, and some hereabouts went to Florida, to the tiny little town known as Pinecraft where Daniel and his parents lived.

"Well, then it's settled." Leah beamed. "You, me, and Naomi. How soon can we leave?"

"Good," Mary Katherine said as Nick left the shop. "It all fell into place."

"*Ya*, didn't it?" Leah tied the doll's black wool bonnet on the doll's head and bounced her on her knees. "God's will is truly miraculous."

Yes, everything had fallen into place. Naomi told herself that she should be happy that her grandmother was going to have a break from the weather, from the enforced confinement because of her injury. Just a few minutes ago she'd offered to go along and make sure her grandmother would be safe and cared for on her trip, hadn't she?

Nick had offered a solution for the trip that made her grandmother happy. So why, Naomi asked herself, did she feel uneasy about the whole thing?

"It's ridiculous. You can't go."

Naomi stared at John. "What?"

"It's unacceptable," he said, wiping his mouth with a napkin.

She knew her cousins—and many people—thought of her as quiet, slow to anger. But she could feel her temper rising at his words.

"It's just for a week or two, for Grandmother—"

"No."

"What do you mean 'no'?"

He glanced around him, then at her. "Keep your voice down. Have you forgotten we're in a public place?"

It had been his idea for them to come here. He'd dropped by the shop, asking if they could have supper. Well, he hadn't asked. He'd insisted. Mary Katherine had pulled her aside and told her she should spend the evening with John since she'd be away for a while.

"I'll be right there at the house tonight with Grandmother," Mary Katherine reminded her. "John's right, the two of you haven't seen each other since Grandmother got hurt."

So Naomi had agreed to have dinner with John when she really needed to be home figuring out what to pack for the trip and that sort of thing.

Now, she watched him as he continued to eat, totally unaware that she was fuming at his pronouncement. "John, I'm not asking you for permission."

John's eyebrows went up and he paused, his fork halfway to his mouth. "Of course you are. We're engaged."

"Even if we were married, we'd be discussing this, not having you tell me what to do like you're my father."

"It's a wife's duty to obey her husband."

She sat there, trying to think of what to say. Where was the charming man she'd fallen in love with who'd seemed so easy-going? She didn't want any unpleasantness before she was going out of town.

"Look, your grandmother will be fine. She'll be back before you miss her."

He glanced at her plate. "Are you going to eat that?" he asked, gesturing at her plate with his fork.

She pushed her plate toward him. "I'm not hungry."

"Waste not, want not," he said, scraping the meat and vegetables off her plate onto his.

When she stayed silent, he looked up. "What? I'm a hungry boy. I worked hard today."

He broke open a biscuit, buttered it, then took a huge bite. "These aren't as good as yours. You should see about making them for this place."

"I'm too busy at the shop."

He grunted and took a second bite before putting it down on his plate.

"Could make some extra money," he said. "Listen, just think about it. We could save faster toward getting a place of our own after the wedding. Then we wouldn't have to move in with my parents for a while."

Her stomach did a lurch. "I can't give you any money this week. I'll need it for my share of the trip expenses."

"We discussed that. You're not going."

The waitress stopped by to inquire about interest in dessert. John ordered his favorite pie. Naomi shook her head when the woman looked at her.

"More coffee, too," John called after the waitress. He stood. "I'll be right back."

Naomi watched him walk to the restrooms at the rear of the restaurant. She stood, reaching into her purse for money. When the waitress returned with the pie and the coffeepot, Naomi asked for the check.

"You're paying?" the woman asked and then just as quickly shook her head. "Sorry, it's none of my business. It's just usually the Amish guys pay."

"It's okay. I'm calling it a treat." There wouldn't be another.

"You're leaving?" the woman asked as she pulled the check from her pocket.

"Absolutely." She handed her a tip and started to walk away, then stopped and turned back. "Oh, but he's not. Don't clear the table. He'd be disappointed if he missed dessert."

While he waited, Nick tried to focus on the book he was reading, but it was no use.

He was crazy to have offered to take Leah and Naomi to Florida. It was bad enough to be harboring a crush on a granddaughter of Leah's—especially one who was engaged. He knew better than to develop feelings for an Amish woman. There was no way that could go anywhere.

Why couldn't he have developed feelings for a woman from his own world? Oh, he knew the answer to that. He'd been restless and disenchanted with so much the last year or two. He'd stopped going to his own church. Just been walking—well, driving—through his life.

Then Leah had become one of his clients. Leah and her three granddaughters. They'd been clients of his father for years.

At first, it wasn't about the granddaughters. Oh, he wasn't someone who was attracted to an older woman. It wasn't like that at all. Leah seemed to recognize that he was feeling adrift. Searching for something.

He suspected she did that with everyone. There seemed to be more to her relationship with her granddaughters than just a grandmother's affection. She had a way of helping someone find this . . . spark in them and bring it out. He'd watched the way she'd encouraged each of the women—and not just with their creativity. Each of them had seemed to blossom not only in their craft but in their confidence too.

Well, except for Naomi. Lately, she seemed to be withdrawing, to be quieter and more serious.

He picked up the book again and tried to concentrate. A shadow fell over him.

"Well, you're looking really calm. I guess a trip's no big deal for you."

Nick looked up at Naomi. "What, me worry?"

Naomi frowned. "Excuse me?"

"Alfred E. Neuman. You know, *Mad Magazine*."

"There's a magazine for people who are angry?"

He chuckled as he got out of the vehicle and helped her load her suitcase into the rear. "Long story. I'd say I'd tell you on the way, but it's really not that interesting."

"I see."

"Is Leah ready?"

"I have her suitcase by the door."

"I'll get it. You climb in."

She reached out and touched his arm. "Nick? I—I wanted to thank you."

"For what?"

"You know. For picking me up last night and bringing me home."

"It's what I do for a living, Naomi. I drive people where they need to go."

"Yes, but I wasn't planning on finding my own way home. I thought that—well, I wouldn't need a ride, and then things changed. And I called you right at supper time and I feel like—"

He touched her hand, and as he did, she jumped back, swiftly withdrawing it.

"Sorry," he said quickly. He frowned. She'd never reacted in such a skittish way to him before.

"No," she told him, looking flustered. "It's all right."

"Who my passengers are and where they go is no one's business," he assured her. "Unless you have the police after you. I charge extra for alibis."

"Police? Of course not." She looked even more flustered, averting her eyes, pretending that her already severely drawn-back hair needed to be restrained under her *kapp*.

There had been something strange last night when he picked her up at the shop. He'd been told she wasn't going home because she was having supper with John, and the lights had been turned off at the shop. He'd pulled up before it and she'd stepped out and looked around, then locked the door and rushed into his car.

"I don't want my grandmother to know—" she broke off and looked toward the door.

"I don't intend to say anything."

"It's not that I'm keeping secrets."

"Naomi, it's your business."

She sighed. "It's just that she'd worry."

"There she is," he warned as Leah opened the door and looked out.

He hurried over and picked up the suitcase sitting by the door. "Anything else?" he asked.

She pointed at the picnic basket just inside the door. "I packed a thermos of coffee and some sticky buns. Sandwiches for midday."

He could smell the coffee and the buns and tried not to groan. Breakfast had been a bowl of cereal and a cup of coffee—and not Leah's coffee, either.

His expression must have been comical because she laughed. "How about we stop in an hour or so for the coffee and buns?"

"Maybe half an hour?"

She grinned. "*Schur.*"

He settled Leah into the backseat and belted her in, then stowed her crutches in the back. Naomi climbed into the front seat next to him and gave him one of her quiet smiles.

"Thanks," she said.

Shrugging, he put the key in the ignition. "You're welcome."

He was carefully backing out of the driveway, cautious of any traffic that could swoop up quickly in this area, when he caught sight of a buggy parked beside the road and a man standing next to it.

Leah caught his gaze in the rearview mirror and shook her head. "Don't stop."

"Okay," he said, shifting gears and stepping on the accelerator to move forward.

"What is it?"

Nick watched Naomi glance back, and her eyes widened when she saw John.

"Do you want me to stop?" he asked quietly.

She turned in her seat and stared forward. "No. Thank you," she said as an afterthought.

Nick gave the rearview mirror a last look and saw that John's hands were clenched.

Something was going on, he thought. Had Naomi broken up with John? he wondered. And why did he feel a sudden lift in his spirits as he headed down the road with her sitting beside him?

He drove and stayed silent after that, concentrating on the road.

Naomi and Leah didn't say a word.

"It's been an hour," Leah finally said from the backseat a little while later. "I thought you said half an hour."

"I'm trying to develop some self-restraint."

"An admirable goal," she said. "But since it's to my sticky buns, I'm not sure I'm happy to hear that."

"It was difficult," he told her. "A struggle of epic proportions. I'm surprised Naomi wasn't pushed out of the front seat by my fight with my conscience."

"We're stopping already?" Naomi asked, coming to attention. "Why?"

Nick wondered if either of them—she or Leah—realized neither of them had spoken for a whole hour as they drove.

"I got a whiff of Leah's sticky buns and coffee when I carried them to the car," he told her, looking for a place to pull over. "She promised me I could have some in a half hour."

"You want to take a break after a half hour on the road?" she asked disbelievingly.

"It turned into an hour."

Naomi rolled her eyes. "Men and their stomachs. Why, I bet it didn't take John—"

She stopped.

"He's not going to forget you while you're gone."

Her expression changed. It was like a lightbulb went out it was such a sudden shutdown. Now what had he said? he asked himself.

She'd had a narrow escape, Naomi couldn't help thinking as they drove.

When she'd looked back at John standing in the driveway, Naomi had thought of the biblical reference to Lot's wife turning into a pillar of salt as she turned to look back.

Thankfully, all Naomi had from doing so were some tears on her cheeks, tears she turned and surreptitiously wiped away.

It hadn't been right to walk out on John at the restaurant last night but she didn't know what else to do. She owed it to her grandmother to accompany her to Florida for a vacation. And she badly needed to think over her relationship with John.

Her grandmother had told her she needed to break up with him, that men like him didn't change. But she wanted to believe he was still the man she'd fallen in love with. That he could be the *mann* she thought he could be.

She couldn't be so wrong about him, could she? Wasn't she supposed to love him as the child of God he was? Weren't the Amish supposed to be forgiving?

He'd said he hadn't meant to hurt her.

"Hungry?" Nick asked, breaking into her thoughts to ask as they helped Leah negotiate the grass surrounding the picnic table.

Naomi shook her head. "I had breakfast."

"So did I."

"I'm not a bottomless pit."

He just laughed. "If you don't want your sticky bun, I'll eat it for you."

She remembered how John had finished her dinner at the restaurant. Men were certainly different from women.

"We're not going to stop every hour to eat, are we?"

He sighed. "Sounds like a great road trip. But no."

"You couldn't have just eaten it in the car while you were driving?"

"Safety's number one," he told her with a grin, setting the basket down on the table and withdrawing the wrapped package of buns.

Leah seated herself, pulled the thermos out, and poured coffee into the disposable cups Naomi held out.

Nick ate two buns in quick succession and then gave Naomi a rueful look. "What can I say? Leah's baking rocks."

"I made them," she told him, swallowing the last of her coffee.

Taking her hand in his, Nick gave Naomi an impassioned look. "Please tell me you'll marry me."

"Very funny," Naomi told him as she got up, tossed the empty cup into a nearby trash can, and walked back to the vehicle.

Leah's delighted laughter followed her.

4

The trip picked up speed from there.

Nick actually drove more than an hour without stopping. Naomi was thrilled. She couldn't take her eyes off the passing scenery.

"Have you ever been out of the state?" he asked.

She turned and smiled at him. "Never gone more than a hundred miles or so for a wedding or a funeral. Always stayed in Pennsylvania."

"I remember some great road trips. Some with my parents, some with my college friends. Why, we'd go on a trip together and . . ." he trailed off.

"I can just imagine what happened," she said dryly.

"You?"

"I have two grown brothers. They're Amish, but they weren't saints."

"I'll say," Leah spoke up from the backseat.

"You doing okay back there?" Nick asked her.

"*Ya.*"

"Let me know when you want to take a break, stretch your legs."

"You too," she said.

They rode for a while longer. Naomi glanced into the backseat a little while later and saw that her grandmother had drifted off.

"We both stayed up too late getting ready," she told him. "I was packing—"

"And making the world's best sticky buns."

He glanced back at the sleeping Leah. "Maybe I shouldn't say that. I thought that Leah had made them until you spoke up."

She smiled slightly. "I'm afraid she's worn out. I caught her up late making notes about the shop for Mary Katherine and Anna. I feel a little guilty. I'm going to go have fun with Grandmother while Mary Katherine and Anna have a lot of responsibility."

"You're making the trip Leah wanted to take possible," he told her. "I'm sure that they're happy to do whatever they can to keep things running."

"They're both just a little too trusting."

"Oh? And you're not?"

She frowned. Did he suspect that things weren't as they should be between her and John? She hoped not. Privacy was very important to engaged couples—to all Amish.

"I just wouldn't want someone to take advantage of them."

He was silent for a long moment and she wondered what he was thinking. "Your parents—not just yours but Mary Katherine's and Anna's—surely they'll be checking in to see if any help is needed. And Hannah Marlowe stops in to teach quilting classes, right? I'm sure she and other women in the community will be available if anything's needed."

Naomi felt a weight lift from her shoulders. "Why, of course you're right." She leaned back in her seat.

Nick glanced into the backseat, then at Naomi, before returning his gaze to the road. "It's a wonderful thing you're doing for Leah."

"The injury's been hard on her. She needs a break."

She shrugged. "Besides, she's done so much for me, for my cousins. The shop's been like a second home for us."

"Are you going to continue working after you get married?"

"Of course. Until we have a family. But even after that I'll be able to continue my quilting and work part-time at the shop."

Nick nodded and kept his eyes on the road. She sensed that he wanted to say something but was holding back.

"What is it?" she asked when he stayed silent.

He raised his eyebrows. "What do you mean?"

"You want to ask me something, but you're holding back."

"Oh, I wouldn't say that." He checked the traffic and merged into another lane.

"Go ahead."

"I dunno. I guess I'm just surprised. John seems pretty traditional to me."

She had trouble repressing a smile. "The Amish *are* traditional. I guess you hadn't noticed."

He laughed. "*Ya*, I'd noticed," he said, using the slight inflection the Amish gave to the language. "I just didn't expect to hear that he'd want you to work outside the home after the two of you married."

"Couples discuss these things and they work them out," she said, and she heard how prim she sounded.

She bit her lip as she thought about how that wasn't exactly the truth about the relationship she and John had. How had Nick guessed that it had been a thorn of contention in their relationship? But what was between the two of them was private, not to be discussed even with someone like Nick who'd become a friend.

The miles sped by. Naomi watched the landscape change as they left the state and headed into the next.

"How good's your geography?"

"It's been a while since school," she admitted. "And it wasn't my favorite subject."

She hadn't been a daydreamer in school, doodling designs like Mary Katherine had, or already certain that she knew who she wanted to marry and followed him everywhere like Anna. But she hadn't really been all that much better at applying herself to subjects she didn't think were interesting or something she'd use later in life.

"Look in the glove compartment," he said and gestured at it with one hand. "I made something for us."

She opened it and looked inside. "Why do they call it that when you don't have any gloves in here?"

"Why do they call it a pocketbook when it doesn't have a pocket and it's really a purse?"

Naomi shook her head and laughed. "I have no idea. I call it a purse."

"My grandmother calls it a pocketbook."

She pulled out a stack of papers with directions and maps. "Is this it?"

He nodded. "I have a GPS but I had AAA make it up for our trip in case you or Leah wanted to follow it. They estimate the trip'll take about seventeen hours."

"Where are we stopping for the night?" she asked, looking up from the trip itinerary. "We *are* stopping for the night, right?" She yawned.

"Yes. When I talked to Leah yesterday, she and I thought we'd stop in North or South Carolina. I was a little concerned about her being cooped up with that ankle and it swelling."

"Sorry," she said when she had to cover her yawn with her hand again. "I was up late."

"Why don't you take a nap?"

"That doesn't seem polite."

He chuckled. "I'm used to having people fall asleep while I'm driving them. I won't mention names but several people do it on their way home from work sometimes after a long day."

Naomi shifted in her seat to get more comfortable.

"Want me to get you a pillow? I packed a couple in the back."

"No, I don't want to wake Grandmother."

"Let me know if you change your mind."

The endless stretch of interstate and the sun shining through the windshield didn't help. She couldn't keep her eyelids open.

In her dream she was running, running from a man. She hadn't gotten a clear look at him, just heard her name spoken and she knew she had to run for her life.

Her heart was racing and her lungs burned as she ran faster, harder than she ever had. It was dark out. No one was around. Her scream for help had gone unheard.

But as the footsteps behind her grew closer she knew she'd never outrun him. Her fear should have outpaced his anger, but his anger was too great. There was no reasoning with him now. She had to run and pray he wouldn't catch her. His hand grasped at her sleeve and she fought it off without slowing.

Sweat ran down her back. Tears ran down her cheeks. She couldn't go on. With the last of her breath she screamed for help, knowing no one was around.

She prayed for God's help, prayed and prayed, but still could almost feel the hot breath of the man behind her breathing down her neck. And then, with a prayer on her lips, she tripped and sprawled on the road, the breath whooshed out of her, and she cried out in pain.

The man yanked her over to face him and her head banged against the concrete. "You're mine! Mine! Do you hear me?"

Jostled awake, Naomi jerked against something that constricted her and she screamed and tried to fight it off.

"Naomi, wake up!" a male voice demanded. She stared in horror at Nick, her breath heaving in her chest.

The vehicle shuddered to a stop as he pulled it over to the shoulder and killed the engine.

"What happened?" Leah leaned forward. "Did we have a flat tire?"

"Naomi had a nightmare," Nick told her, looking over his shoulder at her. "Are you okay, Leah? I tried to pull over without jostling you too much."

"*Ya*, I'm fine," she said, reaching out to touch Naomi's shoulder. "Calm down. You're safe."

Naomi hugged herself for warmth and tried to take a deep breath. The dream had felt so real. But she wasn't lying in the road with a man leaning over her, his hand lifted to strike her.

Glancing over at him, she saw that Nick was staring at her in concern, quietly waiting for her to calm down. He twisted the cap off a bottle of water in the drink holder and offered it to her.

"I'm sorry," she said, taking the bottle from him with shaking hands. "I hope I didn't scare you when you were driving."

"Just a little," he assured her. "A good driver always stays in control."

"Do you need a break?" Leah asked Nick.

"I could stretch my legs," he told her.

"What do you say we do that and then look for a place for supper?"

"Good idea. I saw a sign for a rest area two exits up. While we're there I can check the Internet for someplace local to eat."

He was silent for a moment, studying Naomi. "That was some nightmare. You get them often?"

"I'm fine," she insisted. "Could we go to the rest area now?"

Color rose in her cheeks. Nick winced inwardly. He hadn't thought about asking her if she needed a break when she woke from the nightmare.

"Oh, sure." He started the van, checked that it was safe to get back on the road, and accelerated out into his lane.

She sensed his curiosity, but other than a couple of glances at her, he stayed silent.

Nick stretched his legs by walking around the rest area a couple of times.

He wondered if it was a law or something that all rest areas looked alike: squat concrete buildings without personality; restrooms that smelled of antiseptic but most of the time didn't look so clean. Vending machines full of the same snacks and soft drinks. Parents with children who rushed them into restrooms, and people who walked their dogs in areas where they were allowed—and where they weren't.

A state trooper sitting in his car doing paperwork eyed Naomi and Leah curiously. Nick figured that the man didn't often see Amish in this area.

Getting back into the van, Nick pulled out his iPhone, checked for local restaurants, and jotted them down on a notepad he kept in the car. There were no Amish restaurants in the area but he thought that his passengers might enjoy something different. Just the fact that Leah was enthusiastic about going to Florida for a vacation told him she was a bit of an adventurer. As for Naomi, she usually deferred to wherever the others wanted to go, from what he'd noticed.

He sensed a strength in her today, though, when she'd refused to stop and talk to John. Nick figured he wasn't the only one who saw John's angry expression and his hands clenched at his sides. It must have taken a lot for her to not even wave at him as they left.

She probably thought he hadn't seen her lips trembling and tears running down her cheeks before she wiped them away.

"We're back," Leah announced as she maneuvered with her crutches toward the vehicle. "Where shall we eat?"

Nick jumped out, helped her into the backseat, and opened the door for Naomi.

"I got you another bottle of water," she said, putting it into the drink holder. "Thank you for the one you gave me."

"You didn't need to do that," he said, waiting to shut her door.

"I wanted to," she told him.

Her eyes looked suspiciously bright, as if she'd been crying. She looked away, reaching for her seat belt.

Nick climbed into his seat and got them back on the road. He gestured with his hand at the list he'd made. "You and Leah look at that and decide where you'd like to eat. There are no Amish restaurants around."

"That's fine with us, right, Naomi? We want to experience some new things on vacation, *ya*?"

Naomi nodded. "Southern cooking, steak house, endless buffet, sushi." She leaned around the seat and looked at her grandmother. "Sushi?"

"Raw fish," Leah told her.

Wrinkling her nose, Naomi glanced at Nick. "Why would anyone want to eat raw fish? Even you *Englisch* who are so obsessed with time?"

"It's . . . an acquired taste," Nick told her.

"Acquired, huh?" She thought about that. "Who wants to acquire a taste for raw fish?"

"Lots of people."

"Have you ever tried it?" When he nodded, she asked him, "Did you like it?"

He laughed and shook his head. "It tasted . . . spongy. I kept chewing and chewing and finally spit it into my napkin when no one was looking. My friend suggested I try the next piece with some wasabi. I'd never tried wasabi. It's like inhaling fire."

"So, spongy fish that hasn't been cooked, wasabi that tastes like fire, and it's expensive. I think I can resist that."

Nick grinned at her. "What about you, Leah? Want to try sushi?"

"I'll pass. That all-you-can-eat buffet sounds like a good idea. They should have something for all of us there, don't you think?"

"As long as it's food, it's good enough for me."

"Except for sushi," Naomi said.

"Except for sushi," he agreed.

Naomi leaned back in her seat. The nightmare had faded to a distant memory. It had probably happened because she was so overtired from getting ready for the trip and because she was feeling guilty about not talking to John when he showed up in the driveway.

She had a faint headache from the intensity of the nightmare and the tears she'd shed in the cubicle in the rest area. Washing her face had helped, and she had some ibuprofen in her purse if the headache didn't go away. If Nick had noticed that her eyes were red when she climbed back into the vehicle he'd said nothing.

The all-you-can-eat buffet was a welcome sight. It had been a long time since they'd stopped and eaten the sandwiches Leah had packed for lunch.

A long steam table revolved, offering selections that went into a cutout in the wall so that the cooks in the kitchen could keep the containers constantly filled with hot food.

"Well, this is my kind of place," Nick said with satisfaction. "You know, Leah, this'll make it easy on you. Pick whatever you like as it goes past and I'll fill your plate and bring it to you."

She chuckled. "I think someone just improved on passing a platter up and down the table."

He carried her plate to a table and then joined Naomi at the food. She served herself and sat with her grandmother. Nick joined them a few minutes later, set a loaded plate down, and took a seat.

"Did you get enough?" Leah asked tongue-in-cheek as she grinned at Nick.

"I can always go back," he assured her. "You should see the dessert buffet."

They bent their heads in silent thanks for the meal, then began eating.

"How much further will we go today?" Leah asked.

"It's up to you," he told her. "How's the ankle?"

"Not too bad."

"You'd tell me the truth, right?"

"*Ya*," she said, looking at him.

"Be better if we don't push it too much. We can find a nice place to stay for the night, get some ice on your ankle, and then start out bright and early in the morning."

"Sounds like a good plan." Leah looked up and smiled at the waitress who came to fill their coffee cups. "Tell me, young lady, what's the best thing on the dessert buffet?"

"It's a toss-up between the cherry cobbler and the blackberry pie," the woman said. "How 'bout I go get you a little of both?"

"That would be *wunderbaar*," Leah told her with a smile.

"We don't see many Amish in these parts," the woman told her. "Where you headed?"

"Pinecraft. It's on the Gulf Coast, in Sarasota, Florida. It's a little place some Amish and Mennonites go for vacation."

The waitress turned and looked out the window that overlooked the parking lot. "Y'all got your horse and buggy out there?"

Nick laughed. "No, it'd be too difficult to travel from Lancaster County to Florida," he told her. "They have to settle for my van."

Chuckling, the woman left them and returned with Leah's desserts. "I don't know if this can measure up to yours, ma'am. Paula does nothin' but bake her award-winning pies all day, although I hear there's nothing better than an Amish lady's cooking."

"You've got that right," Nick said. "Especially these two Amish ladies."

The waitress left them and Nick took a bite of the lemon meringue pie he'd gotten. "Not up to the lemon meringue you make, Leah," he whispered, looking around him to make sure he wasn't heard.

Naomi patted his hand. "Try to bear up," she said as he plowed through it with his usual enthusiasm for sweets. "We'll be in Pinecraft soon and there'll be Amish ladies cooking and baking there."

She pulled a paper napkin from the little wicker basket on the table. "Here, you have some meringue on your chin." She dabbed at the fluffy white stuff with the napkin and then happened to look up and saw his eyes darken at her touch. Quickly, she withdrew her hand and focused on her cobbler.

But when she glanced up a few minutes later, he was studying her.

Naomi prowled the motel room, fascinated by everything she found inside it.

She'd settled her grandmother on one of the two double beds with a pillow under her ankle and the ice bag filled with ice from a machine she found down the hall.

Now Naomi was exploring every nook and cranny. An automatic coffeepot sat on a dresser in the room with a basket full of coffees and teas to sample. A small refrigerator was available to store cold drinks. In the closet, she found laundry bags and instructions on how to have your clothes laundered if you wanted the service.

She'd just expected a bed and here was every convenience, so you didn't need to go out of the room.

Finally, done exploring, she sat on the bed in her nightgown and brushed her hair, finding the bedtime routine soothing.

"Aren't you tired yet?"

"Oh, I'm so sorry! You are and I'm keeping you awake."

"*Nee,*" Leah said. "I think having taken a nap in the car I might have trouble sleeping tonight."

"Me too," Naomi admitted.

"Maybe we need to talk about that nightmare."

"Forgot to brush my teeth," Naomi said and ducked into the bathroom.

When she came out a few minutes later, Leah was waiting, her arms folded across her chest.

"Teeth nice and clean?"

Naomi couldn't help but smile. "Minty fresh, too."

"Should be. That's the second time you've brushed them in the last half hour."

She sank down on her bed. "You don't miss anything, do you?" She smiled slightly. "But I don't need to talk about the nightmare. It was nothing. I was just overtired."

"You're sure?"

Sighing, Naomi studied her hairbrush and then looked at her grandmother. "I'm not happy that he showed up this morning to argue—to try to talk to me," she corrected.

Leah shook her head. "I'm sure the two of you will be talking when we get home." A huge yawn overtook her. "Well, maybe I *can* sleep tonight."

Naomi pulled the comforter and top sheet down, climbed into her bed, and scooted around to get comfortable. "Well, the bed is soft but the sheets don't smell like sunshine and lavender."

There was no answer from the other bed. She raised herself on her elbow and looked over. Her grandmother was already asleep. Naomi turned off the bedside lamp and lay back. It felt so strange to be in a motel. She'd slept in bedrooms other than her own but never in a motel room.

The room had been set up to make travelers comfortable and give them a good night's sleep. But the digital clock beside the bed told her she'd lain awake for more than two hours when she turned over and looked at it.

With a sigh, she flopped on her back. She was tired enough to sleep but suspected that the day had just been too stimulating.

Just as she finally drifted off she heard footsteps outside their room and through the gap in the drapes saw a man walk past, then retrace his steps, almost as if he were pacing instead of looking for a room.

She wondered about that for about a second, then sleep overtook her.

Nick knocked once on Naomi and Leah's door. "It's me, Nick. And coffee."

Naomi opened the door. "Coffee? There's a coffeemaker in our room."

"Really? There wasn't one in my room. Maybe someone took it with them and the cleaning staff didn't notice. Anyway, there's a little place right next door. And a Waffle House right down the road a piece."

She removed a cup of coffee from the drink tray in his hand. "A piece? How far is a piece?"

"Mile or two."

"Be right back," she said and turned to go back into the room. When she returned, she took her cup from him. "*Grossmudder* says she'll be just a minute."

Nick gestured at the two lawn chairs placed just outside the room and watched her take a seat, then sat beside her. "Did it work okay for two women to share one bathroom today? Did she give you first chance at getting ready this morning?"

"What?"

"My three sisters always had to take turns to get ready with one bathroom in the house. One of them always got the others mad at her for spending too much time in there putting on makeup."

He glanced at her and grinned. "I know. You don't wear makeup. If my sister had skin like yours she wouldn't, either."

She blinked at the compliment and looked a little flustered. He knew then that he'd gone too far.

"Expect you got it from your mother and she got it from your grandmother," he said quickly.

He took a sip of coffee and it was too hot, burning his tongue and then his throat going down. Served him right, he decided. This was an engaged Amish woman, for goodness sake.

"Ouch!" he said. "Careful, it's a little hot."

He watched her blow on the coffee and test it carefully before she took a sip.

Leah came to the door. "*Danki* for the *kaffe*, Nick."

"Ready to go get some breakfast?"

"When you've finished your coffee," Leah said. "We're on vacation, remember? No need to rush."

Nick watched Naomi's enjoyment of the coffee and the quiet, contented way she was taking in the sight of the sun rising. Leah was right, but he thought remembering his place right now might be a good idea.

"Have a seat while I get the luggage," he told her. "I can finish the coffee in the van."

5

Too bad we're driving straight through," Nick said as they walked to the van after lunch in a small restaurant off the interstate. "I found some great places to visit on a road trip going to Florida."

"Like what?" Naomi asked him as she helped her grandmother into the backseat.

"All sorts of little roadside attractions, unusual and strange things to see. I was on the Internet and made a list. I know we aren't going to any of them but I got a kick out of seeing what was on the way. Maybe I'll do it sometime. It's in with the map."

After fastening her seat belt, Naomi picked up the list. Virginia: "The Fletcher Farm Rhino? Someone has a rhinoceros on a farm?"

"Yeah. Don't see that on an Amish farm, do you?"

She laughed. "I doubt you see it on any *Englisch* ones, either. The ABC Cemetery?"

"Now that was a man who was really organized. He wanted everyone buried in alphabetical order, so he'd move people's coffins to keep it that way."

"And changed his name to one starting with Z when he knew it was his time to go," she said, reading the printout. "A car that runs on Kool-Aid—oh, I loved that stuff as a kid. *Mamm* let us have it once in a while in the summer. And there's a chunk of meteorite you can visit."

"Don't forget Gilligan's Island Bed and Breakfast." He looked at her. "It was a television show. These people got stranded on an island."

"So then why would they want to go back?"

He thought about it and then laughed. "People who watched the show loved it. They like to go to the B & B. Just like *Star Trek* show fans. They visit The Spock—the World's Only Church of Star Trek."

"The NASCAR Cap Museum. Guess we could go get you another cap."

"A man can never have enough."

"I saw five in the back of the van."

"I know. I didn't bring all of mine. Had to leave some room for the stuff you ladies needed to bring."

Naomi laughed and rolled her eyes. "The World's Largest Ten Commandments."

"North Carolina?"

"The world's largest strawberry. And the largest strawberry building. Why would anyone build something that looked like a strawberry?"

"Because they can?" he said, grinning. "What about South Carolina?"

"World Grits Festival. Oh, wrong time of year to go."

"What about Pinecraft?"

"Pinecraft Park has shuffleboard and all kinds of sports to play like volleyball," Naomi said, reading from the computer printout Nick had provided. "Siesta Key is the beach just a short distance away. The neighborhood of Pinecraft is really small—less than a mile in each direction—but it says here that in the winter the population swells to thousands. Guess we're adding three to those numbers."

Leah leaned forward, "Anything interesting in Florida?" she asked. "I mean, other than Pinecraft?"

Nick heard the irony in her voice and he laughed. "A castle made of coral. Weeki Wachee Springs, which is an attraction with real live mermaids. Jungle Gardens in Sarasota."

"Well, maybe we can visit one of those fascinating places in those places on the way back," Leah responded dryly. "So what are you going to do after you drop us off, Nick?"

He glanced at her in the rearview mirror. "First, I need to thank your friend Ida for finding me a room to rent. Then I'm going to spend some serious time at the beach. I haven't been to one in years. Got a whole lot of books to read."

Naomi had noticed that Nick was a reader, often finding him with a book or his e-reader when he arrived a little early to pick them up at the shop. Today, a Bible lay on the seat between them.

She glanced out the window and watched the scenery. Too little sleep the last two nights, the monotony of the interstate, and the lunch she'd eaten were combining to make her sleepy.

"Tired?"

"A little. It was hard to get to sleep last night."

"Excited about taking a vacation?"

She nodded, not willing to tell him what a country mouse she was, never having stayed in a motel—or, probably a bigger reason, that she was feeling guilty about John.

He glanced in the rear seat, then looked at her. "Try to relax and have a little fun even if you're going there for her."

She smiled slightly. "I'll try."

"Oh, the enthusiasm," he said with a laugh. "Try to calm down."

"Did you have trouble sleeping last night?"

"No. Slept like a log. Why?"

"Someone was walking back and forth in front of the room. I thought maybe you were having trouble sleeping."

"Nope. Maybe it was someone having trouble finding his room. Maybe he went out and had a few too many at a local bar after getting a room, then couldn't find it when he came back."

"Oh."

"Sorry, I shouldn't say such things in front of you."

"And why is that?"

"You don't need to know about matters not of your world."

"I'm hardly innocent."

"What does that mean?"

Naomi rolled her eyes. She'd forgotten about her grandmother in the backseat. She turned and looked into the back- seat. "You know what I mean. Just because we're Amish doesn't mean that we don't know about drinking and such."

"How much do you know about drinking?"

"I just mean it's not like we don't know about the *Englisch* world. We hear things, we read things. That's all. I certainly didn't drink when I did my *rumschpringe*."

She shrugged when Nick glanced over. "You know it's just the *Englisch* media that thinks Amish youth run around being wild and drinking on their *rumschpringe*."

"You don't have to convince me," Nick told her. "Remember, I've lived in Pennsylvania for a decade."

"You said something about a road trip yesterday," she said after a moment. "About how you and your buddies went on them during a break from college."

His smile was reminiscent. "Yeah. Great times." Then his smile faded. "Sorry, there weren't a lot of PG moments."

"Pig moments?"

He laughed until tears ran down his cheeks. "No, PG. That's short for saying something's clean enough to be discussed in front of kids."

He glanced at her. "Or in front of Amish *maedels*."

She sniffed and folded her arms across her chest. "You seem to enjoy telling me how backward you think I am."

"I don't think you're backward," he said seriously. "It's just fun to tease you."

"I don't remember you doing it this much before," she said.

"No. Guess that's the perk of having more time with you. And not having Anna in the car. Teasing her's like teasing your younger sister."

A car slowed in front of them and Nick braked quickly. When the car picked up speed, he did the same.

"So what's teasing me like?" she asked.

He glanced at her, then back at the road ahead. Opened his mouth and then shut it.

Interesting, she thought. She'd never seen him at a loss for words.

She'd become quiet again, thought Nick.

Usually it was refreshing when people were quiet in the vehicle after all the chattering some people did. But he liked to talk to Naomi.

Maybe too much.

"Are you warm enough?"

She smiled and nodded. Turning, she started to ask her grandmother if she was comfortable. But Leah was sleeping.

"She nodded off a few minutes ago," Nick told her.

"I'm afraid her ankle is hurting her. She tossed and turned a lot last night."

There was silence between them as the miles sped by.

"You're sure you're warm enough?"

"Yes."

"Not too warm?"

"Nick, I'm fine. What's going on?"

"You're being awfully quiet."

"I'm a quiet person. You know that." She grinned. "Sometimes it's hard to get a word in edgewise with Anna in the car, remember?"

"I wouldn't know," he said, returning her grin. "A driver always exercises great discretion. We never talk about a passenger."

"Right," she said, drawing out the word.

"Just seems like you're unusually quiet today."

"I'm okay."

But he noticed that she was massaging her forearm. "Did you hurt yourself?"

She nodded. "Bumped it last night."

He glanced at her, then at the rearview mirror. Leah was still napping.

"What would you like to talk about?" Naomi asked him.

"What makes you think I want to talk?"

She cast her eyes heavenward and blew out a breath. "You sounded like you wanted to talk."

"Nope. S'okay."

Naomi folded her arms across her chest and stared at the windshield. "Well, no surprise," she muttered.

"Huh?"

She bit her lip. "Nothing."

"Naomi."

Shrugging, she looked out her window. "It's not like I'm a—a scintillating conversationalist anyway."

"Scintillating?"

She glared at him. "And no remarks about my education. I know I didn't go to college like you."

"I'm impressed. I know some professors who don't use the word *scintillating*."

"You're just saying that."

He gave her a brief glance. "I don't flatter, Naomi."

"Some men do," she muttered.

He almost didn't catch her words. He'd recognized John as a charmer. "Well, I'm enjoying talking to you."

"Anna's the talker of the three of us at the shop."

"I know."

She grinned.

"So you're not going to say that it's hard to be in a car with four women who like to talk?"

He said nothing. But he wasn't able to hide his grin from her and she returned it.

Speaking of her grandmother . . . she thought he was doing her a big favor driving her to Florida. But the truth was that he really was looking to take some time off. The fact that Naomi had said she was going along to take care of her grandmother was just icing on the cake.

He just hadn't realized just how much being close to Naomi was both a pleasure and a torment.

Naomi was enjoying talking to Nick entirely too much.

Her grandmother had even told her that Nick refused to take anything for driving them and was only willing to take half the cost of gas. He didn't know it yet, but Naomi intended on making him take some money when it came time to pay.

Considering everything, it seemed like the least she could do was talk to him. Maybe it was boring to drive endless miles on the interstate.

She, at least, could spend time looking at the signs he called billboards but could only give a glance since he was driving the speed limit.

"Alligator Farm just ahead," she read aloud and then she laughed.

"What's so funny?"

"The python painted on the sign says, 'No waiting. No pressure,'" she told him.

"Ha-ha."

"Is that one of those places you two want to visit on the way home?" Leah asked.

Naomi shivered. "I don't think I want to see pythons. Or alligators. You, Nick?"

He chuckled. "They were fun when I was a kid, but I can skip them now."

Naomi went back to looking out her window, searching for something to say. A SUV pulled up alongside them and she found herself captivated by the antics of the children in the backseat.

There was some pushing and shoving between a boy of about eight and a teenage girl. She was trying to keep him from getting into an overnight bag and pulling things out.

Then the boy looked over and saw Naomi staring at him. His glance went to the window behind her. Leah must be watching too, she thought.

Turning, he reached into the overnight bag and pulled something white out—a bra, she realized. He popped it on his head, tied it under his chin, and gazed piously toward heaven.

No amount of being hit on the head by his sister deterred him from his antics.

Naomi stared, too shocked to react, and then she collapsed in giggles. Turning in her seat, she peered at her grandmother. "Did you see—" she stopped.

Leah had her arms wrapped around her middle and she was laughing.

"You too?" she asked Naomi between giggles.

"Yes."

"What's so funny?" Nick wanted to know. "What's going on?"

Naomi turned back in her seat and looked for the vehicle. "Speed up a bit and you'll see," she told him.

The boy was still wearing his sister's bra on his head, imitating the Amish *kapps* Naomi and Leah both wore.

Nick accelerated and caught a glimpse of what was going on. Naomi could tell the moment he did without even asking him. Nick's guffaw was all she needed.

"I'm sorry," Nick said quickly. "I'll signal the driver that his kids are being disrespectful—"

"You'll do no such thing," Leah said, laughing. "He's rather funny."

Naomi wiped the tears from her cheeks.

"Besides, look at that poor man," Leah said. "It can't be easy driving with a herd of *kinner* all excited about going somewhere."

The turn signal flicked on and the driver guided the SUV down the exit to Alligator Farm.

"I hope they don't let that boy hug the python," Naomi said. "I'd fear for it."

"I remember my dad taking me places like that when I was a kid," Nick said. "We drove him crazy. 'Are we there yet? Are we there yet?'"

Leah leaned forward. "Are we there yet?"

Nick laughed and made a check of the traffic to his right and then moved into the lane to take the next exit. "Let's go get some coffee."

He took them to one of those restaurants that advertised country food as well as a gift shop.

Leah made short work of her coffee and pie and then headed off to the gift shop, insisting that she'd be fine walking with her crutches and that he and Naomi should stay where they were and finish.

"Not much longer now," Nick said, leaning back in his chair. "We'll be there by nightfall."

Naomi rubbed at the side of her neck. "Good."

"Headache?"

"More a little stiffness, that's all. From the enforced sitting. I'm used to moving around more."

"Do you want to take a walk before we drive some more?"

"No. I'd rather keep going. Unless you need a break."

He took another sip of coffee. "I'm fine. I'm a little more used to sitting in a car seat for a long time than you are."

"Don't know how you do it." She reached for the check but he snatched it up before she could and stood to pull out her chair.

"Grandmother wouldn't be happy to find out you paid that."

"So don't tell her," he said casually. Then he stopped. "Sorry, I didn't mean to joke. I know you'd never lie."

She looked at him. If only he knew. Pretending that nothing was wrong . . . that was a lie, even if she never said anything, that was a lie. Wasn't it? Not that Nick needed to know about what she'd been going through with John.

Her grandmother hadn't needed to hear about it, either. Naomi felt she'd burdened her by telling her that John had hurt her. Now, Naomi watched Leah making her way toward her carefully with her crutches and felt an overwhelming rush of guilt.

If her grandmother hadn't been upset that day—first by her and then by Anna—she would have been watching her step as she went after Anna. She wouldn't have injured herself. Her face wouldn't be drawn with pain.

The minute Leah looked up and saw Naomi, her face changed. She smiled, and it was as if someone had wiped away the pain.

So her grandmother knew how to hide her feelings, her pain, Naomi thought.

"Wait until you see what I found," Leah said, holding up a plastic shopping bag. "Pecan praline candy."

Nick took the bag from her hand. "Let me carry that for you."

Nick enjoyed watching Naomi's interest pick up as he signaled to exit the interstate.

He had to admit he felt pretty interested himself. He'd been to Florida just once, on a family vacation, and it had seemed like a strange and wonderful place to a ten-year-old boy. As he'd gotten older, his father hadn't always been keen on a vacation that involved getting behind the wheel of the car. He was too tired of ferrying other people around, he'd said. It had taken a lot of persuading by Nick and his mother to get his father behind the wheel for a road trip. By the time he had become a teen, Nick had lost interest and wanted to stick around and have fun with his pals in the summer.

His father was fascinated with what he called the "real" Florida—the places that were a unique mix of the old, eccentric Florida that drew the curious. The places unlike those in any other state.

Nick had been a little bored seeking out anyplace but a beach. That was before he saw his first roadside alligator attraction near the Everglades, where they watched a man actually climb into a pen to be near one and not run screaming like a girl as Nick would have done. Nick had sat, entranced, as the trainer grasped the reptile and not only managed to not get eaten but actually talked to it and stroked the gator's throat and stomach until it went to sleep!

They explored swampy places in the Everglades with trees that dripped strands of something called Spanish moss that looked like the gray beards of old men—and with shifting pools of quicksand that were said to have caught men unaware.

There were Native Americans there who didn't dress like the ones he'd seen in other states. The women wore bright cotton skirts and shirts with intricate pattern bands on them and arranged their hair in an unusual topknot. The men wore long shirts and trousers, not feathers like in other states.

Those road trips and being around his father's business had led to Nick's interest in making transportation his career after community college. He'd joined the business in driving the Amish and the tourists who came to visit the area and had taken over when his father died two years ago.

He'd remembered that long-ago Florida trip when Leah began talking about Pinecraft. So it had been intriguing to him when Leah mentioned Florida. He'd always wanted to come back and hadn't found the time or the money. Then suddenly, it seemed it all worked out for both Leah and him to have what they wanted. And Naomi coming along hadn't hurt.

He had to admit to a strong attraction to Naomi. But it was just that—a strong attraction that couldn't go anywhere. He wasn't looking to break up her relationship. Even if he'd wanted to, something couldn't happen between them.

Then, too, he was pretty realistic about why a woman might or might not be interested in him. He surely didn't have the looks, personality, or money as enticements to have a relationship—not that Naomi could ever be considered someone interested in him for money. The trip had shown him that. She'd been upset when he paid for their coffee and snack yesterday and had asked a number of times how they were going to reimburse him.

He glanced in the rearview mirror. Leah was glued to her window. When she realized he was looking at her, she grinned. "Do you need directions to the cottage?"

"Already got them in the GPS," he told her.

They traveled down a wide boulevard with waving palm trees and then Nick turned at a light.

"I see I won't have to miss Amish food," he said with satisfaction as they caught a glimpse of Yoder's Amish Restaurant to the right.

"You know you're going to be eating with us a lot," Leah told him. "We wouldn't let you starve after you went to all the trouble of driving us here."

"That's hardly a vacation for you if you're cooking," Nick said.

"But I love to cook," Leah protested. "And here I'll have more time than I do after a workday."

"You're staying off that ankle," Naomi told her firmly.

Dozens of charming little houses came into view, all with scrupulously tended lawns. Brightly colored flowers bloomed in pots everywhere. Nick half-expected to see little bluebirds fluttering from the trees.

"They look like little fairy tale cottages," Naomi mused. "Don't they look like the ones in the storybook I had when I was a girl?" she asked, turning to her grandmother.

"They do," Leah marveled. "What a pretty place to vacation."

"There are some year-round residents, I'm told," Nick said. He wasn't as fanciful as Naomi, guessing these were the smallish cottages built in Florida after World War II. But he'd never seen homes so meticulously kept up.

He drove slowly around the streets—they were packed with visitors dressed in Amish and Mennonite garb—past the shuffleboard court where people played one last game as dusk fell. Others were cleaning up from what appeared to be a community barbecue dinner. Nick had opened the windows on the van and the sweet, smoky flavor hung on the warm air.

Nick was being so careful of pedestrians that he must have turned down the wrong street, because the GPS spoke up, saying, "Reconfiguring" in its flat, almost metallic voice.

He drove a little bit longer—the community wasn't that big, more a neighborhood or village in Sarasota than an actual town—and as he pulled into the drive of a little cottage painted a sunny yellow, the GPS announced that they were at their destination.

Turning to Naomi, he saw her staring at the house. Curious, he glanced back and saw nothing unusual.

"Someone left a light burning."

"Yeah. Nice of them, since we weren't sure if it'd be dark when we arrived."

"Does this mean the place is wired for it?"

Nick spied a window air conditioning unit. "Yes. And that's an air conditioner—probably for when the place is rented during the summer."

Naomi gave the house a doubtful glance. "I doubt we'll use the electricity."

"It's easy as pie," he told her. "You just flick a switch."

Her eyes narrowed. "You're not making fun of me, are you?"

"Teasing," he said. "Sorry. Do you need me to go in with you both and see if you need anything?"

"I think I can manage," she said dryly.

They got out of the car. Naomi thought she could smell the scent of the ocean on the cool evening air. But maybe that was her imagination.

Leah just stared at the cottage. "I can't believe we're really here."

Nick nodded as he opened the rear of the vehicle and began taking out their luggage. "We are indeed, ladies."

He carried the suitcases into the house and set them down by the front door. Then, looking around, he leaned in and whispered in a conspiratorial tone, "Before we left I heard one of the Lancaster County men who's visited here say that what happens in Florida stays in Florida."

There was a steady stream of visitors the next day, starting with Ida, Daniel's mother.

Naomi watched the two women embrace and knew she'd done the right thing helping her grandmother travel here to visit her longtime friend.

Ida held out a basket of oranges. "I picked these for you from my own tree."

She placed them on the kitchen counter along with a coffee cake and some farm-fresh eggs.

"The cottage is perfect," Leah told her, gesturing for her friend to take a seat at the kitchen table. "But there was no need for you to stock the refrigerator and cupboards with food."

"Of course there was," Ida said, accepting a cup of tea from Naomi. "How's the ankle?"

"She always says 'fine,'" Naomi told her. "I'm hoping she'll stay off it for a few days before we start exploring."

"Maybe a day or two," Leah said, pulling the coffee cake over and cutting pieces for them.

"So what's on the agenda?" Ida wanted to know.

Leah held up her hand and began ticking off on her fingers, "Naomi and I read the copy of the *Pinecraft Pauper* newspaper you left on the table. We're looking forward to all sorts of activities, starting with Nick driving us to Pinecraft Park tonight for shuffleboard—"

"Shuffleboard?" Naomi nearly shrieked. "What? What's he thinking? You can't be playing shuffleboard right now!"

"I won't be playing, I'll be watching," Leah said mildly. "Really, *liebschen*, do you think I've lost my senses as well as my ability to get around?"

Naomi bit her lip. "No."

Leah tilted her head to one side. "Did you think Nick would let me do something like that?"

"Well, I think Nick's smarter than that," Naomi said slowly, thinking about it. "But I know you, and you do what you want to do."

Ida laughed and set down her cup of tea. "She knows you well, Leah."

"*Ya*, indeed she does." She put a slice of coffee cake on a plate and set it before Naomi. "But if you're worried, then maybe you'd like to go along and make sure that I don't do something foolish."

Naomi stared at her grandmother. "Well," she said finally, "I did see you take a flying leap out of the store not so long ago."

Her grandmother pursed her lips, and then the crinkles around her eyes deepened and she chuckled. "I am quite the athlete, am I not? Who knows what I could do on the shuffleboard court!"

6

Before Ida left, she had a surprise for them.

"My cousin is coming in on one of the chartered buses today," she announced. "Everyone turns out to see who's on a bus from up north. Sometimes they have a relative or friend, but even if they don't, it's fun to see the new arrivals and say good-bye to those going back home."

There was a knock on the door. "That'll be Caleb," she told Naomi.

Caleb, her husband, had a surprise of his own. "I brought a wagon for you, Leah, if you'd like to come with us," he said. "*Kumm*, see how you like it."

Naomi helped Leah with her crutches and they walked outside.

Leah laughed. "Well, it's no coach, but it's no pumpkin either."

Caleb had fixed up a small wagon—bigger than a child's wagon, one that a small woman like Leah could fit in—and lined it with a pillow and blankets to make it more comfortable to sit in.

"You don't have to go if you don't want to," Ida told her. "Caleb just wanted you to have a chance to if you wanted. It's one of the social events here, seeing who's arrived."

"*Schur*, I'm willing to give it a try," Leah said and let Naomi and Caleb help her get seated.

"Take or leave?" Naomi asked, holding up the crutches.

"Leave," Leah said without hesitation. "I doubt I'll want to get out and walk around if there's a crowd of people."

Caleb picked up the handle and began pulling the wagon along the sidewalk.

They'd traveled just a few feet when Leah burst out laughing. "I bet I make quite a sight."

Ida's laugh was rich and deep. "*Ya*. But wait until you see how everyone gets around here. There are no horses and buggies so we use three-wheelers and bicycles and wagons like Caleb's to get groceries. Neighborhood seems too small to do anything else."

She shot a glance at Caleb. "Until you go to haul some Yoder's produce home. Then you're grateful for the wagon, eh, Caleb?"

Leah laughed. "Just pretend I'm a load of produce, Caleb."

Naomi smiled. It was wonderful to see how much her grandmother had cheered up. She couldn't wait to tell her cousins.

People were hurrying toward the spot where the chartered bus, its side decorated with a mural of a train, sat. If you were a little nearsighted, you could almost think a train had pulled in and passengers were stepping down from it.

"My cousin from Indiana is on the bus," Ida said. "I can't wait to see her."

Female passengers wearing a variety of dress styles and *kapps* descended the steps, some of them carrying tired-looking children who blinked in the glare of the bright Florida sun. The men went to retrieve luggage from the belly of the bus.

Greetings were exchanged and the visitors were escorted off to stay with relatives and friends or went to places they'd rented for their stay.

Ida went off to get her cousin settled at her place and Caleb pulled Leah home in the wagon.

"Hey, stealing one of my favorite passengers?"

Naomi's eyes widened as she saw Nick strolling up. Her heart lifted and the day seemed just a little brighter.

Caleb turned and chuckled. "*Ya*, and I'll be taking her all the way back to Pennsylvania in my fine conveyance here when she's ready to go home."

Nick reached out his hand and helped Leah up from the wagon.

"Let me get her crutches," Naomi said quickly.

"No need," he said, scooping up a surprised Leah and carrying her up the walk.

Naomi fished in her pocket for the key and unlocked the front door. Nick set Leah down inside and handed her the crutches that Naomi had left nearby.

"You do love the grand gesture, don't you?" Leah said and reached up a hand to pat his cheek affectionately. "Would you like a cup of tea?"

"Love one."

Naomi rushed into the kitchen so her grandmother wouldn't have the chance to get near the stove. Nick winked at her, showing her he was aware of what she was doing.

He pulled out a chair and got Leah settled at the table with her ankle on another chair, seated himself, and gave his attention to the plate of cookies Naomi set before him.

"I came by to see when you wanted to go to the shuffleboard court this evening," he said around a mouthful of cookie. "Mmm. What's in these?"

"Butterscotch chips, oatmeal, walnuts." Naomi pulled a plastic baggie from a box and slid half a dozen inside before handing it to him.

"Well," he said. "I'll have to stop by more often."

"Have you left yet?" she asked as she met his gaze.

He laughed. "You just love to zing me, don't you?"

She just smiled.

"So. Shuffleboard court?"

"I'm game anytime," Leah said. "But Caleb just took the wagon."

"I can do better than that." Nick took another cookie from the plate. "My wheels are parked outside. Guess you didn't see when you came home."

Naomi hadn't. She'd been too happy to see *him*. It had been a little boring that day, she told herself. She wasn't used to being so idle. To not have Mary Katherine and Anna around. To not have her quilting. And while the visitors who stopped by were nice, she felt a little cooped up.

In the very next moment, she felt a stab of guilt. The reason she was here was to help her grandmother. Any fun was a bonus.

"So what do you say? Shall we go check out the shuffleboard?"

"This can't be exciting for you," Leah said as they climbed into the van a little while later.

"I'm enjoying everything," he said, at ease behind the wheel as he threaded the vehicle through narrow streets and watched out for people suddenly jaywalking without looking. "Besides, I'm going fishing later in the week."

Naomi started to say that she loved fishing—that she always tagged along with her older brother. But that might look like she was trying to get herself invited along. Maybe Nick was even going with someone.

She sighed.

"What?"

Looking at him, she shook her head. "Nothing."

Pinecraft Park seemed like it was the place to be. Dozens and dozens of Amish and Mennonite visitors swarmed the place playing shuffleboard, chatting in groups, and just generally enjoying the balmy temperature. Back home in Lancaster County it was in the thirties, and even colder in other parts up north.

Nick dropped Leah and Naomi off at the courts and had to drive around and around to find a parking place. When he returned, he found Leah sitting on one of the wooden benches that surrounded the court, her foot propped up on an upside-down pail someone had found.

And Naomi was deep in a discussion with Daniel Kurtz, Ida and Caleb's son who he'd met back in Paradise. Daniel was a big strapping blond Amish guy who seemed to be paying a little too much attention to Naomi as far as Nick was concerned.

Nick's stomach sank. Which was really stupid when he thought about it because he had no claim on Naomi. After all, she was engaged to John Zook. Was he going to be jealous of two men now?

He strolled up casually. Daniel appeared to recognize him. He stood and offered his hand.

"Nick, right? You have a transportation company in Paradise? Are you enjoying your vacation?"

"Having a great time."

"*Gut*. So glad you could drive Leah and Naomi down." He waved a hand at the bench. "Saved you a seat."

They watched the action for a while. The Amish loved sports, enjoying volleyball, basketball, and softball—back home and here. The shuffleboard court seemed especially popular, and not just with the older crowd.

"Naomi's catching me up on what's happening back in Paradise. We went to *schul* together." He gave a heavy sigh. "Says she's engaged."

"It's not flattering to have you acting like that when I know you were interested in my cousin Mary Katherine," Naomi pointed out.

He grimaced. "Sorry. But think how I feel. We have a small Amish Mennonite community here, so when all the visitors come down during the winter I try to meet someone. But they're only here for a week or two and then they go back home. It feels like my time is spent with the 'tourist of the week.'"

"Someone *female*," she inserted, grinning.

"I'm ready to get married," he said earnestly. "Maybe you know someone. Look around," he told them, gesturing at their surroundings. "What could be a more beautiful place to live?"

Naomi had to agree. What she'd seen of Florida so far was lovely. The sky seemed a more vivid blue here. There were warm temperatures and flowers blooming in the midst of winter. It was truly paradise.

Thinking of the word made her think of home—Paradise, Pennsylvania. And John. She hadn't talked to him since she came here. Nick had offered her the use of his cell phone on the trip—and since—and Leah had taken him up on the offer and checked in with Mary Katherine and Anna at the shop during business hours to see how things were going.

But even though Nick looked curious at her refusal, he said nothing.

"Excuse me," Daniel said as he stood. "Mary Graber said she'd bring her niece tonight after she came in on the bus."

Naomi saw an older woman gesturing from the other side of the court. Beside her stood someone Naomi's age. The young woman smiled shyly at Daniel as he hurried over to her.

"That's tough about Daniel. I hope this girl isn't the latest 'tourist of the week.'"

The crowd shifted as games ended and new people took to the court. Naomi felt a prickling at the back of her neck, as if the hairs rose. It was the strangest feeling—as if someone was watching.

She glanced around but no one seemed to be paying attention. People chatted with one another as they watched the shuffleboard action and generally milled around. A man's hat bobbed as he walked behind the line of spectators, but she couldn't see his face. Naomi frowned and then shook her head. Must have been her imagination, she decided.

"I think I'll take a walk," she told her grandmother and Nick.

He dragged his attention away from a game. "Mind if I go with? I have a hankering for some ice cream at Big Olaf's."

"Who says I'm going that way?"

"Don't be silly," he said. "You need ice cream."

He rose and turned to Leah. "What can we bring you?"

"Maybe a root beer float?"

"Turning wild and crazy there, Leah," he said, and her chuckle followed them as they walked away.

Nick slid a glance at Naomi as they moved through the crowd. "You okay?"

"Fine."

"You looked a little rattled there for a minute when we were at the court."

Naomi shrugged. "I thought I saw someone I know, that's all."

He scanned the crowd. "It wouldn't surprise me. A lot of people here came down from Lancaster County. I'm getting better about recognizing what area of the country they come from by the clothing."

Naomi's prayer covering was made of a rather delicate material that was translucent so that her hair showed beneath, and it had a back that was shaped rather like a butterfly. The *kapps* worn in other parts of the country were opaque, sometimes with a sort of cylindrical shape made of stiff, tucked cotton.

There wasn't a lot of difference in the men's clothing, she noted: dark pants, shirts, suspenders. Children wore a miniature version of their parents' clothing, and since it was so warm here, many of them ran barefoot.

"Looks like we have a wait," Nick told Naomi as they neared Big Olaf's. "Do you want to go someplace else?"

He saw her eyes widen as a young boy walked past with a strawberry sundae. The strawberries were a rich, deep red, and huge.

"I don't think so," she said. "It looks like it's worth the wait. And the line's going fast."

When their turn came, they ordered—the strawberry sundae for Naomi, a banana split for Nick, and Leah's root beer float—and then they walked back to the shuffleboard court to enjoy them.

Nick's cell went off and he set the banana split down on the bench between them to take it. One of Nick's drivers had an important question about work that was soon resolved.

Nick started to put the phone back in his pocket and then turned to Naomi and Leah. "Would either of you like to call home? The shop's still open."

"Maybe tomorrow," said Leah. "I don't want Mary Katherine or Anna to think I'm checking up on them too often."

She continued to drink her float and they heard a gurgling noise as she sipped the last of it. Grinning, she set it down. "My, that was good. Makes me remember my childhood when my *mamm* made them as a special treat for us."

Nick turned to Naomi. "Would you like to call your fiancé? I can get his number at his work, if you like."

"No," she said quickly, a little more quickly than he expected.

"Okay." Tucking the phone in his pants pocket, he picked up the banana split and resumed eating.

There it was again, he thought. The quick snap of Naomi's head as she turned to look at something to the far right, her eyes scanning the crowd.

"What is it?" Leah asked, looking curiously at her granddaughter. "Naomi?"

"It's so strange," she said. "I feel like someone's watching me."

"I don't see anyone doing that," Leah told her.

Nick glanced around and saw nothing out of the ordinary. "Do you want me to take you home?"

She shook her head. "No, it must just be my imagination."

"Maybe it's because we're not usually around so many people at one time," Leah offered, patting her on the back.

"Maybe."

But even though she brushed off the offer to take her home and seemed to go back to watching the shuffleboard players and eating her sundae, Nick noticed that she was merely stirring the ice cream and strawberries on top until it was a melted puddle in the dish.

Nick finished his split and disposed of the container in a nearby trash can. He took his seat again and looked at her sundae. "You gonna eat that or stir it to death?"

She laughed. "It was a little too much for me, I guess."

"Here, I'll finish it for you," he said.

"I'll go get you another spoon," she said, starting to rise.

He gave her a look. "I'm not afraid of you having cooties."

"Okay," she said, sitting again.

But maybe he shouldn't have spoken so soon. As he put the spoon in his mouth, he thought about how she'd slid the utensil between those perfect pale pink lips of hers and tried not to let his reaction show on his face. He didn't want to shock Naomi's sensibilities.

The strawberries were tart on his tongue, a contrast to the sweet vanilla ice cream. He wondered if the taste lingered on Naomi's lips.

"So have you been to the beach yet, Nick?" Leah asked him.

"I was thinking about going tomorrow. You two want to go with me?"

"I have plans with Ida."

"Naomi?"

The beach. She'd never been to one. Never seen an ocean.

Nick saw emotions chase across her face: desire, longing.

"C'mon, it'll be fun."

Leah nudged her. "Go. You've never seen the ocean."

Nick knew that an engaged woman—especially an Amish engaged woman—had to avoid all appearance of inappropriateness. "You don't have to worry about me chasing you up and down the beach."

She regarded him primly. "I know that." Sighing, she nodded. "I'd love to go."

Naomi slipped out the front door, trying not to wake her grandmother.

Nick was standing beside his vehicle and opened the door for her. "Leah didn't change her mind about going?"

"No."

"Shuffleboard wasn't too much for her last night, was it?"

"No, of course not. She's been good about sitting with her foot up on something." She got in and waited for him to get in his own seat. "But I have to admit I was worried she'd try to play a game when I first heard that she was going to go there."

He started the car. "Is that why you came?"

"No. I realized I was being overprotective. I went because I wanted to see what was happening."

"Hot spot of Pinecraft from what I hear."

She fastened her seat belt and sighed. "I'm so looking forward to this."

He'd dressed casually on the trip, foregoing his usual white dress shirt, dark pants, and subdued tie. Instead, he'd worn khakis, polo shirts, and sneakers.

Today, he wore a pair of baggy knee-length shorts and a loose tank top. And a Miami Dolphins cap and leather sandals. He looked relaxed and comfortable.

Meanwhile she was sitting here in her usual dress and black stockings and shoes, already feeling a little warm.

He got in his seat and handed her a cup of coffee from a take-out place before starting the engine.

Surprised, she took it and found that it was fixed just the way she liked—extra milk and sugar. "You didn't have to do this."

"Got donuts too," he said, gesturing at the bag on the seat between them.

"Well, that's certainly worth getting up early for," she said, opening the bag to peer inside.

"And this is all nothing compared to your first glimpse of the ocean."

He glanced down at her legs. "Oh, I hadn't thought . . ." he broke off and frowned. "Listen, I bought you something, but maybe you need to go back inside and change."

"I'm not wearing a bikini to go to the beach," she said tartly.

Nick laughed. "I know that." He handed her another bag with the label of a gas station chain.

She pulled a pair of flip-flops from the bag. Her eyes widened. "I've never worn sandals like this."

"Later, you'll see nearly all the women and the teens and kids wearing them," he told her. "It's really warm here still, so you won't want to wear shoes and your—um—stockings."

She studied him in the growing light. "Why Nick, are you blushing?"

"'Course not," he said. "Men don't blush."

"Uh-huh. Whatever you say. I'll be right back."

She slid out of the vehicle and ran inside, where she kicked off her shoes and pulled off her stockings and then slipped on the flip-flops. It felt strange at first to feel the plastic thong between her big toe and the next one, to feel the bounce of rubber beneath her feet. And how cool they were. It could be addictive to feel the breeze across your bare toes.

She was grinning when she returned to Nick.

"Looks like you like them."

She looked down at her toes and wiggled them, then felt herself blush when Nick glanced over. Even though she went barefoot a lot growing up, and even did so now when she was at home, it felt almost immodest to wear these after having her feet cooped up in shoes for months now.

It was continuing to grow lighter outside. "We're on the west coast of the state so obviously the sunsets are supposed to be better here than the sunrises. I don't know about you, but I think a sunrise on a beach after the weather we've had in Pennsylvania is going to be pretty great."

Nick parked and they headed to the beach, Naomi carrying her coffee and the bag of donuts, Nick with a blanket he kept in the van. Seagulls flew overhead and followed them, one with a beady eye fixed on the donut bag. She breathed in the scent of the ocean and felt her heart beating faster with excitement.

He was so right about how she'd feel when she caught her first glimpse of the ocean. The water glimmered like a milky opal stone, pink and blue and green, growing blue as the sun rose. Nick spread the blanket on the dry sand and they sat. He opened the bag and offered her first choice of the donuts. She chose a plain cruller with cinnamon sugar and he pulled out a big chocolate frosted bar filled with cream.

She wrinkled her nose. "I can't believe the stuff you eat."

"C'mon, Amish food is hardly low calorie."

"True, but you don't do farm work and yet you don't gain weight from the way you eat."

"Oh, so you've noticed?" he teased.

She bit her lip. If she hadn't felt so comfortable with him she'd never have said something so personal.

"Hey, it's okay, I'm joking," he said. "I don't always eat the way I have the last couple of days. But it's vacation. Gotta have a little fun."

He was right. She pulled out another donut, this time with blackberry jam inside—too much blackberry jam. It oozed into her mouth, and though she swallowed quickly, she couldn't keep it from dripping down her chin and onto the front of her dress.

Grabbing a napkin, he wiped at her chin, but when he went to dab at the blobs of jam on her dress she waved her hands and took the napkin from him.

"Oops, sorry!" he said quickly when he realized what he'd done.

Her own cheeks suffused with color. "It's okay."

She did the best she could and would just have to hope soaking and washing the dress would get rid of it later. "Why is it you can eat those things and not get messy but I do?" she complained as she put the empty cup into the paper bag.

Sighing, she ate the rest of the donut and washed it down with now lukewarm coffee.

"It's a gift," he told her, grinning. "Guys learn these things at an early age."

She got to her feet. "I want to see what the water feels like."

He put his empty cup into the bag and stood. "It's probably a little cool to go swimming."

She gave him a look over her shoulder. "I'm not going in."

"Not even if I got you a bathing suit at the gas station?"

She stopped and stared at him. "You can't buy a bathing suit at a gas station."

"You can at a tourist location."

When she continued to look at him disbelievingly, he shrugged. "Okay, maybe not in Amish-land. But you can here in Florida. They have everything you need in a place like this. Vacation in a box."

Turning, she continued walking down to the water's edge. "You didn't buy me a bathing suit."

"Didn't," he agreed cheerfully, coming alongside her. "But could have."

"Did you buy a swim suit?"

"Trunks."

"Trunks? You're not an elephant."

He laughed. "Oh, you are something else. You look so quiet and serene. But you say the darnedest things sometimes."

"I do not."

"You do. Anyway, most guys call them swim trunks. And no, I didn't buy any. Already had these, although they don't get much use back in Pennsylvania."

She gave the long, loose shorts another look, then, as she heard voices behind her, she turned and saw people arriving to spend time at the beach. Sure enough, a number of men were dressed as Nick was. She wished one man had worn as many clothes. He looked like he was wearing underwear—and not the kind that Amish men wore. At least not what her *dat* and her *bruders* used to throw in the laundry for her and her *mamm* to wash each week.

She thought she couldn't be shocked by the clothes the *Englischers* wore, but she was wrong.

Her face flamed.

"You're looking a little pink already," he said. "I think maybe you should put on sunscreen."

"It's not from the sun," she said, not wanting to move. With a slight tilt of her head, she gestured at where to look.

"Oh," he said. "You don't see men wearing Speedos much anymore."

"That's *gut*," she told him, lapsing back into Pennsylvania *Deitsch*. She sighed. "Sorry, that sounds judgmental."

"No, I agree."

Two young women ran past them, and there was little left to the imagination with their revealing attire. Naomi hadn't seen a bikini in person before but she knew that's what the women wore. They screamed when they hit the water, so she imagined that the water temperature wasn't balmy.

Children ran up and down the waterline like little sandpipers, screaming with delight and dancing as the water swirled around their toes. A couple of them settled down to start building sandcastles.

A group of people their age began setting up a volleyball net further down the beach. They looked familiar and yet she couldn't think where she'd seen them.

Then she realized that both the men and the women were very pale-skinned. The men wore shorts *Englisch*-style like Nick, but had bowl-shaped haircuts. The women were dressed—or nearly undressed—in one-piece swimsuits and had their hair covered with white kerchiefs.

Her jaw dropped and she stared. Then she turned to Nick and saw him studying her.

"Did—did you see—" she stammered.

"Uh-huh."

"But they're—I mean, they may well be on their *rumspringe*, but still—"

"Uh-huh."

"You're not surprised?"

He shook his head. "Remember, I told you what that Amish man said who'd been here: 'What happens in Florida stays in Florida.'"

"Well, I'm not wearing a swimsuit," she responded, and heard how prim she sounded. "It's just . . . immodest."

"Aren't you a little warm in your dress?"

"I'd like to get my feet wet," she said.

"Sounds good." He turned and walked with her down to the water's edge.

Her feet sank in the sand and it drifted over her toes and tickled as they walked down to the water's edge. A wave swept up and the water slid over her feet like silk. When it retreated, it sucked at the sand under her feet and caused her to lose her balance.

Nick grabbed her arm to steady her and she yelped and stepped back.

"What? Did I hurt you? I barely touched you!" He moved closer.

She held up a hand. "It's okay. You just touched where I hurt it the other night."

"Naomi."

"I want to walk a little bit," she told him and hurried ahead of him.

He must have taken the hint because he left her alone to walk by herself. Finally she turned around and walked back. Nick was sitting on the blanket, staring out at the ocean.

"C'mon, sit down and let's talk," he said quietly.

She sank down on the blanket and did as he'd done—watched the waves sweeping up, then back, on the shore.

"Show me," he said.

She shook her head. "It's okay. Really."

Something didn't feel right. He started to insist but there was a flash of something in her eyes—a mute plea to stop asking questions, to let it go.

He dropped his hand to his side. "You'll let me know if it doesn't get better and you need to see a doctor? I can drive you to see one here, no problem."

"I know," she said, avoiding his concerned gaze by staring out at the ocean. Then she realized he'd just been trying to help and she might not sound very friendly. "I appreciate it. Really."

7

They sat there, watching the waves rolling in and out, neither of them speaking.

After a long while, Nick heard Naomi sigh. He glanced at her.

"It's so beautiful," she said, and she gave him a shy smile. "Thanks for letting me come."

"I didn't *let* you come," he said, frowning. "I invited you. That's different. I wanted you to come."

"Okay. Thank you." She smoothed her hand over her skirt as the wind ruffled its hem.

Nick studied her face. Naomi possessed the glowing, flawless skin of so many Amish women. Hers was a little paler, more porcelain, and now, when he looked at her, he thought she looked a little pink. And not because she was blushing as that man walked by again in the European swimsuit.

He dug out the bottle of sunscreen and held it out to her. "You need to use some of this, otherwise you're going to get sunburned."

"I never get sunburned."

"But the sun's stronger here. And we've been here for—"

"Nick! I didn't know you were such a worrywart!"

"I just don't want you to burn."

"I won't. And if I do, I'm not going to blame you."

"Naomi, please put some on."

"I don't need it," she insisted, frowning at him. "Can we please change the subject?"

He hated the thought of that exquisite skin burning, peeling. Causing her pain. But she turned back to stare at the ocean, her posture rigid, her chin thrust out. He recognized the signs that she wasn't about to budge.

Nick liked to think he was a smart man who knew when not to argue with a woman. If she was right, well, she wouldn't burn. But if she was wrong, she was going to suffer, and he didn't want that to happen.

Her stubbornness surprised him. He'd never seen that before. Of course, he told himself he hadn't ever spent that much time around her before—just driving her and her cousins and grandmother to and from work.

He asked himself why he should care so much if she learned an unpleasant lesson. Why wasn't he repelled by this stubbornness? Who wanted to be argued with when you were just being concerned?

Was this how she behaved with her fiancé? he wondered. Not that he blamed her. He didn't know much about John Zook, only that he'd moved to Paradise from another Amish community on the other side of the state. He seemed . . . charming, but the funny thing was, the time he'd met him at the shop he'd gotten the distinct impression that Anna didn't like him. Although some people assumed that because the Amish led a traditional lifestyle the husbands might be more controlling than *Englisch* husbands, Nick hadn't found that to be true. They seemed to be better about working in partnership together.

He thought back to that day when he picked up Naomi and Leah. John had been standing at the end of the driveway of Leah's home that morning. He'd offered to stop and let Naomi talk to him, thinking she wanted to say good-bye.

But he remembered how Naomi hadn't wanted him to stop. She hadn't wanted to say good-bye to John. He'd wondered about it at the time, but now he remembered how her chin had been thrust out stubbornly, how her arms had been folded across her chest. And how she'd stared forward, refusing to look at John.

Now, he wondered again if they'd had an argument, wondered if John was too controlling.

Well, it didn't matter why Naomi resisted his advice just now and turned so stubborn. All he had to do was say that it was time to get lunch or head home.

He looked over at her and saw that she was watching a family near them. A mother and father were playing with a little boy who looked about two years old. The Amish loved children but Naomi looked sad, not happy.

This was a woman who was supposed to be getting married soon. He'd have thought she'd be thinking of her wedding, of children in the near future.

The little boy jumped up and down, excited as his mother rooted inside a picnic basket. When she held out a treat, he wrapped his arms around her neck and kissed her, reaching for it at the same time.

Naomi stood abruptly and brushed the sand from her skirt. "I'm going to go take a walk."

"Okay," he said, and by the way she started off, got the message that she didn't want company. "I'm hungry. Back in fifteen?"

"Back in fifteen," she called over her shoulder and continued striding down toward the shoreline.

He watched her stop and slip off her flip-flops, dangling them from her fingers as she walked, her head bent.

Anyone who thought that because they lived a simple life the Amish were simple was dead wrong. Naomi was one complicated lady.

Her face was on fire.

Groaning, Naomi turned her face into the cool fabric of her pillow. But the material chafed like steel wool against her cheek and she moaned.

She got up and padded to the bathroom. Sure enough, her face was shades and shades pinker than when she'd gone to bed. She turned off the light and went into the kitchen for a glass of water, then a second. Her throat was so parched. Maybe there was something there she could put on her skin.

She ran an ice cube over her cheeks and her nose until it melted, and then another and another. They cooled her skin a little but then the heat would return. Frustrated, Naomi looked in the cupboards for vinegar, opening and closing the doors quietly so she wouldn't wake her grandmother. Home remedies were passed down from generation to generation in her community. Plain people didn't run to the drugstore every time they got a sunburn or a bug bite or their *boppli* developed a diaper rash.

But there was no vinegar in the cupboard. She went back to the refrigerator and stood there, staring into its depths, enjoying the cold air that emanated from it. There was a cucumber. That might work. They had cooling properties. She pulled it out, washed it, then used a knife and cutting board to slice it. Sitting down at the kitchen table, she rubbed the slices all over her nose and face. Her face felt a little cooler but there had to be something that worked even better.

Another foray into the refrigerator yielded a jar of mayonnaise. She scooped a little out and smeared it across her face and nose. Maybe it wouldn't do anything to cure the sunburn, but it surely felt nice and cold. She relaxed back into her chair and closed her eyes.

That reminded her of an article she once read in a women's magazine. *Englischers* liked to go for beauty treatments in spas and beauty shops. Often they put cucumber slices on their closed eyelids to reduce puffiness. She opened her eyes and picked up two slices, then closed them again and applied a slice over each eyelid. Well, the article was right. It felt nice and cool.

"Midnight snack?" her grandmother asked.

Her eyes snapped open and the cucumber slices went flying. "*Grossmudder*! You scared me."

Leah had her hand pressed to her chest. "You think you didn't give me a fright when I walked in here and saw your face?"

But Naomi saw her lips twitching. She grinned. "I guess I look a little silly."

"*Ya*, you look a lot silly," Leah agreed, chuckling.

"I couldn't sleep. The sunburn really hurts." She touched her cheek tentatively and winced, then went looking for the cucumber slices. After tossing them into the trash, she screwed the lid back on the mayonnaise and put the jar and the uncut portion of the cucumber back into the refrigerator.

"Whose remedy is mayonnaise? Your mother's?"

"No. I just thought if it was cold it might help. After all, some women use cold cream."

Leah pressed her lips together to keep from smiling. "Not the same thing at all, *kind.* Wash your face and we'll try what my mother used."

Naomi did as her grandmother requested and gently patted her skin with a kitchen towel. Though the material was a soft terry cloth, she still winced from the pain.

"It got worse pretty quickly," Leah said, examining it. "When we ate supper you looked a little pink but now you're red as a *rotrieb.* I don't think I've ever seen you get sunburned."

"I told Nick that."

"Oh?"

"He said I should put sunscreen on. I told him I never burned."

"Hmm. So he offered sunscreen and you didn't take it?"

She glanced at her grandmother, then away. "No."

"Hmm."

"Hmm?"

Leah shrugged. "Just wondered why you didn't take it—the sunscreen. We *are* in Florida."

"That's what Nick said. But it's the same sun we have in Pennsylvania." She paused. "Isn't it?"

Leah drew a bowl from a cupboard, filled it with water and ice, and then soaked some tea bags in it. "What did Nick say to that?"

"What does it matter?" Naomi said, and heard the irritation in her voice. "Anyway, he was just being so . . . pushy about it. I might have listened to him if he hadn't—" she stopped.

"If he hadn't made you think he was John imposing his will."

Naomi bit her lip. "*Ya.* Men!"

"Sit down and tilt your head back," Leah instructed, using her fingertips to squeeze excess water from several tea bags. "Naomi, he's not John."

Naomi took a seat and let her head fall back onto the back of the chair. "I know. He's the exact opposite," she whispered, knowing she'd argued with him and generally not behaved like herself over it. "He's going to say, 'I told you so.' "

"Nick's not like that." Her grandmother draped a tea bag across Naomi's nose and applied several others to her cheeks and forehead. She stood back. "There, how does that feel?"

"Better," Naomi said, and her breath caused the tea bag tags to flutter and tickle her nose. "Oh my, if I looked silly before, I can't imagine what I look like now."

Leah pulled open the bottom drawer of the stove and retrieved the lid to an aluminum pan. She held it in front of Naomi to use for a mirror. Naomi took one look and burst out laughing. The tea bags slid from her face, one of them slipping down the front of her chest to land inside the neckline of her nightgown.

"Cold!" she cried, and quickly pulled it out. She leaned her head back again and reapplied the bags to her face.

"This is *gut*," she said, nearly swooning with relief. "You should go back to bed now. No need for you to lose sleep over my foolishness."

"I don't mind," Leah said, taking a seat beside her. "You've sat up with me when my ankle was troubling me."

"It was no trouble at all. That's what families do. By the way, I got us some postcards today. Nick stopped at a gas station he said had everything for vacations. I thought we could send some to Mary Katherine and Anna and my parents tomorrow."

She moved a tea bag from one eyelid and checked the kitchen clock. "Well, today. I didn't realize it was so late. Now, you really should go back to bed. I'm going there in a minute."

"I think I will," Leah said.

Naomi heard the scrape of her chair on the kitchen tile, felt her grandmother's lips on her cheek when she kissed her good night, and heard her uncertain shuffle down the hall to her room.

She knew from the one time she'd experienced sunburn that the next stage was little clear water-filled blisters, followed by peeling, and she wondered if she could avoid Nick for a few days.

He was going to enjoy telling her "I told you so!" She just knew it. And she wouldn't be able to blame him for it.

She'd known he was right about the sunscreen. Something about the way he'd insisted that she use it had just gotten her back up. She'd never been that way before. But he'd just sounded like John for a moment and she'd felt compelled not to back down.

Well, she'd just have to put up with him telling her that she'd been wrong and he'd been right. She wouldn't even mind, if God would just take away the pain of the sunburn. Gathering the bags from her face, she dunked them in the ice water again, squeezed them, then reapplied them to her face.

She felt something under her chin—something sticky. She rubbed at it and looked at it. Mayonnaise. She pulled a paper napkin from the holder on the table and wiped her chin clean.

Her grandmother's words when she'd walked into the kitchen came back to her. She got to her feet and looked into the refrigerator again.

Suddenly she felt like a midnight snack.

Nick regarded Naomi and shook his head. "Your nose looks like a strawberry."

Naomi rolled her eyes. "I know. Don't rub it in."

"If only you'd done that."

"What?"

"Rubbed in some sunscreen the other day."

She folded her arms across her chest. "Go ahead. Say, 'I told you so.'"

He sighed and leaned against the doorjamb. "Naomi, I would never do that."

She stared at him, searching his face for something—he didn't know what. "*Grossmudder* said that," she admitted finally.

"But you still thought I might." He watched as a reluctant smile tugged at her lips.

She nodded.

He stepped closer and touched the back of his hand to her cheek. His eyes widened when she flinched. "Easy. I'm not going to hurt you. I just wanted to make sure you don't have a fever."

"I have a sunburn, not a fever."

Peering into her eyes, he saw that they were bright, not glassy. "Some people get sun poisoning from a bad burn."

She touched her nose and it felt less tender. "Well, I don't have sun poisoning, whatever that is. Just a simple sunburn."

"Nothing simple about sunburn. Or anything else," he muttered, troubled by the way she'd pulled back from him.

Nick heard female laughter from inside the house. "Sorry, I shouldn't have dropped by. You have company."

"I'd invite you in, but we're quilting."

Nick backed away from the door, holding up his hands. "No, thanks."

"There are men who quilt."

"I'm sure. I'm just not one of them."

He turned to walk away and heard her call his name.

"Did you have a reason to come by?"

He'd heard the wistfulness in her voice when he mentioned fishing. "Yeah. Thought I'd see if you wanted to go fishing for a couple of hours. But I guess not, since you're sunburned."

Her bottom lip thrust out. "I love to fish."

He jerked his head in the direction of the house. "You love to quilt."

"I can do that anytime," she said. "You know how long it's going to be before we're going to get to fish again in Pennsylvania? They're all wearing little overcoats right now."

He laughed. "Well, that's an image I've never thought of before."

"I'll cover up."

He looked at her dress—a Plain dress with a high, modest neckline, cape, long sleeves, and skirt past her knees—and weighed his words. "You were pretty covered up the other day."

She stamped her foot and glared at him. "You know what I mean. I'll wear a hat and put some stuff on my nose."

"I'll find you something," he told her. "Go back inside and get out of the sun. What time shall I come back?"

"Two."

"Okay." He watched her walk back toward the house, a spring in her step. Who knew just offering to take her fishing would make her that happy?

Naomi stitched on a section of quilt and tried not to watch the clock on the wall.

"So wonderful to get your help with the quilts for the auction for Haiti," Ida said as she threaded her needle.

She smiled up at Naomi as she set a cup of tea on the table for her. "I can't wait for you to attend after all the quilts you and the women in your area have donated."

"We had such fun making them," Naomi said. "When I was younger I thought it was kind of strange that people who lived in such a warm climate needed quilts. I didn't know back then that the quilts were sold to people here and the money got sent to Haiti to feed and shelter and clothe those who needed it."

Naomi remembered being at the quilting where the Trip around the World quilt had been sewn for the Haiti auction and Jenny had said she wondered where it would end up. She couldn't stop herself from smiling as she remembered seeing how curious Jenny, a former *Englisch* television reporter, could be.

That day, Jenny had watched a friend's child crawl under the quilting frame. Jenny had followed. Her feet and the child's had stuck out from under the frame as the two watched the needles dipping in and out of the fabric.

Naomi's thoughts wandered back to Jenny at home in a Pennsylvania farmhouse, a far cry from the New York City apartment where she lived before becoming Amish in order to marry Matthew Bontrager.

She heard more about the Amish becoming *Englisch* than the *Englisch* like Jenny—and Chris Marlowe—becoming Amish. But right now, thinking about how she felt about Nick, she couldn't help wondering what it would be like to be *Englisch*.

The thought lingered for only a moment. When she was twenty-one, she'd joined the church and never looked back. The *Englisch* world held no appeal for her. She loved her church, her family, her community.

Both she and Nick went back and forth between their two worlds, but at the end of the day they each went to their own. It was where they belonged.

Naomi got up and filled the teakettle for about the dozenth time, and as she did, she gazed at the little bowl of shells sitting on the shelf above the sink. She'd found them on the beach and tucked them into her pocket to take home. They weren't fancy. Some of their edges had been broken as the surf tossed them up on the sand. She didn't care. They'd be a reminder of her time here.

Who would have imagined a vacation place where you could walk outside in the morning and pluck an orange for your breakfast juice? Where you could meet other Plain folk from all around the country in one place?

And instead of being in Paradise watching her grandmother—always such a cheerful, encouraging influence on her life and that of her cousins—become more and more depressed as she contemplated another dreary Pennsylvania winter, she could see her laughing and talking with the quilting circle now.

She closed her eyes and spoke a silent prayer for His plan for her grandmother. The shrill whistle of the teakettle startled her and she reached quickly to lift it from the stove.

"Need any help?" her grandmother asked.

"No, thank you."

She'd found a pretty teapot in the cupboard and scrubbed it earlier. Now she brewed some orange spiced tea she'd made from the oranges in the front yard and walked around filling empty tea cups.

"So how are the wedding plans coming along?" Ida wanted to know.

Naomi raised her brows and glanced at her grandmother.

"Don't blame your grandmother," Ida said quickly. "Daniel told me after he returned from selling the farm."

She tied a knot at the end of the thread and began sewing again. Naomi hoped that was the end of it. She didn't really know what to say. Once she got back to Pennsylvania, it was almost certain she'd be breaking up with John.

"We haven't made many plans yet," she finally said. It wasn't exactly the truth, but it wasn't a lie either. She sent up a quick fervent prayer that God would forgive her for it.

"I always wondered about the two of you—you and Daniel, I mean. I always liked you." She smiled and shrugged. "Well, it wasn't God's will."

"So, I know you quilt for a living, and you and your cousins and Leah have a shop," Mary from Ohio said as she paused from her stitching to take a sip of tea. "Have you designed a special wedding quilt?"

Naomi felt a momentary panic. She just hadn't expected questions about this and didn't know what to say. She looked at her grandmother, hoping for guidance.

"We've been so busy we haven't had a chance to discuss that," Leah said.

That was the truth, Naomi thought. She'd been so busy with commissions. Stitches in Time had received some nice publicity when Mary Katherine spoke at the college, and holiday business had been bigger than usual.

The teapot was empty. Naomi went to make more tea, grateful for the chance to escape more questions. Even though she was in the same room, she hoped that looking busy would discourage them. Once again, as she stood at the sink filling the teakettle, she found herself looking at the shells. The question about designing her wedding quilt made her think about how she could make a quilt with colors and shapes that would remind her of her time here in Florida with her grandmother.

Maybe she'd make some sketches while she fished with Nick in . . . she checked the clock. Less than an hour now.

Remembering how Nick loved to eat, she decided to pack a picnic lunch. She quickly made sandwiches with the leftover roast chicken from dinner, adding some carrot sticks and a handful of cookies. Iced tea was a staple in Florida all year 'round, she'd discovered. Sweet tea, they called it, and she knew Nick liked it. She filled the small jug they'd brought along on the trip and set it in the refrigerator until it was time to leave.

Her grandmother watched her but didn't ask any questions in front of the other women. When she brewed more hot tea and made the rounds of the room pouring it, Naomi whispered to her that she was going fishing for a few hours with Nick.

"Are you sure you should go out again with that nose?"

"It's the only nose I have," Naomi said with a straight face. "I've had it all my life."

"Oh, you," Leah said, chuckling. "You know what I mean."

"Nick promised he'd bring something so I wouldn't make it worse."

"Very funny!" Naomi said, glaring at Nick when she climbed into the van and saw what he'd brought for her nose.

Nick wiggled his eyebrows and modeled a nose protector for her. "You don't like it?"

"Where did you find a clown nose?" she demanded, pretending to be offended but having trouble keeping a straight face.

He pulled his off and took the one he'd handed her. "I was just kidding. Here, I bought you something else." He pulled a package from a bag and gave it to her.

"This is still pretty silly looking," she said, hesitating as she read "Surfer Nose Protector" on the packaging and opened the triangular hard plastic thingy.

She sighed, but since she wanted to go fishing she applied the thick white cream to her nose and face before applying the plastic piece.

"And here's the final part of the disguise," he said, reaching into the backseat for a big, wide-brimmed straw hat.

She hesitated at putting it on but then nodded. "There's enough shade under here for two people," she told him, then realized it sounded like an invitation for him to get closer.

Fortunately, he didn't take it as such, instead starting the car and moving out onto the road. The Pinecraft speed trap was in effect: several police officers patrolled on horseback, making sure there was no speeding with so many pedestrians and bike riders around.

Phillippi Creek ran beside the shuffleboard court, and today a few people stood or sat along the shore and dropped their lines in the water. Nick found a place to park and they walked down to the water's edge, Nick carrying their fishing poles in one hand, Naomi carrying their picnic lunch in one of hers. When Naomi stumbled on a tuft of grass, Nick reached over and took her hand in his.

The contact with his hand felt electric and she glanced over at him. He gave her a half smile, his eyes dark, but she couldn't read his expression. His fingers grew firmer on hers and he continued to hold on while they walked down the incline, and she didn't withdraw her hand.

She told herself she appreciated the help so she wouldn't trip and fall—after all, they didn't need two women with sprained ankles—but she felt troubled by how she felt when he broke contact when they reached the water.

They spread out an old quilt that Naomi had tucked in the back of the van for the trip and Nick got their lines in the water. Other people nearby nodded a welcome but there was little talking. Naomi's brother had always told her that fish were scared away by noisy conversation. She'd believed him but suspected her brother liked her being quiet as well. When she was younger she'd been quite the talkative younger sister. Now, she realized he might have been telling the truth.

She chuckled at the memory, and when Nick glanced over, she whispered what she'd remembered.

"You were lucky he took you," he whispered back. "Guys don't like to drag their sisters along anywhere. That only changes when they get older and having a baby sister along can get girls interested in them."

Naomi laughed and shook her head. Then, as he continued to stare at her, she felt her face grow warm, her mouth grow dry.

It was the sun, she told herself. She wasn't attracted to Nick.

She couldn't be.

8

"You've got a bite!"

Naomi blinked. She'd been sketching a quilt design on a pad of paper and saw that her line was bobbing. Jumping up, she began reeling in the fish that splashed in the water.

"Easy, easy," Nick cautioned at her side.

A flick of the wrist and Naomi pulled the fish from the water and dropped it to the grassy bank where it flopped around. She looked up at Nick and found him grinning.

"Good job! I wasn't sure when you said you liked to fish if you were good at it," he told her.

"Too small, have to toss it back," she muttered. Naomi unhooked the fish and saw his surprise when she looked up. "What?"

"Nothing," he said.

"Were you expecting me to be squeamish and say, 'Oh, please, Nick, I can't touch it!' and make you do it?"

"Well . . ."

"I can't speak for all Amish women, but we're not wimps," she told him. "We help with farming, milk cows, anything and everything we have to do."

"I know, I know," he said. "You are woman; I hear you roar."

"What?"

"Nothing. Just something from a song. About women being strong, independent. "

She gave him a skeptical look as she tossed the fish back into the water. "You are a strange man, Nick."

He laughed. "You have no idea."

Naomi dropped the line back in the water and sat down again on the quilt. "Would you please get the hand sanitizer out of my purse for me?" She held up her hands and made a face.

"Sure."

"Not that one!" she exclaimed. "That's the lunch bag."

Nick regarded the striped bag with the shoulder strap. "Really?"

"Figures you'd pick the lunch bag," she said as he rooted through her purse and found the sanitizer. "I think you have a hollow leg."

"Only when I'm around good food." He opened the sanitizer cap and squirted some of the gel into her hands.

Naomi rubbed her hands together and then wiped them on a tissue from her purse. "I brought sandwiches and cookies. I had the feeling you might get hungry."

"Speaking of hungry," he said when his line bobbed. He reeled the fish in, a nice-sized one, and after unhooking it, put it in a bucket he'd brought.

"You said something about lunch?"

She shook her head. "Men. All about their stomachs."

A little while later, fellow fishers began going home. Naomi sketched and didn't catch anything else. Nick caught four more fish in quick succession—all big enough to join the fish in the bucket. He checked her nose, suggested she apply more sunscreen, then plopped himself on the quilt.

When she finally got a nibble on her line, Naomi jumped to her feet in a surge of excitement—and promptly slid on the grass and into the water.

She stood there, up to her ankles, stunned speechless. Laughter rang out. She raised her eyes and saw that the laughter came from Nick.

"Very funny!" she said. "The water's not exactly warm."

And she wasn't the only one in it. Something brushed against her leg and she let out a yelp. Just a fish, she told herself, taking a cautious look. Not a snake. She tried to lift her foot and found the mud clung and wouldn't let go.

He rose and hurried toward her. "It's okay, you're in shallow water. Just step out."

"Be careful!" she cried. "That's how I ended up in here!"

He held out his hand. "Here, let me help you."

But when she tried to lift her foot it was like being in an awful nightmare of being caught in quicksand. She looked down and tried to pull her foot out again but felt herself sinking, the mud sucking at her.

"Nick, I can't lift my foot," she said, starting to get panicky.

"Give me your hands," he said.

Something bumped her again, something that was cold and slimy. She started to look but Nick jerked her hands.

"Look at me," he commanded, and she raised her eyes and looked into his.

The thing in the water scraped her skin.

"Don't look," he said. "I've got you!"

When it touched her again, she looked down. The *thing* that swam around her foot looked prehistoric—a big greenish-brown fish with a long snout.

And row upon row of jagged teeth.

She never knew if it was the sight of the fish or Nick's strong hands that lifted her from the water. She only knew that she was a quivering mass of nerves as he led her to the quilt.

"What *was* that?"

"Garfish."

She looked up. An Amish man had strolled up with his pole.

"I hear some of 'em can get to be three, maybe four feet long," he said, nodding and stroking his long beard. "Up to two hundred pounds. They'd make a meal for a lot of folk but they don't taste *gut*."

Speaking of tasting, thought Naomi, checking the ankle the thing had brushed against. Her skin wasn't broken but she couldn't wait to get the mud off and put some disinfectant on it anyway. The water hadn't looked clean.

"It's time to go home," Nick said.

It wasn't really a question. He was already picking up her purse and the lunch tote and pulling at the corner of the quilt she sat on.

"I just need to get my breath back," she said.

"Do it in the car," he said in a curt tone. "I just saw a log move in the water."

She looked up and sure enough, what had looked like a log now had protruding eyes and a length of scales. And it was moving across the creek under its own power, leaving a rippling wake behind it.

"It's okay, the gator won't bother you if you don't bother him," the Amish man called behind them.

Naomi made it back to the van in under five seconds. Only when she'd slammed the door shut did she realize that she'd left her flip-flops behind in the creek.

Nick jumped into the driver's side, throwing their things into the backseat once he'd closed his own door.

"Well," he said. "That was a fishing trip I won't soon forget."

"Me, either," she told him, her hand pressed to her chest. "Sorry for the mud."

"No problem," he told her, starting the van. "Sorry, I dropped the lunch bag."

"The alligator will be disappointed," she said dryly. "You ate everything."

Then her hand flew to her head. "My hat! I lost the hat!"

Nick chuckled. "I wonder if the alligator is wearing it right now."

The image made her laugh. "The whole thing is funny. Now."

"Yeah," he agreed. "Now that we're safely in the car."

Nick drove her home, and as he pulled up to the curb of the rental cottage, Naomi gasped. She'd thought the afternoon couldn't get any worse.

She'd been wrong.

John Zook sat on the steps of the cottage, a bouquet of flowers in his hand.

Nick laced up his running shoes and then rested his forearms on his thighs as he sat on his bed. He felt hung over from a bad night's sleep and figured a run might help clear his head.

Why had John Zook come here anyway? Had he missed Naomi and figured he'd spend time here with her? Or was he going to try to convince her to go home with him early?

And why was he torturing himself wondering about this when Naomi was someone else's?

It was just starting to get light out when he stepped outside. He ran his usual route, up and down the quiet streets. The

Amish and Mennonite residents were early risers and were already stirring. People were sitting in lawn chairs, sipping coffee in the mild weather, stopping to chat, filing into local restaurants to eat breakfast.

As he passed Leah and Naomi's rental house he saw Leah outside reaching for an orange in a tree, balancing herself on her crutches.

He stopped, walked up to her, and plucked the orange she was reaching for. He dropped the fruit into a plastic bowl sitting on the sidewalk near her.

"*Guder mariye*," she said, smiling at him.

"You should let Naomi help you with this," he chided as he pulled more fruit from the tree. "We don't want you to have another accident."

"I was managing just fine," she said with a little tartness in her voice. "No need to worry."

"Uh-huh."

"Besides, she's sleeping in a bit. She was up late last night what with John coming to town."

"I gathered that Naomi was surprised. He was sitting on the steps when I brought her back from fishing yesterday."

"Yes, it was a surprise."

When he saw her frown, Nick had the answer to his unspoken question of how Leah felt about it.

"I think that should be enough," she said, and he nodded and carried the bowl into the house for her.

If he had hopes of seeing Naomi come out of her room, he was disappointed.

"Would you like to come by for supper later, Nick?"

"Thanks, Leah, but I have plans," he said.

He hated lying. Well, it wasn't a complete lie. He'd be finding someplace for dinner, then sitting around reading a book. Hardly big plans that couldn't be changed.

But he didn't want to sit and watch John with Naomi.

Waving a hand at Leah, he continued on his run. Just the thought of John here to see Naomi had him pounding the pavement for another street, then another and another.

"Practicing for a marathon?" Daniel called from the porch of his mother's cottage.

Nick slowed, bent, and put his hands on his knees. His lungs ached.

"Why don't you have a seat and I'll get you some water?"

When Nick hesitated, Daniel walked toward him and looked him in the eye. "Sit down before you fall down. Believe me, you can't outrun your thoughts."

Glancing behind him, Nick measured the distance back to his rented room and decided he wouldn't make it if he didn't take a break. He dropped into one of the lawn chairs and swiped at the sweat on his face with the back of his forearm.

"Thanks," he said when Daniel returned with a chilled bottle of water. "I'm not trying to outrun anything."

"Not even the local gator?" Daniel teased, grinning as he took his own seat.

"You heard about that, huh? Amish grapevine?"

Daniel shrugged. "Small town. Word gets around." He sipped from a mug of coffee he'd brought out. "I don't know this John Zook. He didn't go to school with us."

"Moved to Paradise last year."

They sat there, silent, Daniel drinking his coffee, Nick gulping his water.

"So, how long have you been in love with Naomi?"

Nick choked on the water, half of it going down, half of it coming up through his nose and mouth. "*What*?"

Daniel merely continued to sip his coffee.

Then Nick's shoulders slumped. "Oh, no," he groaned. "Don't tell me it's that obvious."

"To me," Daniel said, and he set down his mug. "Takes one to know one."

"You're in love with Naomi, too?"

"No, not really. Well, years ago, maybe. I just know what it's like to want someone and not be able to have her."

Now Nick was even more depressed. But Daniel was right. It wasn't just that John Zook was engaged to Naomi. She wasn't a woman he could have ever had anyway—even if the charming Zook hadn't come along. She was Amish and he was *Englisch.*

He'd never stood a chance with her.

When he finally roused from his little pity party, he glanced over at Daniel and saw that he sat there looking as if he had succumbed to an even bigger funk.

"We're pretty pathetic."

Daniel nodded. "I'd like to disagree with you but I think you're right." He rested his chin on his chest. Finally he sighed. "Have you eaten breakfast yet?"

"No. You?"

"No."

Nick dragged himself out of his chair. "Give me half an hour to shower and change and I'll meet you at Yoder's."

"Deal."

"And bring your cash. You're treating."

"Me?" Daniel stared at him. "How do you figure?"

"I think I know someone I can introduce you to. I just saw one of my clients on vacation here. She's single and about your age."

Daniel grinned. "Now you're talking."

"You don't seem happy to see me."

John was a handsome man, but with the corners of his mouth turned down, he looked more like a sulking child.

Naomi hadn't been happy to see him, but she didn't realize it had been that obvious to him. "It was just a surprise, that's all. And I don't understand why you came. We were returning in a week."

John leaned over and took her hand in his. "I told you. I missed you." He smiled at her.

Naomi stared at him. There was something familiar about his smile.

"Your nose is peeling."

Sighing, she nodded. Why did he need to state the obvious? "I was out in the sun a little too much when I first got here."

Then she looked closer. "You look like you got a little sun, too. When did you get here?"

He touched his nose and winced a little. "I told you. Yesterday. I sat waiting for you quite a while yesterday." He sounded aggrieved, as if she should have been waiting for him.

She knew that a bus from Lancaster County had come into Pinecraft yesterday, but she hadn't gone with her grandmother and her friends to see who'd come. She and Nick had been on their infamous fishing expedition.

"Strawberry stuffed French toast for you," the waitress who appeared said as she put the plate before Naomi. "And Amish scramble for you, sir," she told John. "Anything else I can get you?"

"No, looks good," John said, smiling up at her. "*Danki*—er, thank you."

Naomi watched him dig in. A huge plate of stuffed French toast sat before her. Yes, she loved it and knew John knew that, too. But he'd actually ordered it for her without asking.

She was mad at herself for not speaking up and telling him that she was capable of ordering her own meal, but the restaurant was crowded and it wasn't worth it to fuss. Not when they had bigger issues to settle.

"Eat," he said as he dug in.

"I will."

She concentrated on her cup of tea and watched him. The dish he'd ordered featured eggs and fried potatoes scrambled together and topped with cheese. Normally it looked good—she'd even had it once. Right now though she didn't think she could eat anything. Her stomach felt too tense.

Something else was bothering her. She added more hot water to her cup and dunked a new tea bag in it. Something seemed off.

Then she realized what it was. John had ordered their breakfast without looking at the menu.

"*Gut*," he said, nodding. He wiped his lips with his napkin and drained his cup of coffee before returning his attention to the eggs.

"I want you to go home, John."

"Why?" he asked. "Why don't you want me here? We're engaged to be married. Why don't you want to spend time with me?"

"I came here to make sure my grandmother got to have a vacation. I owe her this, John. You know that."

"We can do both," he said persuasively. "I love you. I want to be with you. You can spend time with us both."

She lifted her eyes and looked into his. "John, I want you to go home. I want you to go back to Pennsylvania."

Looking down at her plate, she wondered how long it would take him to eat. She had no appetite—hadn't had one since she'd come home to find him sitting on her doorstep. Maybe she could have her breakfast boxed up and take it home to her grandmother.

"Naomi, nice to see you."

She glanced up and saw Daniel and Nick standing near the table. "Oh hi, Daniel. Nick."

Turning to John, she said, "Daniel and I went to school together. He helped his parents sell their farm not long ago. And, of course, you know Nick."

John stood and shook their hands and flashed a smile at them. And suddenly Naomi was reminded of that garfish that had scraped along her ankle yesterday when she was stuck in the creek mud.

"I have a table right over here for you," the hostess said behind them.

"See you later," Daniel said, and Nick nodded and followed him.

John sat again and thanked the waitress, who was pouring him more coffee. "So, which one of them is it?" he turned and asked Naomi. He smiled at her and acted like nothing was wrong.

But his smile didn't reach his eyes.

"What do you mean?"

"Which one of them have you been seeing?"

"Neither of them," she told him quietly. "Not in the way you mean. You have no reason to be jealous. Daniel's a childhood friend and Nick's our driver."

"Maybe I should stick around and see if you're telling the truth."

Temper rose up in her. How dare he accuse her of not being faithful to him. Deliberately she tamped down the temper, the righteous anger. She reminded herself that there were people all around—

Wait a minute. That night at the shuffleboard court she'd felt like someone was staring at her. Had he been here that night?

She started to ask him but then reason took over. If he'd been here earlier than he said and had been spying on her, she doubted he'd tell her. Better to find out herself.

"Is there something wrong with the food?" the waitress stopped at their table to ask.

"No, no, it's great," John said, picking up his fork again. "We just spotted some friends and talked with them."

He resumed eating, as if the tense moment he and Naomi had just had never happened.

"Could I get a box for mine?" Naomi asked. "It's a lot for me to eat at one time."

"Of course. Be right back."

"I'm staying for the auction. Besides, there isn't another bus for a while."

She sighed inwardly.

The day of the Haiti benefit auction dawned bright and clear.

Nick arrived to pick up Naomi, Leah, and John. Naomi noticed that John behaved politely despite his suspicion about Nick that he'd stated at breakfast that day.

Then again, a ride was a hard thing to get, with so many Amish and Mennonites wanting to go to the event in Sarasota. Naomi suspected that once John had found that out he'd taken up Leah's offer of a ride there.

A huge white tent had been pitched and row upon row of chairs had been set up inside. Hundreds of people were already showing up early.

"Leah! Over here!" Ida called, gesturing to seats she'd saved them next to herself and Caleb.

They walked over and Leah sat down, tucking her crutches under her feet.

"I'm going to look over the quilts," Naomi said.

"You go ahead," Leah told her, and then she turned to chat with Ida.

Naomi made a beeline for the quilt section. Dozens of them in many different patterns had been donated. Naomi had been quilting since she was a young girl but she figured she could always learn something by studying the work of others. Besides that, there were some truly beautiful quilts sent here by Amish women from around the country.

She loved the traditional ones that had been part of her heritage for years, made of the scraps of clothing materials in rich tones of blues, greens, purples. There were quilts that the *Englisch* liked to decorate their homes with, most made of brighter fabrics and prints and designs not used in Amish homes.

And then there were some very unique quilts donated to the cause by ladies from several quilting guilds. Maybe next year she'd donate several of the quilts that the bishop back home had thought were "not Amish enough."

Maybe she'd sew some quilts based on the sketches she'd made while she waited for the fish to bite that day, designs with all the tropical wildlife and colors of this exotic state she was visiting. Hmm . . . she found her mind racing as she walked around the handicraft of other women.

John and Nick disappeared in the direction of other donated items: farm equipment and handcrafted furniture and tools.

The scent of food drifted through the tent. Those who'd come early and skipped breakfast back at their own places drank coffee and ate bacon, egg, and cheese sandwiches as they sat at tables—*Englisch* shoulder to shoulder with the Amish and Mennonite attendees.

One little girl with blond wisps of hair escaping her snowy *kapp* clutched a fresh glazed doughnut so big she'd slipped her chubby fingers through the hole and had difficulty stretching them to grasp it. Sugary icing crusted her mouth as she chewed. A churn cranked out homemade ice cream and loud popping came from a cast-iron skillet being used for kettle corn.

Naomi hadn't eaten much for breakfast—John had come early to wait for his ride—so the little girl's glazed doughnut looked so good she couldn't resist buying one. It tasted heavenly, sweet and sugary on the outside, the inside light and fluffy, melting in her mouth. She accompanied it with a cup of coffee instead of a juice box like the little girl drank.

The tent filled rapidly. People knew to come early to inspect the goods and get the good buys. An auctioneer welcomed them to what he said was the seventeenth annual auction sponsored by the Amish and Mennonites to benefit Haiti, then began his rapid-fire urging for bids, shrewdly encouraging the members of the auction audience to bid more and more.

Nick came to take his seat, but Naomi didn't see John. She frowned when Nick grinned at her. "What?"

"You have something sugary around your mouth. What have you been eating?"

She reached into her pocket and found a tissue. "A glazed donut," she admitted.

He gestured at her mouth. "You missed a place. No, the other side."

When he started to reach to show her where, she stiffened. He quickly dropped his hand. "Sorry."

"It's okay," she said and swiped at her mouth again. "Gone?"

"Gone." His dark eyes were intent on hers. He dragged his gaze away and looked around. "By the way, where's John?"

"I don't know. I thought he was with you."

"He was, for a while. Then he saw someone he knew. Some guy."

She didn't know he knew anyone here. At least, he hadn't said anything.

"Naomi, look!" Leah jerked her head to the front of the tent where two young Amish men held up a quilt. "That's one of the ones you donated!"

"Really?" Nick sat up straighter and checked it out. "Nice!"

"Nice?" Naomi asked him.

"You know. Looks good." He shrugged and looked a little sheepish. "Hey, I'm a guy. I don't wax poetic."

"Wax?"

"Never mind. Sssh."

She wanted to ask him why he wanted her to be quiet. It wasn't as if he cared about quilts. His eyes widened and he whistled at the figure the auctioneer started the bidding at.

"You don't think it's worth it?" she asked, unoffended.

"No—I mean, I'm sure it is," he said. "I just had no idea."

He raised the numbered paddle in his hand.

"What are you doing?" she cried.

"Bidding. What's it look like?"

Scandalized, she pulled at his arm. "Stop that!"

"Hey, I like it and the money goes for a good cause."

"You can't afford it!" she hissed as someone outbid him.

He gave her an affronted glance but winced when he heard a second bidder go higher. Still, he started to raise his paddle. Naomi pulled at his sleeve and turned to her grandmother.

"*Grossmudder*, make him stop!"

"What's going on?" John asked as he appeared.

He frowned as he looked at Naomi's hand on Nick's arm.

9

Nick could sense the tension emanating from John.

Maybe he'd have felt the same way if he'd walked up and seen his fiancée touching another man's arm. Especially since the Amish were careful about that type of thing—about public displays.

"Nick's trying to bid on my quilt," Naomi said.

John took a seat next to Nick. "If you like the quilt I'm sure Naomi will make you one for a lot less money when you get back home."

He sounded bored but Nick sensed that he was hiding a discontent. He started to suggest that he could switch seats with John so that he could sit next to Naomi, but something held him back.

He hoped it wasn't jealousy on his part.

"Please, Nick, I'll make you a quilt."

Nick heard the auctioneer calling, "Going once, going twice!" and the final bid. He gulped. Any illusions that he could afford the quilt had just been shattered.

"They cost that much?"

"Not the one I'll make you," she said, laughing. "Besides, you did my grandmother and me quite a favor driving us here."

John's head snapped up. "What, you're not paying him?"

"Nick wouldn't let Grandmother and me pay him what we should," Naomi said quietly. "And he's constantly asking us if we need him to drive us someplace or pick up anything."

John shot him a look that Nick could only describe as disbelieving.

Shrugging, Nick focused on the auction. Every so often he cast a surreptitious glance at Naomi, who appeared to be enjoying the selling of the quilts. Only when they were gone did she seem a little restless.

Nick moved a seat closer to Leah to make room for a woman looking to sit down. He turned to Leah. "Having a good time?"

"*Wunderbaar*," she said, smiling. "It's a great auction."

John had looked at the handcrafted furniture and tools that were for sale, since he was a carpenter by trade, but Nick noticed that he didn't seem interested in bidding on anything. Maybe that was because he didn't want to have to haul it back with him on the bus to Pennsylvania.

Naomi asked if anyone wanted anything from the food concessions, and when she got up and left them, John followed her.

At first, Nick thought that the other man went along to help carry food back, but it seemed John was saying something to Naomi that put an unhappy expression on her face.

Nick decided that he had even more reason to dislike John. Not that he'd needed any. When he felt a tug on his sleeve, he glanced over and found Leah staring at him.

"Aren't you having a good time?"

"Sure."

Had she noticed that he was tracking her granddaughter? He hoped not.

"I'm just not interested in farm equipment," he told her. "I think I'll stretch my legs for a while."

Leah smiled and patted his hand, then turned her attention back to the auction.

Nick walked through the crowd that milled around the auction and went outside. Dozens of people were outside talking. Such an event would have been fun enough in this little town, but coming together to help out the people of one of the poorest countries in the world—something this community had been doing for years—appeared to lend an air of excitement.

Many of those he passed exchanged a smile with him; it didn't seem to matter if they were Amish or Mennonite or *Englischer.*

He didn't know it was possible to be surrounded by so many people and feel so lonely.

It wasn't rational, he told himself. Even though he spent most of his working day ferrying people around—most of whom either chatted with someone with them or spent much of the time talking on a cell phone or doing paperwork or just enjoying some quiet time—he was a solitary man.

He was nearly thirty, and while he hadn't been in a rush, on his last birthday he'd been surprised that he hadn't been married by now. Somewhere along the way he'd thought he'd meet someone in his work—after all, he didn't just drive the Amish around—but he guessed it was like Daniel had told him: he met mostly tourists.

Then, one day Leah had called him and asked if she could arrange daily transportation between work and home for herself and her granddaughters.

The three granddaughters had similar looks as cousins and, of course, wore similar Plain dress. But that's where the similarity ended. Mary Katherine stood taller and her hair had auburn tones to it. She'd seemed more withdrawn, less confident when he'd first met her but had really blossomed as her ability at her loom grew—and as she fell in love with Jacob.

Anna was the smallest of the three and yet exuded such energy that she seemed the most vibrant. Her moods swung from one end of the spectrum to the other so quickly. And he'd never known anyone so curious . . . well, downright nosy.

And Naomi. She'd become quieter and more introspective in the past few months.

He'd always thought that instant attraction was the stuff of those romances women read. The whole thing was ludicrous in any event. Amish and *Englisch* might mix as friends and often did. But they didn't marry. Naomi had been baptized and, he quickly found out, was engaged to an Amish man. They would have been married by now but the *Ordnung* dictated that they couldn't marry until after the harvest.

They'd become friends—even more so traveling here. She'd never indicated any kind of interest in him. Ever. And even if he'd suspected she wasn't happy with John, she continued to stay with him. He'd even come here to see her.

Nick considered himself a realist. Even if he'd wanted to go out to a club and meet a woman, he knew if it got around that he visited a drinking establishment he might put his career as a driver at risk. Besides, he wasn't really comfortable with the dating scene. His friends often teased him for being bookish. Introverted. And, like the Amish he drove, born into the wrong century.

He supposed that they were right. Although he loved his personal car and the bigger vehicles he used for transport, and technology like his e-reader and his cell phone, he tended toward quieter activities like reading. Recently, he'd tried dabbling in writing the occasional short story. His idea of an ideal evening? Dinner with friends. Good conversation.

Such an evening, Nick reflected with some irony, wasn't really much different than an evening his Amish counterparts might enjoy.

Matter of fact, once a friend had even teased Nick that he seemed more Amish than some Amish he knew.

"I hope you're happy."

Naomi looked at John standing there, his hands shoved into the pockets of his jacket. She often saw other women staring at him, thinking he was good-looking. They often flirted with him, even after she and John had announced their engagement.

But right now, when he was . . . there could be no other word for it than *pouting*—his bottom lip was thrust out and he glowered like a little boy who hadn't gotten his way.

She sighed. "I'm not happy, John. But if you'd asked me about coming here, I could have saved you the trouble."

"Are you saying I needed your permission?" His tone was quiet because there were people nearby. But his mouth thinned and his eyes went cold.

"Are *you* saying I can't go on vacation with my grandmother without having you come, too?" she asked him, keeping her voice level. "We're not married yet."

Instantly his expression changed, and he took her hands in his. "I just wanted to spend some time with you."

This wasn't doing anyone any good, she thought. They were just going around and around.

She used the excuse that her purse slipped off her shoulder to pull her hands from his. He resisted at first, tightening his fingers around hers, and then finally let her go.

"I'll be back in Paradise before you know it," she said lightly as people milled around them.

He bent to kiss her and when Naomi turned, he grasped her forearms and she gasped.

"You're hurting me!" she cried.

"What a fuss," he said, letting her go. "All I wanted was a good-bye kiss," he told her. "Is that too much to ask?"

"John, you know we don't do that in public." Naomi rubbed at her forearms and frowned. "You hurt me."

He took off his hat and ran his hand through his hair. "I didn't mean to. You know that. You just get me so upset. Why do you do that?"

It was her fault again.

"There's no reason you don't want me around here, is there? Aside from wanting to spend time with your grandmother."

"Of course not."

"You're *schur*?"

"Of course. Why wouldn't I want you around?" She told herself she had no reason to feel guilty. But she did because she didn't want him around right now. And she did because she'd had impure thoughts about Nick. She hadn't acted on them though, so she had no reason to feel guilty.

"What about this Nick who drove you here?"

"Nick drove my grandmother and me here. He's our driver. You know that."

"Is that all?" His eyes were intent on her. Tension radiated from him.

"I've been faithful to you, John," she said quietly. "In Pennsylvania and here."

He looked at her for a long moment and then he seemed to relax.

She glanced over his shoulder and saw the bus filling up. If they talked anymore he wouldn't get on and then who knew how much longer he'd be here? The bus didn't run on a daily basis back and forth to the north.

"John, you need to get on the bus. We'll talk when I get back home."

His eyes were dark and troubled as he stared at her. "*Ya*, we'll talk."

She frowned. The way he said it, it didn't sound like a promise that such a talk might work out the differences between them.

It sounded more like a threat.

Then he clapped his hat back on his head and strode toward the bus. She watched him go, troubled, yet not knowing what else to do. Just before he reached the front of the bus he was hailed by someone, a young Amish man, and the two of them stood talking.

Naomi frowned as she tried to catch a better look at the man. She didn't know John knew anyone here and yet he seemed to be talking to the man as if he were a friend.

She shielded her eyes from the bright sun, trying to see better. Just then, a cloud passed over the sun, and as the glare went away she recognized him. She'd seen him around several times, walking up and down the street and in a restaurant when they were eating.

The man slapped John on the back in a friendly fashion and strolled off, and John got on the bus.

She watched him walk to the rear of the bus and find a seat. He looked out the window and raised a hand to wave at her. The remaining passengers boarded after stowing their luggage and their various boxes and totes and carry-ons. Quite a number of mesh bags of Florida oranges and grapefruit were going home with them.

The plain wooden coffin that Naomi had seen off-loaded wasn't traveling back up north. At least not on this trip.

Finally, the driver climbed aboard, shut the door, and started the bus. He drove out of the lot and his passengers and the people seeing them off waved good-byes.

Naomi searched the row of windows, looking for John as the bus passed her. She didn't see him and her breath caught. For a moment, she thought he'd somehow gotten off the bus without her seeing him and he'd pop up in front of her.

Then she saw him staring at her through the third to last window. She waved and he waved back, but he wasn't smiling. And neither was she.

The crowd that had come to send off their family and friends walked away slowly, as if reluctant to lose sight of the bus.

But Naomi's steps were brisk as she walked back to the rental cottage. She flung open the door and saw her grandmother look up from her sewing, surprised.

"He's gone. I saw him off on the bus myself!"

Someone stood and Naomi realized that it was Nick. He'd been sitting there opposite her grandmother and he'd not only heard what she'd said—he'd heard the lift in her voice.

Naomi sat on the beach, writing letters and postcards while Nick dove in and out of the waves like a dolphin.

"*Wish you were here*," she wrote Mary Katherine and Anna, and she meant it. "*I'm sitting on the beach in Florida. In the middle of winter. And I'm not even wearing a sweater. Nick is swimming right now. He says he'll take some photos to bring back.*"

She paused and chewed on the plastic cap of her pen. Then she began writing again. "*We've had a great time.* Grossmudder *has been spending a lot of time with her friend and we've both been quilting a lot. There are many women here who have some time to rest and enjoy themselves after all the gardening and harvesting of summer and fall, and they're enjoying some time off. Of course, they find lots to do. You know how Amish women stay busy."*

A little boy ran past, kicking up sand on her skirt and the quilt she sat on, too absorbed in having fun to see what he'd done. His mother chased after him, slowing a little to apologize to Naomi, and then picked up speed, catching him and swinging him around, both of them giggling.

Naomi just smiled and brushed it off. She continued, *"Tomorrow Nick's driving us to several quilt shops and then we're taking a drive around Sarasota. We've done some things I never thought I'd do here: eaten alligator (yes, it does taste like chicken), which was much better than being chased by one—more on that later—attended the big Haiti auction, and best of all, walked on this beach."*

Some not-so-good things had happened since the last time she'd written her cousins and talked with them on Nick's cell phone. She almost wrote, *"John came to see me and I asked him to leave."*

But it didn't seem right to talk about John like that. It felt . . . disloyal. If she wanted to share that, she'd do it later, in person, with her cousins.

A few drops of water fell on her. Startled, she glanced up and saw that Nick had walked up and was shaking his wet hair on her. She hadn't heard him approach on the soft sand.

She flicked away the drops and turned the letter over so he couldn't see what she was writing.

"Water's great," he said, shaking his head so more drops flew.

"Stop that!" she cried. "What are you, a puppy?"

He grabbed up his towel and scrubbed his hair with it, then ran it over his chest.

His chest. She felt a blush creep up her neck and wash over her face. When he'd shed his shirt earlier, her mouth had gone dry. Beneath it was a muscled chest with a dusting of curling brown hair on it. The loose white dress shirts he wore for work, sometimes with a tie, and the polo shirts he'd worn here on vacation—well, they'd never really hinted at the toned muscles beneath.

Was that because the shirts had been loose and that's why she hadn't ever noticed? Or was it because something had changed between them? The enforced closeness in the car, being thrown together as he drove her and her grandmother around doing fun things?

She had been attracted to John or she never would have accepted his proposal. But now, she was realizing that she felt much more physically aware of Nick than she should.

The thought disturbed her. She frowned as she tried not to look at him and flipped over the letter to finish it. After adding a few more lines, she signed the letter, folded it, and stuffed it into an envelope. She sealed it, found a stamp and affixed it, then put the envelope and her pen in her purse.

The water was such a beautiful clear blue today. Time was flying by and there wouldn't be that much more time to enjoy this, to feel free of all cares.

She knew she needed to talk to John when she returned. When she and her grandmother talked before they came on the trip, her grandmother had said she needed to break off the engagement. Naomi knew she was right. But just the thought of doing so made her head ache. She felt like such a failure, such an utter, utter failure.

She didn't want to deal with it, but she wasn't willing to stay with him rather than make the break. As her grandmother had told her, men like John didn't change.

"You okay?"

Naomi nodded. "I was just thinking we don't have that much time left."

He didn't need to know that it wasn't just that she'd miss this place and the time she'd had here. What she needed to do about her relationship with John was their business and no one else's.

She glanced over at the e-reader in his hands. "What are you reading?"

He held it out for her to see. "I found this cool book. Look at what sand looks like under a microscope."

"That's sand?" she asked, leaning closer to look at the screen.

A surprising array of dozens of multicolored shapes appeared on the screen—a mixture of crystals, shells, and volcanic rock combined to make the sand.

Like snowflakes, each was too tiny to see how unique it was. Like snowflakes, they formed a bigger whole.

"I never met anyone who loves to read as much as you."

Nick laid the e-reader down on the quilt. "I've been like this since I was a little kid. I loved climbing up on the top bunk of our bunk bed and reading. I was hiding out, too. Sisters can drive a guy nuts."

"I was the youngest," she told him. "Apparently I drove my two sisters crazy. They were in their teens when I was born. The last thing they wanted was a baby sister."

"I thought the Amish loved children."

She smiled. "Kids are kids wherever they are. I was constantly in their things. As the only two girls in the family I think they were hoping that there wouldn't be another girl sharing their room by the time they got to be teenagers."

"You don't talk much about your family—your parents and your siblings."

Thoughtful, Naomi scooped up a handful of sand and let it drift through her fingers. "My *mamm* died several years ago and I'm not close to my *daed's* new wife. And my brothers and sisters are much older than me."

She looked up at him and shrugged. "That's probably why I feel closer to Mary Katherine and Anna. We were all born within a few months of one another. We've always felt more like sisters."

She sighed. Lately, she'd been feeling guilty that she'd neglected her family to spend more time with John. She'd neglected some of her friends, too. He had a way of drawing her away by saying she wasn't with him enough.

Aware that he was watching her, she glanced up and smiled. "It'll be nice to get home."

"But . . ."

"But?"

"It sounds like you'd like to stay longer."

He was doing it again, that way he had of seeming to know what she was thinking.

"No, it'll be nice to be back in Paradise."

He gestured at the ocean. "So you didn't think this was paradise, huh?"

She pulled her legs up, wrapping her arms around her knees. "It's felt a little unreal. I know people live here full time but I guess it seems too far removed from what I'm used to. Besides, I love my work at the shop. And my friends and family. I'll be happy to go back."

Except for seeing one certain person, she thought, but kept her expression neutral.

"You're getting freckles!" he said, sounding surprised.

"I am not!" But she reached into her purse and withdrew a small mirror to check.

Sure enough, there was a scattering of them across her nose. "Oh no!"

"I think they're kinda cute," he said, leaning closer and studying them. "They're kind of like little flakes of gold."

"You're getting fanciful," she told him. "Maybe you've been reading too much fiction." But she felt a funny little catch in her chest when her eyes met his.

"I know you're not supposed to think about looks. Vanity and all that. But you've grown prettier since we've been here."

Her—pretty? She didn't know what to say to that. Oh, John had complimented her now and then. Particularly in the beginning. But he'd never said something like this. It flustered her a little, made her face feel warm—and it wasn't from the sun.

"You've got a tan now and you glow," he said. "But I don't think it's just the sun you've gotten since we got here. You're more relaxed. You were getting a little stressed-looking there at the end, before we left Pennsylvania."

She wasn't surprised to hear that. After all, she'd finally broken down and talked to her grandmother about John.

The breeze toyed with her hair and tugged a strand free. Before Naomi could raise her hand, Nick reached over and tucked it behind her ear. Her breath caught and her skin tingled as his fingers slid down her jawline.

He leaned forward and she felt herself doing the same, drawn wordlessly to him, entranced. She focused on his mouth, wondering what it would be like to kiss him. His touch was gentle, irresistible, his fingers stroking her cheek, luring her closer until their breath merged. Her eyes closed and she felt his lips touch hers, tentative at first, and then with growing passion.

A gull shrieked overhead, startling her into drawing back. She touched her fingers to her lips, feeling them tingle from his kiss.

Nick looked stunned. He shoved a hand in his hair. "I'm sorry," he said quickly. "I have no business kissing you. I—"

"It's not all your fault," she finally managed to say. "I kissed you back."

He stared at her for a long moment and she felt her face grow warmer and warmer.

"Yes, you did," he said. "Why?"

10

Naomi glanced around nervously. What if someone she knew had witnessed the kiss? It didn't even have to be someone she knew. If any of the Amish or Mennonites in the community had seen it, they'd know that Naomi shouldn't be kissing an *Englischer.*

"Relax," he told her. "No one was looking."

The beach was nearly deserted. The lone woman who sat on a nearby blanket looked engrossed in a book.

"I know why I kissed you," Nick told her. "Why did you kiss me?"

"What kind of question is that?" She stuffed her sketchbook into her tote bag and looked around for her pencil. When she couldn't find it, she gave it up for lost and stood.

"What's your hurry? I'm not going to kiss you again."

"Well, good."

"Ouch. You still didn't answer my question."

"It was just a— What do you call it? A spontaneous reaction, that's all."

"You're an engaged woman."

She straightened. "You're just now remembering that?"

Nick stood. "Maybe *you're* just now remembering it."

Her face flamed. He was right. After all, he didn't know that she intended on breaking things off with John when she returned to Pennsylvania.

She reached down to yank up the quilt with her left hand and cried out.

"You're still having pain in that arm?"

"No. Yes." How did you answer? He'd notice it was a different arm than the one that had pained her when they first left for Florida.

"Let me see it."

"It's fine."

"Naomi."

"I appreciate your concern," she said carefully. "But you're not a doctor."

His expression grew shuttered. "No, I'm not. But I'm obviously someone who cares about you."

He bent down, plucked up two corners of the quilt and shook the sand from it, then folded it. Ignoring her when she reached for it, he grabbed his e-reader and walked away.

Naomi stared at his retreating back and then scrambled after him. "I'm sorry, I didn't mean to hurt your feelings."

Nick stopped so suddenly that she nearly ran into him. A vein throbbed near his temple and his eyes were stormy.

"When is it going to stop, Naomi? When are you going to stop letting him hurt you?"

When she started to speak, he held up a hand. "Don't!" he said sharply.

Then, shaking his head, he took a deep breath. "Look, I don't want to yell at you. I'm just frustrated. I know these things are complicated. But you have to break it off with him before he really hurts you."

"I know." When he continued to stare at her, disbelieving, she lifted her chin. "I know what I have to do."

With that, she walked past him and proceeded to the car.

"She's going to go back to him. I just know it."

"Maybe not," Daniel said.

"C'mon, if there's one thing I'm certain about, it's that the Amish are known for their forgiving nature."

He looked up and smiled at the waitress as she set a piece of peanut butter pie before him. Stabbing his fork into the pie, he grimaced. "I wonder how much weight I've gained since I came here. These people ought to be arrested for making this pie."

Daniel cut a bite of his own Dutch apple pie. "Better than back home, huh?"

"That and I'm resorting to stress eating."

"And running."

"And running." He wiped his mouth on a napkin and took a sip of his coffee.

"So what are you going to do?"

Nick stared down into his coffee cup as if its contents held some kind of answer to his dilemma. "I'm going to have a talk with Leah this afternoon. If I can just get Naomi out of the house."

Daniel clapped him on the back. "I'll be happy to help there."

"You?"

"I'll take her shopping. You know, souvenirs, that kind of thing."

Nick narrowed his eyes. "Am I supposed to tell you that you're a pal? You'd better not be thinking of putting the moves on her."

"Thinking of her being your girl?" Daniel asked him mildly.

"Wouldn't matter if I did." Nick pushed the pie aside and concentrated on his coffee, but suddenly it tasted bitter. "I had no business falling in love with her."

"No, you didn't."

He jerked his head up. "You don't need to rub it in."

"I know." Daniel pushed aside his empty plate and leaned his elbows on the table. "I shouldn't poke fun at a man in love."

"That's an apology?"

Daniel shook his head. "No. You've got it bad. I can relate." He leaned back in his chair. "I know in your culture that sometimes two people of different religions marry. A Catholic man and a Jewish woman, that sort of thing. But it's not the same concept with the Amish and the *Englisch*. It's not just a matter of religion. It's a different culture, a totally different way to live when you're Amish."

Daniel cocked his head and studied Nick. "Although you certainly do blend in. You dress plain for an *Englischer* and you're constantly getting involved in the community. You even attend services from what I hear."

He grinned as Nick's eyebrows went up. "Yes, I checked you out. Naomi's a childhood friend. I care about her."

Reaching into his pocket, he pulled out some bills. "Now it's time for me to take Naomi out for a ride."

Their waitress approached with the check and smiled at Nick. "You remembered your frequent pie card, right?"

Daniel snickered. "Do you need to ask? You know he's addicted to your peanut butter pie."

She grinned at him. "But the fact that you're in here almost as often for Dutch apple is okay, right?"

"Right." Daniel returned her grin.

"Say, how is it that you Amish here can drive but it's not okay in Lancaster County—or any other Amish community

I've heard of?" Nick asked as they waited in line to pay at the cash register.

"I'm Beachy Amish Mennonite," Daniel told him.

Nick watched Daniel pay for his pie and coffee and waited, wanting to know more.

Determinedly he looked away from the baked goods conveniently placed nearby for sale. Maybe he'd stop in for some homemade breakfast rolls and other baked goods when they left for home. Just to tide them over.

After all, he wanted to reciprocate for what Leah and Naomi had baked and packed for the trip. He was just that kind of guy. He grinned. He was justifying getting more treats, that's all.

"So tell me more," Nick said after he paid his bill and they turned to leave.

"Most people don't want the history lesson about the founding of the church, so I'll just say this," Daniel said as he held the door open for Nick. "The Beachy Amish Mennonites—named after Moses Beachy—have been around since the 1920s or so, and we're very progressive compared to the Old Order Amish you know in Lancaster County. The original settlers to that part of the country have been there since the 1600s."

They strolled down the sidewalk. "I drive, my home's wired for electricity, and I have an inside phone," Daniel said. "All things you have."

A line had formed for the restaurant. Nick walked with Daniel to his car parked nearby. It was a good thing they weren't in a hurry, because there were a lot of people moving around.

A mounted police officer stood on the corner, watching traffic and pedestrians as they moved past.

"Our version of a speed trap," Daniel told him. "Want a lift to your van?"

"I'm not parked too far away. I'll walk."

"Well, then I'll go see if I can persuade Naomi to go for a drive," Daniel said, and he shoved his hands in his pockets as he walked away.

Nick frowned. He hoped he hadn't just asked a wolf to go pick up a lamb.

Leah opened the door when Nick knocked on it a little later.

"Why, what a nice surprise," she said with a smile, holding the door wider so that he could enter.

"You might not think so in a minute," he muttered.

She pressed a hand to her heart. "Oh my, do you have bad news?"

"Can we sit down?"

"*Schur*," she said. "What's wrong? It's not Naomi, is it? She just left with Daniel. There hasn't been an accident?"

"No, no, I'm sorry, I'm just making this worse," he said. "Come, sit down, and let me talk to you."

He told her about how Naomi had reacted at the beach not once but twice, the latter time right after John had returned home. She listened but didn't react with surprise.

Then she reached over to touch his arm with her small but firm hand. "I know about John," she said quietly.

"And you think it's okay for her to marry him?" he nearly yelled, jumping up from the table so impulsively that his chair fell over backward, the noise jarring in the small house.

"No, no, of course not," Leah said quickly. "I've spoken to Naomi about it and I was glad when she came here with me so that she'd have a chance to think about what she needed to do."

Nick closed his eyes and then opened them. Relief left him feeling dizzy. Then he realized that just because Leah wanted her granddaughter to break off her engagement, it didn't mean that Naomi would do so.

"Would you like some coffee or tea?" she asked.

"Only if you put that ankle up on a chair and let me make it."

"Always thinking of other people, aren't you, Nick?"

"I'm no saint," he muttered, pulling out a chair and gesturing at it.

Only when she put her foot on it did he move to fill the teakettle and set it on the stove burner.

"Tea?"

He shrugged. "You've gotten me to liking it. Sometimes."

She stared at him, a thoughtful expression on her face.

"What?" he asked as he returned to the table.

"Have you come to care for Naomi?" she asked point-blank.

She made him think of his own grandmother. It was unnerving the way she reminded him of his mother's mother—gone now—and the way she'd always known when he'd gotten into mischief. He'd sworn that Grandma Iris had known he'd done something before he'd actually had a chance to do it.

"You know I think you have three fine granddaughters—well, the ones I know," he said carefully. "I'm aware you have many more, but I'm talking about Mary Katherine, Anna, and Naomi. I'm fond of all three of them."

"But you don't look at Mary Katherine or Anna the same way."

The teakettle hissed. He turned off the flame, poured hot water into cups, and brought them to the table.

"Good thing," he told her lightly. "I doubt Mary Katherine's husband would put up with that. And Anna would just laugh at me if I started looking at her . . ." he trailed off. Romantically? He was afraid to even say the word.

He pushed the bowl of tea bags toward her and then chose one for himself. Opening it and dunking it into the hot water provided a nice diversion. But when he finally had to look up, she was still staring at him.

"I'm just worried that John will hurt her," he told her. "I swear that's all I care about. I know that any feelings I have can't go anywhere. She's been baptized. She'd be shunned. I couldn't let that happen. Her faith, her family and friends . . . I couldn't—"

Leah laid her hand on his and it was cool and dry and firm. "Does she know how you feel about her?"

He remembered the kiss on the beach and he didn't dare look at her or she'd know what happened. "I think she's guessed I'm attracted to her," he said honestly, meeting her gaze. "But I promise you I won't pursue a relationship with her, Leah. Just help her break things off with John. I beg you."

Leah's eyes widened and she blinked. "Oh my," she whispered. "You're in love with my *grossdochder.*"

Groaning, he put his head in his hands and slumped in his chair. Lifting his head, he stared at her. "Are you related to my grandmother?"

"It's written all over your face," she said sagely.

They sighed in perfect unison.

The door opened and Naomi breezed in, then stopped as she saw Nick sitting in the kitchen with her grandmother. "What's wrong? Something's wrong."

"No, it isn't," he said quickly. "We were just talking about how sorry we are that we're going home soon."

"Yes, well—" Naomi looked like she couldn't think of anything to say.

"Why are you home so soon?" he asked her.

"I forgot my money," she said, and then she frowned. "How did you know I'd gone anywhere?"

"Because you weren't home when I got here."

"Oh." She appeared to think about it. Then she shrugged. "Well. Okay. I should get my money. Daniel's waiting." She headed for her room.

Leah started to say something but Nick quickly shook his head and touched a finger to his mouth, indicating she should stay silent.

Naomi came out of her room, tucking some bills into her purse. "*Grossmudder*, Daniel wants to know if we'd like to have supper with him tonight. He says I should invite you too, Nick."

Daniel walked inside. "I thought we could go to this great sushi place."

Nick watched Naomi make a face. "Will they cook mine if I ask? I don't think I'd like raw fish."

Daniel laughed. "I was just joking. Nick, you joining us?"

"Sure. Thanks."

"He doesn't even care where we go," Daniel teased.

"Hey, I'm a guy," Nick said with a shrug. "I like to eat."

"We'll be back around six and figure out where we'll go then. Okay with you two?"

"Not earlier?" Nick pretended to complain. "I'll be really hungry by then."

Leah patted his hand and smiled at him. "I'm sure we can find something for a snack for you, Nick. No one goes hungry in an Amish home. You know that."

He waited until Naomi and Daniel left, then turned back to Leah. "I'm sorry I wasn't truthful with Naomi. I just didn't expect her to walk in. I didn't know what to say."

"You're not very good at lying," she said.

Nick fidgeted. "That's a good thing, right?"

She regarded him sternly. There was that reminder of his grandmother. "*Ya*, that's a good thing," she agreed dryly.

"If you don't mind me saying so, that's why I'm worried about Naomi," he said. "Amish girls are sheltered. Naive. And there's pressure on them to conform to tradition. John is probably using all those things to get her to stay with him. Abusers are smart. They're manipulative. They know how to work on women—make them feel guilty. Damage their self-esteem. Make them think everything is their fault."

"How is it you know so much about this?" she asked quietly as she refilled their cups.

She leaned over to snag the cookie jar and slid it across the table to Nick. He thanked her but shook his head. His stomach was knotting up more and more as they talked.

"A friend of mine had the same problem years ago when we were in college," he told her. "And I read a lot. It's a big problem."

So many women hid the abuse for months. Years. What if Naomi's arm wasn't the only place she was injured? Plain dress covered a woman; if he hadn't innocently touched her, he'd never have known she was hurt.

"If you weren't so worried, I wouldn't have talked about this with you," Leah said after a moment. "It's between Naomi and John—"

"Are you saying you won't do anything if she doesn't break it off with him?" he demanded, frowning at her.

"*Nee*, I'm not saying that at all," she hurried to assure him. "I can talk to her again. I can ask the bishop to . . ." she trailed off. "Well, it might not be a good idea to consult with him," she mused, and became lost in thought. "But let's see what she does when we go back home."

She brightened. "Maybe John will decide that she's not *fraa* material after all," she said. "He didn't look happy when she wouldn't stop to talk to him that day when we left. And Naomi said he didn't like that she told him to go home when he surprised us with a visit—"

She stopped and grimaced. "Please forget that you heard that from me. I doubt she wanted me to share that."

"She won't hear it from me."

Hmm, he thought. Maybe it was a sign of hope. It showed some backbone on Naomi's part. Then again, John might not appreciate it and might see it as a sign that she was rebellious. Disobedient. Noncompliant with his wishes.

Who knew how he would behave?

Leah glanced at the kitchen clock. "Well, the quilting circle is coming in a half hour. Would you like to stay and help us?"

Nick scrambled to his feet. "Thank you for the invitation but I have to run."

"Is that the truth, Nick?" She regarded him sternly.

"Yes, really, I have to run," he said. "I had my daily slice of peanut butter pie at Yoder's. I need to run off the calories."

He jogged for the door. "See you back here at six."

11

It was a good thing their vacation was ending tomorrow, thought Naomi, because she thought she might become a beach bum.

Well, as much as an Amish girl could be. Relaxing on the beach was still a little hard . . . at first. Once the sun had begun warming her skin and she watched the waves for a few minutes, though, pure bliss set in and she felt herself unwinding and not urging herself to get something useful done.

Nick and Daniel were out deep-sea fishing today—she'd declined, not interested in going out on a boat—and her grandmother and Ida wanted to spend the day just relaxing at home.

Naomi wanted to be out in the sun. So she did a little research and found out she could catch a bus to the beach. While she didn't intend to go so far as to wear a swimsuit, she'd picked up a light cotton denim skirt that barely hit the knees and a T-shirt on one of her shopping forays. It felt totally different to walk out of the house today wearing them, along with a kerchief tied over her head instead of her *kapp*. She slid her feet into the new flip-flops Nick had bought her after the incident with the gator, and her outfit was complete.

No one gave her a second glance on the number nineteen bus crowded with passengers from Pinecraft. They seemed to want to bring everything with them—not just totes with food and insulated containers of drinks, but a volleyball net and ball, lawn chairs, and toys for any children who came along.

Daniel had warned her to get there early to get a seat, and so she sat on the bus, watching as people piled on with their things. The bus driver occasionally shook his head and rolled his eyes at all the paraphernalia but stayed good-humored about it.

The ride didn't take long and the view was worth the crowded conditions. Naomi carried her tote down to the sand, set it down for a moment to shed her flip-flops, and then walked to a place where she could spread her quilt.

She plopped down on it and gave a big sigh of pleasure. The sky didn't have a cloud in it and there was a warm breeze blowing off the ocean. Perfect day.

Remembering that first day when she hadn't used sunscreen and had gone home looking like a lobster, she pulled out the bottle and slathered it everywhere there was skin showing. Then she set the little kitchen timer she'd brought from the kitchen. No way she was going back with a nasty sunburn. One thing she knew about herself: once she'd learned a hard lesson, she didn't repeat it.

She hoped. Please, God, don't let me ever fall in love with another man like John, she prayed.

The tiny cottage they'd been staying in had two very small bedrooms, and in one she'd found a shelf of books left behind for guests. Most weren't really of interest to her, but a little, dog-eared copy of *Gift from the Sea* by a woman named Anne Morrow Lindbergh caught her attention with its cover featuring shells scattered on a beach.

She quickly became engrossed in the short essays within that centered on a message the author had gleaned from studying a shell she'd found on the beach during a vacation from her family.

It was an odd concept, taking some extended time away from family, since Naomi's whole experience had been so focused on being with so many, many members of hers since she'd been born.

At first, she thought she'd feel that the author didn't love her family enough or that she was selfish. But as she read about women needing to have some alone time to renew their emotional strength in order to have it to give to family, Naomi could see the sense in it.

She looked up from the book and watched the ocean. In the beginning, she'd been so in love that she'd wanted to spend every minute she could with John. Then when she had gotten some complaints from her family that she wasn't seeing them enough, she'd tried to back off a little. Now she could see that she felt drained by his constant demands. And tired of the way he became more and more critical.

As much as she enjoyed having family and friends around—and as much as she'd loved the time she'd spent here with Nick—she thought it was kind of nice to be by herself a little today to read and to think about . . . well, everything or nothing at all. It was her choice.

She went back to the book and kept reading. The story about the chambered nautilus shell fascinated her the most. They'd all gone to a shell shop one day—Nick insisted that the three of them had to take some shell souvenirs back home. It was required, he'd said, and the shells could be plain or they could be made into all sorts of things, from a mermaid to a vase. Actually, the more elaborate the decorations the more he seemed to enjoy looking at them.

Naomi just didn't know anyone who she thought would want to decorate their house with a pirate ship made of shells.

The one item she'd bought herself was a chambered nautilus that was sliced so that all the interior chambers could be seen. So she was fascinated by Lindbergh's story of how as the animal inside the shell outgrew the home—the chamber—it moved into a bigger one and now it used a gas to create a buoyancy to propel itself up and down in the ocean.

She thought about the example of the nautilus having many homes and remembered the passage in the Bible about how in God's house there are many mansions. Wasn't even one of His lowliest creatures using something from its past to learn how to lift itself to something higher?

She couldn't blame God for her making a mistake with John. If anyone had made a mistake, maybe it was she, because she'd wanted to believe so badly that he was the one for her. She needed to pray for guidance and know that all was working according to His plan.

Ding! went the timer. She laughed, thinking it sounded like she'd had a brilliant idea.

"Man, this is the life," Nick said, leaning back in his chair on the boat and gazing at the cloudless sky. "I have to say I don't usually envy anyone, but to be able to do this most days where you live . . . wow."

"You could move here," Daniel said casually.

"Yeah, right." Nick tilted the brim of his ball cap to shield his eyes.

"I'm serious."

"I don't think I'd find as much work."

Daniel tested his line and decided he had no bites. "I'm serious. You could come work for me."

"I'm no farmer."

"Me neither."

Nick was taken aback. "I thought your family farmed."

"We used to. Sold the place in Pennsylvania. Remember?"

"But I thought that was so you could just farm here. So what do you do here?"

"I own a landscaping business," Daniel told him. He reached into a cooler, pulled out two soft drinks, and handed one to Nick. "And I have a growing business installing solar panels."

"Solar panels?"

Daniel grinned. "Yeah, kind of ironic, huh? Even more so if I were Old Order Amish—not Beachy Amish Mennonite."

He climbed back into his chair and popped the top on his drink. "Think about it. Solar energy is a green business that helps the environment. No coal messing up the air and no transporting oil. No worrying about nuclear power. I always thought it made no sense to be using up a resource heating or cooling our homes when especially in the South the sun is there to use."

"There'd be less sun some days up north," Nick said slowly. "But I see the possibilities. I don't plan to move, though."

"Yeah, wonder why," Daniel said with a grin as he took another gulp of his soft drink.

Nick's line bobbed. He put his drink in the holder on his chair and fastened his seat belt, then took his rod and began reeling in.

A huge marlin burst from the water and yanked at the line as it plunged back down into the ocean. He'd always thought it was an amazingly beautiful sport fish with its silver and blue colors, curving sculptured tail, and long pointed snout.

Daniel jumped to his feet, spilling his soft drink. "Wow! Look at that!"

One of the crew came to advise Nick on how to bring the fish in, and for the next twenty minutes Nick held onto the rod and wrestled the fish. It took two of them to bring it to the side of the boat.

And then Nick broke their hearts when he shook his head and insisted that they return the fish to the water.

"I'm going to cry," the crew member said as he walked away. "Who doesn't keep a fish like that after he landed it?"

Nick looked at Daniel. "You think I'm nuts, too, don't you? I just couldn't let it die. It's too beautiful."

Daniel clapped him on the back. "You're a strange dude, my man."

"Dude?" Nick laughed. "You're calling me a dude? Who does *that*?"

Nick whistled as he drove home a couple of hours later.

Ten pounds of less attractive fish that he'd caught were tucked into the insulated carrier on the floorboard of the front passenger seat, all cleaned and filleted.

If Leah and Naomi wanted, he thought he'd fry up the fish for supper. He'd see if one of them would make some cole slaw and that Southern delicacy known as hush puppies. Amish women knew how to cook all kinds of food. Surely, they knew how to make hush puppies

He passed several people walking from the bus stop. They were younger than him, in their late teens, and already their skin looked bright red. He remembered how Naomi had gotten burned that first day. She'd said she was going to the beach today. He hoped that she'd remember and use the sunscreen he'd bought her.

Then he realized that the woman behind the teens looked familiar, although she wasn't dressed in Amish clothing. He looked closer, careful of traffic, and saw that it was Naomi.

Pulling over, he honked. She stopped, saw it was him, and when it was safe, crossed to the other side of the road.

"Like a lift?"

"That would be nice, thanks." She got in.

"I almost didn't recognize you."

She glanced at her clothes then up again and colored a little. "I noticed some of the girls wore things like this when they didn't want to wear swimsuits."

He'd thought she was an *Englisch* girl at first. That would have been so much easier for them, he reflected. There wouldn't have been any conflict over them dating.

However, he'd never have met her and become attracted to her if he hadn't been driving her because she was Amish and couldn't drive herself.

Besides, if he were honest he'd have to say that he'd been attracted to her because of her spiritual beliefs, her nature—all the things that she'd become because of her culture.

"You look nice," he told her. "You always do."

"Did you have a good time going deep-sea fishing?" she asked, clearly trying to deflect attention from herself.

"Great time. Caught a blue marlin."

"One of those big fish with the huge fin on the back and the spear thing on its face?"

He laughed as he drove her home. "That's quite a description."

She turned in her seat and looked in the back. "Where is it?"

"You mean like am I having it mounted?"

She wrinkled her nose. "Yes, I guess so." She tried not to shudder.

"You can relax. I let it go."

"Too small, like the fish I released?"

"No."

"Why? I don't understand."

Nick pulled into the driveway and stopped. "One of the crew members thought I was nuts to let it go. But I thought it was too beautiful to let it die, so I put it back." He shut off the engine. "I guess I didn't look like a 'manly man' or something, you know?"

"That's silly."

"I did catch some nice fish and thought I'd fry them up for dinner for us. Would you and Leah be interested?"

"She's having supper with her friends."

"Oh." Nick leaned an arm on the steering wheel. "I guess that's out, then."

He watched indecision flit across her face. But he knew that a single Amish woman didn't entertain a man, especially a single *Englisch* man, without someone else present. They didn't need to have anyone comment on it.

"Maybe we could put it in the refrigerator for lunch tomorrow and cook it then?"

"Great idea. Why don't we get cleaned up and I'll take us to Troyer's for the buffet tonight. I promise I won't go back for thirds."

"That's good. I'd hate to see you bankrupt them before we leave."

"Very funny," he said, not making it out of the van before she got out on her own. "If they haven't gone under with Daniel eating there, they never will."

12

Maybe it was her imagination, but it seemed to Naomi that Nick was driving slower going home than he had on the trip down.

She glanced over at the speedometer and saw that, sure enough, he was.

"Nervous? I can drive slower."

"How?" she asked, looking pointedly at the speedometer.

He shrugged. "I didn't know you were in a hurry to get back."

"At this rate, it'll take twice as long."

She bit her lip. Why was she complaining? She was dreading going to see John. Then she thought, *I wonder if Nick isn't in a hurry to go back, either?* He'd joked on the way to Florida that they should stop off at some roadside attractions, tourist things to see off the beaten path, and her grandmother had said if he was really interested maybe they'd do that on the way home.

But Nick said nothing about them now and Naomi wasn't about to do so.

Nick checked the rearview mirror in preparation to change lanes and saw Leah watching him.

"Sorry, I'll speed up." A few minutes later he glanced over. "Better?"

"Hmm?"

"I'm driving the speed limit."

She stared at him blankly for a minute, wondering why he was telling her that, and then realized she'd been so totally involved in her thoughts that she'd complained about him driving too slowly. He must think she was an idiot.

"I see. Good."

Naomi went back to looking out the car window. She'd been so mixed up about what to do about John when she'd left Paradise. Now, on her way back, she knew deep inside that she didn't want to be with him anymore. But she still didn't know how to break up with him.

And why had it proven to be necessary? She'd thought John was the man that God had set aside for her. Even as other girls in her community had wondered—sometimes worried—that it was taking so long for God to send a man to them, she hadn't.

When Mary Katherine and Jacob started seeing each other, then gotten married, it just confirmed to her that God's will was manifest and all was working as it should.

Then one Sunday, a new man in the community came to the service, and just like the romantic novels she and her cousins had read years ago when they had a sleepover, he'd been perfect for her. He was handsome and charming, and it was kind of nice that he wasn't someone she'd grown up with.

That had been a kind of bonus—her not knowing him from childhood. It made him a little . . . mysterious. Nearly always, the girls knew the boys from *schul*, and friendship made the strongest foundation for a good marriage.

It was different being with John, almost like being *Englisch* since they didn't have all those years of knowing each other forever. They'd spent a lot of time learning about each other.

She told herself that must be why it seemed she couldn't do anything right in John's eyes. It hadn't taken long for her to notice that when she packed a picnic lunch for them to enjoy on a drive in the country he said it wasn't what he was used to eating. He complained that she wasn't putting him and their relationship first when she refused to drop everything to go somewhere with him when he got off early. She wouldn't spend enough time with him and needed to see her father, his new wife, and the family less. What a complaint; she had so little time with working so much at the shop that she seldom saw them.

And she made him so angry sometimes. He accused her of flirting when she was simply talking to a former classmate who happened to be male. Why, she didn't even think of most of them as men. Often they were the boys who'd always pulled her pigtails and eaten her lunch and made fun of her every time they could. She really didn't see any of them as having grown up much. And she certainly didn't see them as possibilities for marriage.

She'd told John he didn't need to check that she was at work. And she hadn't forgotten her date with him that one afternoon. She'd simply been delayed while she and Anna were mailing some packages at the post office. She winced as she remembered how he'd stormed at her, saying that she'd hurt his feelings.

She rubbed at her forehead as she remembered the list of her wrongdoings.

"Headache?"

Her fingers stilled. "A little."

"There's aspirin and ibuprofen in the first-aid kit. Want me to get some for you?"

"Maybe when we stop next."

How ironic, she thought. Nick wasn't engaged to her but noted an action like her rubbing her forehead and asked if she was all right. She turned slightly and studied him. They'd spent a lot of the last two weeks doing things together, and there hadn't been the tiniest complaint from him.

She blushed as she remembered what had happened instead—how he'd kissed her, cared about her when he found that her arm was hurt. And he'd been angry when he realized that John had hurt her.

"I could use some coffee," he said. "How about you two?"

"That would be nice," Leah said. She reached forward to pat Naomi on her shoulder. "Coffee always helps your headaches too, *liebschen*."

Nick pulled off the interstate and located a restaurant. Once they were settled at a table, Leah excused herself to visit the restroom.

John stirred his coffee, then looked up at Naomi. "So how long have you been having headaches?"

She shrugged. "I don't know. Maybe six months."

"About the length of time you've been with John?"

Naomi froze and carefully set her spoon down beside her plate. "I don't want to talk about it." She rubbed at her forehead again. When was the ibuprofen she'd taken going to kick in?

"Here y'all go," said the waitress, setting down a plate in front of each of them, then setting Leah's on the table.

"Maybe I should check and see if *Grossmudder* is okay," Naomi said as she stood. "It's not easy to get around on crutches."

"I see her," Nick said. "She's making her way back now."

He stood when Leah approached the table and held out her chair, then took her crutches to lean them against a nearby wall.

"I'll be right back," Naomi said, and headed for the restroom.

Splashing some cold water on her face helped. She wet some paper towels with cold water and held them to the back of her neck.

When she returned to the table, it seemed to her that Nick and her grandmother stopped talking suddenly, but when she looked curiously at them, she wondered if she was imagining it.

Nick, always the gentleman, stood and helped her with her chair.

Her grandmother patted her hand. "Try to eat. It might help."

"It's already getting better," she told them.

"I think we should find a place to stay a little earlier tonight," Nick said as he buttered his biscuit. "Let you get some sleep and get rid of that headache."

"I'm fine."

"You're looking a little peaked," her grandmother said. She put the back of her hand against Naomi's forehead.

Naomi moved away. "What are you doing?"

"Checking for fever."

Shaking her head, Naomi began eating her chicken and dumplings. "I'm not sick. I just have a bad headache. I think we should drive for a while longer."

So they did. The ibuprofen and the food helped—well, they helped her get drowsy.

"Why don't you just give in and take a nap?" Nick asked quietly. "Leah is."

Naomi looked back and saw that her grandmother was indeed sleeping. But she was half afraid to try to sleep. When she'd fallen asleep on the way to Pinecraft she'd had a nightmare.

Back then she'd been emotionally upset about John and she hadn't had enough sleep. This time she felt rested from the time off, but she knew her headache had developed from the stress of thinking about seeing John again. She didn't want to chance another nightmare.

"They must have put something in our food," she said. "Aren't you tired?"

"I'm fine. Got revved up on the coffee. I figure I'll call it a day in about an hour and find us a motel."

Night fell. Nick switched on the headlights.

She peered into the darkness ahead. "You can't see very far in the dark, can you?"

"I can see as far as the headlights," he told her. "I can make a whole trip that way."

He glanced at her. "E. L. Doctorow. He's a writer I admire. He said, 'Writing a novel is like driving a car at night. You can only see as far as your headlights, but you can make the whole trip that way.'"

"I don't know anyone like you," she said quietly.

"Well, we're all individuals," he said, shrugging. "I don't know anyone like you, either."

"So you don't think we Amish are all alike?"

"Don't be ridiculous. Just because there's conformity to a dress code and behavior and religion doesn't mean you're not a snowflake."

"Snowflake?"

"My mom always said everyone's different."

She smiled. "Like snowflakes. Or grains of sand on the beach," she said, remembering the beautiful photo he'd shown her in the book that day.

"Right."

He was silent for a long time. Then she saw him glance in the rearview mirror. Naomi looked too and saw that Leah still slept. A faint snoring could be heard from the backseat.

"I just want to say something."

She straightened and looked at him. "What?"

"You don't need to worry about—about what happened on the beach that day. When I kissed you," he elaborated.

"I know what you did." She compressed her lips. "What I did," she added primly.

"It's between us, Naomi. I'm never telling anyone." He sighed, glanced at her briefly, then back at the road. "And I'm never doing it again."

That was best. She knew that. But deep inside she realized that she felt . . . disappointed.

It was disheartening that she felt so attracted to Nick. The more she'd been with him, the more she'd realized that what she felt for him was so much more than what she felt for John. Even if John's actions hadn't caused her to reconsider their future marriage—well, it would have been obvious to her just how much she wanted to be with Nick.

Why couldn't he have been the man God had set aside for her?

13

Naomi got into the van the morning after they returned and regarded Nick with a faint smile. "Well, long time, no see."

He laughed. "Never figured you'd use that expression."

"Yes, well, I've been hanging around with an *Englisch* man a lot lately."

Leah joined them, climbing into the backseat and closing the door. "I don't know about you two, but I'm looking forward to work today. Vacation was nice but it's *gut* to be back."

It was back to business as usual. Nick picked them up and then swung by to pick up Anna. Mary Katherine's husband, Jacob, liked to take her to work these days.

Anna sat waiting on the front porch of her home and squealed the minute Nick pulled into her drive. She opened Naomi's door and hugged her, then climbed into the backseat to throw her arms around her grandmother. Belatedly, she said hello to Nick and then clicked her seat belt.

"Hello to you, too," he said, grinning at her.

Then the questions started. Nick tuned out the excited female chatter. The drive seemed over before it started—probably because he'd just made a two-day road trip so recently that anything less than that might seem short.

Nick turned down the street of the shop and saw a familiar male figure standing in front of Stitches in Time. He didn't need to glance over at Naomi to know the moment she spotted her fiancé waiting on the sidewalk, a bunch of roses in his hand.

"Shall I go around the block?" he quietly asked her.

"Why would you go around the block?" Anna asked, breaking off her conversation with her grandmother. "What's going on?"

"We'll talk about it later," Naomi told her.

She gathered up her purse and tote bag and looked at Nick. "Go ahead and drop us off. But thanks for the offer."

Nick pulled to the curb and watched Naomi release her belt and get out.

"Have a good day," she told him.

His stomach clenched at the despair he saw in her eyes. He wanted to protect her, shield her from pain, but he had no right to do so.

"*Ya*," said Leah, giving Nick's shoulder a pat. "We'll see you later."

"Nick?"

He met Anna's gaze in the rearview mirror. "Yeah?"

"What's going on?"

"Naomi said you'd talk later."

She made a face at him and got out of the van, shutting the door with a little more force than necessary. Then she glanced over her shoulder and shot him an irrepressible grin.

Nick laughed and shook his head. That was Anna. Always curious. Always pushing. But never bad-tempered. He was a little surprised at how he'd missed her while he was gone.

He sat there in front of the shop, watching Naomi accept the flowers from John. Watching the man give her a chaste kiss on her cheek. And watching her shake her head and gesture at the shop.

There were other people Nick needed to pick up. A schedule to keep. But he realized he was waiting because he didn't want to leave Naomi alone with John. Not after what he knew about him now.

Naomi could be heard saying she had to get inside for work. John argued with her but Naomi remained firm. When he reached for her arm, she backed away, and he didn't pursue touching her.

Good thing. Nick had his hand on his door and would have intervened.

Nick could hear parts of their conversation because Naomi had rolled her window down. But he didn't need to hear their voices or all of their words. Just one surreptitious glance at their body language and he could see that both were tense.

He sighed, knowing he couldn't protect Naomi if she wanted to stay with John. When Naomi suddenly glanced over at him Nick pretended to be occupied with his clipboard. She was probably curious why he hadn't left yet, since he usually had pretty full days with his business. He reminded himself again that he had other clients he needed to pick up. It was important to maintain his reputation for promptness.

Reluctantly, he set the clipboard down, checked for traffic, and got back on the road.

As he drove, he thought about how he and Leah had done a lot of talking about God's will the past few months. She understood about his search for something more in his life, his desire to understand what God wanted of him.

All he could do at this point was try to be a friend to Naomi since he couldn't be more. And he could pray for her.

Come to think of it, that was a lot. Feeling better about things, he continued on his route.

"Naomi!"

She glanced up and saw Jacob pulling up in the buggy with an animated Mary Katherine sitting beside him. Naomi had never been so glad to see Mary Katherine as at that moment.

"I'm so glad you're back!" Mary Katherine cried, climbing down quickly and flinging her arms around Naomi. "I missed you so much!"

Jacob got out of the buggy and gave Naomi a big hug. "Nice to have you back."

He acknowledged John with a nod, then gave his wife a quick kiss on the cheek. "See you later."

Mary Katherine watched him leave, then turned to John. "*Guder mariye.*"

"*Guder mariye*," he said. "Naomi, we have to—"

"Get to work," Mary Katherine said breezily. "I'm afraid we got a little behind with Naomi and Grandmother gone."

She turned to Naomi. "So, are you ready to get back to work?" she asked Naomi, wrapping a companionable arm around her waist and leading her toward the front door of the shop.

"But—" John began.

"Time to open," Mary Katherine called over her shoulder.

Once inside, Naomi looked out the window and saw John standing there scowling, his hands on his hips.

"That was really rude of you," Naomi said under her breath, smiling and waving to John.

He hesitated for a moment and then when he saw she wasn't coming back outside, he began walking away. Naomi breathed a sigh of relief.

"I just wish you were engaged to a man like Jacob."

Naomi rolled her eyes. "When are you going to come down from your honeymoon?"

Mary Katherine smiled dreamily. "I hope I never do."

They went inside and put their things away. Naomi wanted to throw the flowers John had given her into the trash but that didn't seem fair to the poor flowers.

The blooms hadn't done anything wrong and deserved to be appreciated for their beauty. Instead, she found a vase, filled it with water, and arranged the hothouse roses in it.

She'd never liked red roses. But John never seemed to remember that. She sighed as she set them on the table and walked back out into the shop.

Mary Katherine hugged her grandmother and then went to stand at the front counter.

Local customers streamed in all morning, welcoming Leah and Naomi back. Fellow Amish wanted to know about their vacation. What was Florida really like? How was the weather? What had they done?

"I always wanted to go to Florida," Katie Stotzfus said, ooh-ing and aahing over the photos Nick had taken.

"You should go." Leah told them about walking outside to pick an orange for breakfast, about playing shuffleboard in the middle of January, and about the sugar-white sand on the beach the day Nick carried her down to sit on a quilt and gaze at the ocean.

It was so good to see her grandmother in a totally different mood from the almost depressed one she'd worn before the trip. At noon, with the last of the morning rush out the door and the Monday quilting circle gone home for lunch, Naomi locked the door and turned the sign on it around to "Back at 1 p.m." Then they gathered in the back room for lunch.

Leah gave a happy sigh as she sat in a chair and put her injured foot up on another.

"I'm happy to be back, but that was a busy morning," she said.

"I brought cold fried chicken," Mary Katherine told them, taking it from the refrigerator and placing it on the table. "I made potato salad and baked beans too."

"That's a lot of trouble on top of running the shop while we were gone," Naomi told her as she set the table with plates and forks.

Mary Katherine shook her head. "I just doubled the recipe for supper last night. And Jacob helped. I think he really enjoys cooking."

"Wouldn't it be wonderful if he convinced other men in the community to do so?" Anna said.

"He told me Chris, Hannah's husband, cooks because he learned how before he became Amish," Mary Katherine told them.

She opened up the containers of potato salad and beans and put serving spoons in them. "He and Chris actually swapped recipes when Chris and Hannah stopped by. Can you believe it?"

"I can just imagine what the bishop would think of that," Naomi muttered.

Anna clapped her hand to her mouth. "We forgot to tell them."

"Forgot to tell us what?" Leah asked, the chicken leg she'd just chosen suspended on the way to her mouth.

"The bishop came down with a nasty case of pneumonia a few days after you left," Anna told her. "He's still not doing well."

"I'll stop by his house and talk to his wife on the way home," Leah said.

She placed the chicken on her plate and helped herself to potato salad and beans, then passed them on to Naomi.

"You're going to go by his house?" Anna asked. "Really?"

"We've had our differences recently, but still, he's served our community faithfully."

Naomi listened to the conversation at the table. She couldn't help feeling relieved that she wouldn't have to accompany her grandmother to the bishop's house, especially after the way their last conversation. She was still upset that he'd thought he should make comments about what goods they offered in the shop when he didn't do that with what men sold in their stores. He wanted only traditional crafts and that was contrary to Leah encouraging new, creative crafts by her three granddaughters.

However, Naomi would have preferred visiting him over having to talk to John after work.

What a sad state of affairs to think that way, she thought. Right now, she just wanted to go home and hide under the covers— and the day was only half over.

She wished she could have the kind of forgiving attitude her grandmother had about the bishop. If she did, maybe then she could have a better attitude than she did about John. All she wanted was to break off the relationship she had with him. She didn't want to hurt him, but she was so tired of him turning everything around on her when it was actually him hurting her.

When she realized that the room had gotten quiet, that Leah was staring at her, she realized she was absently rubbing at her forearm, which still ached from where John had hurt her when he unexpectedly visited her in Florida. She shook her head in a silent message to her grandmother that she didn't want to talk about it and placed her hand on her lap.

They heard the shop door open and then close. Hannah walked in, her key in her hand, her husband, Chris, at her side.

She bent and hugged Leah. "So glad to see you!"

"I'm glad to be back," Leah said.

Hannah turned to Naomi and hugged her too. "Are you glad to be back? Did you have a good time?"

Naomi nodded. Well, that was mostly true, she thought. She'd had a wonderful adventure in Florida and she was glad to be back and happy to see everyone.

Except John.

Chris pulled out a chair and helped Hannah into it, then stood beside her, his hand a silent gesture of support.

She patted his hand. "Why don't you go find something to do for an hour while I teach the class?"

"We talked about this."

He met her gaze and an unspoken message moved between them. Neither backed off.

"Hannah, we have some juice if you'd like it," Naomi suggested.

She glanced at the coffeepot sitting atop the stove. Her bottom lip jutted out. "I want coffee."

"I know, I know," Naomi soothed. "But it won't be much longer."

Hannah rubbed her protruding abdomen. "I can't drink coffee even after the baby comes. I'll be nursing."

Naomi turned to Chris. "Can I get you something to drink?"

He gave his wife a sidelong look. "I'll have whatever she's having."

Hannah's pout vanished. "You don't have to do that." She looked at the other women. "He said he wouldn't drink coffee since I can't have it."

Chris reddened. "No big deal."

Anna reached over and gave his forearm a squeeze. "That's really sweet of you, Chris."

"Long as I don't have to give birth," he muttered.

He stuck around after the women cleaned up the remains of lunch, sipping a cup of decaffeinated tea like Hannah.

The ladies taking Hannah's quilting class began arriving. Naomi knew most of them, but one woman was new—a police officer who wore her uniform. She thought she'd seen her before.

Chris greeted her when she walked into the back room looking for coffee. "Kate, how's everything?"

"Good," she said, leaning against the kitchen counter. "You coming to the wedding next month?"

"Wouldn't miss it. Can't wait to see you put a ball and chain on my old friend Malcolm."

"Ha-ha," she said, rolling her eyes. "There's that guy humor about marriage." She glared at him. "I'm getting enough of it at the station, thanks. And if I hear anything said about me being here for a quilting lesson, I'll know who to go after."

Chris held up his hands. "What happens in Stitches in Time stays in Stitches in Time," he said, grinning.

Naomi jerked her head to look at him when he said it, but he wasn't directing his comment to her. It reminded her of what Nick had said about what happened in Florida stayed in Florida. But no one was looking at her. There was no deeper meaning.

"So are you here for a quilting lesson?" Kate asked Chris.

"Me? No."

"I've heard some men quilt."

"Well, I do my part cooking, when most of the men around here don't. That's all the girlie stuff I'll do." He winked at Naomi to show he was joking, that he was enjoying teasing Kate.

Naomi rolled up her sleeves and plunged her hands into the dishwater. Sometimes they had the time to clean up right after lunch and sometimes it had to wait until they closed the shop. It all depended on how busy the shop was.

Chris brought his cup over and handed it to her. Then he frowned. "That's quite a bruise you've got."

She glanced at it and nodded.

"How'd you get it?" he asked.

"I don't know. Probably bumped it."

Chris reached out and took her forearm. He peered at it. "Don't think so. Looks like somebody grabbed you—you can see separate finger marks."

Naomi pulled her arm away from him and pushed her hands back into the soapsuds. "It's nothing."

"Naomi—"

Glancing over her shoulder, she shook her head. "I'm taking care of it."

"How?"

Sighing, she leaned her elbows on the edge of the sink and met his concerned gaze—so concerned that he deserved to know.

"I'm breaking up with John, if you must know," she said quietly.

"Good. Mary Katherine has told me she's been uncomfortable around him for some time. But she didn't suspect that he'd hurt you."

He picked up a dish towel and began drying the dishes that were draining in a rack.

It did her heart good to see how easily he shifted into helping mode. It wasn't easy to run a farm, and yet he obviously helped Mary Katherine inside the home, just as she tried when she could to help outside with his chores. And his help would be needed so much when she delivered their second child.

"When are you doing it?"

"Today. Right after work."

"Where?"

"What do you mean where? Are you going to check up on me?"

Her breath hitched and she heard the edge in her voice. Then she felt contrite. "I'm sorry, I'm just a little tense about it."

"If you're afraid he's going to get angry and hurt you—"

She bit her lip and finally nodded. "I'd be stupid if I didn't think it could happen."

Chris threw down the dish towel and walked over to close the door. "You know I used to be in the military. C'mere, I'm going to show you a little self-defense. Just in case."

Naomi dried her hands on the towel and walked over to him.

The door opened.

"Oh, my!" Hannah cried out.

Chris pulled his arm from around Naomi's neck. "It's not what you think! I can explain!"

Hannah was jostled aside by Kate, who raised her gun and held it pointed at Chris.

"What's going on?"

"Easy, Kate, easy," Chris said, holding up his hands.

"He's just showing me some self-defense moves," Naomi rushed to tell them. "Really, everything's okay."

Kate lowered her gun and holstered it. "Any reason for you to need self-defense lessons?" she asked Naomi.

Naomi saw the woman's sharp eyes take in the bruise on her forearm as she started rolling down her sleeves.

Hannah wavered on her feet and Chris reached out and grabbed her. "Dizzy," she said as he lowered her into a chair. "I'm okay," she said as he bent over her. "Just a little too much excitement."

"Now you know how I felt when your brother found me in your hayloft," he said, patting her back. "Let me get you some water."

He straightened and turned to Kate. "Was it necessary to flash your gun? You knew it was just Naomi and me back here."

"The shop has a back door just like most of them do. I didn't know what I'd find when your wife cried out."

Mary Katherine and Anna filled the doorway, their eyes wide.

"What's going on?" Leah called behind them.

Kate sighed. "I'll go out and explain," she said, glancing back briefly at Chris. "You stay with Hannah and take care of her. No delivering early again," she told Hannah sternly. "That was a little too much excitement for me, helping Malcolm deliver your last kid."

"Yes, ma'am," Hannah said with a faint smile as she rubbed her abdomen.

Anna followed Kate, eager to find out what had happened. Mary Katherine hesitated, then, when Naomi nodded, left them.

Chris straightened. "I'm going to see if our driver is here."

"Self-defense?" said Hannah, studying Naomi. "What's going on?"

When Naomi didn't answer, Hannah's eyes widened and she covered her mouth with her hand. "Oh no, is John hurting you? Is that why Chris was teaching you self-defense?"

She got to her feet awkwardly and winced, but shook her head when Naomi tried to help her. Naomi went to the door to watch to make sure that Hannah made it safely to Chris's side. They held a whispered conversation she couldn't hear.

Hannah glanced back at Naomi, looked doubtful, but then left the shop.

Kate approached. "Naomi? I'd like to talk to you."

Naomi moved about in a daze the rest of the day.

She helped customers, rang up sales, swept the floor, and gave the shelves one last straightening.

Mary Katherine watched her, looking worried. Anna tried asking questions a couple of times, but after a stern look from their grandmother she subsided.

"Should I lock up now?" Naomi asked as she glanced at the clock.

Her grandmother nodded and gathered the day's receipts. "Naomi, I'd like you to help me with the deposit."

"But Mary Katherine and I've been doing it," Anna protested.

"Then all the more reason Naomi should be helping now," Leah said calmly. "If you could finish taking care of those mail orders, I would appreciate it, Anna."

Anna didn't look happy about it but she did as she was asked.

"*Grossmudder*, I just don't think I can talk about it anymore," Naomi said as she sat down at the table in the back room.

Leah gave her a gentle smile. "I know." She set the receipts aside and grasped Naomi's hand in hers. "I'm not going to tell you what you need to do. You know. And I believe you'll do it."

The tears came then, surprising Naomi. "Oh, *Grossmudder*, I loved him."

"I know. You still love him."

Naomi nodded, sobbing now. She reached for a tissue in her pocket.

"If you didn't, you could have walked away easily. You have a generous heart. A forgiving one. But that's not enough sometimes."

"I don't know what happened. He changed."

"Maybe he did. Maybe he didn't. He may have always been like this but he just knew how to hide it from you." She was silent for a moment, looking at Naomi with damp eyes. "Let's pray."

They sat there, hands clasped, and prayed, and then her grandmother took a fresh tissue from a little pack she carried in her pocket and wiped Naomi's eyes.

"Why don't you go wash your face and then we'll take you by the restaurant on our way home."

Naomi nodded. She got up, then bent down and hugged her grandmother. "Thank you."

Leah patted her cheek.

Nick parked a short distance from the restaurant and walked around to open her door. Naomi pretended that she was meeting John for a welcome-home dinner, but her cousins were so quiet she didn't think she was fooling anyone.

"I'll be back in an hour and I'll wait outside for you," Nick told her quietly. He slid a cell phone into her hand. "Put this in your purse."

"I can't take your phone."

"It's an extra one I keep for emergencies. Take it so you can call me if you need me sooner."

Naomi tucked it into her purse, then waved to her grandmother and her cousins. "Okay, have a good night, everyone. See you tomorrow."

She walked into the restaurant, trying not to drag her feet. The sooner she got it over with, the sooner she'd be home.

The hostess led Naomi to John's table. He was already there, drumming his fingers impatiently. "You're late."

She wasn't, but what was the point of arguing?

A waitress came with menus and John ordered supper, but when Naomi only ordered coffee, his eyebrows went up. "Did you eat before you came here tonight?"

"Of course not. There wasn't time after we closed the shop."

She stared down at the cup of coffee when it arrived, wishing she could figure out what to say.

"Did you enjoy your vacation?" he asked abruptly as he waited for his food.

"It was very nice."

John fiddled with his silverware, arranging it to his satisfaction. "I was quite disappointed that you weren't more appreciative of the trouble I went to in coming to see you."

"It was unexpected, John. I was there to be with my grandmother." She sighed. "We've already discussed that."

"You weren't there just to be with her," he said, frowning. "You were there to spend time with Nick."

"He's a family friend and driver," she told him. "That's all. You have nothing to be jealous of."

The minute the word *jealous* slipped out of her mouth, she was sorry. His expression darkened and he set his fork down with a clatter.

"That's not what I hear."

She'd wondered but hadn't been suspicious up until now. "I saw you talking with a man before you got on the bus," she said slowly.

"I—"

"And I saw him sitting in restaurants and such when *Grossmudder* and Nick and I sometimes went somewhere together," she continued.

She held her breath and waited for him to tell her that she'd been seen kissing Nick. If he did, she had no defense. She'd kissed him. It hadn't been intended, of course, but when it happened, she'd responded to Nick.

Which told her that even if she hadn't been sure she should break off her engagement with John, she knew she had to do so now.

Apparently John didn't know, because the accusation never came. He said nothing more about Nick.

The sense of relief was massive. That combined with the dread of coming here to talk to him and all the drama at the shop made her realize she felt drained.

"You didn't trust me," she said flatly.

"You can't blame me. If you hadn't—"

"Stop," she told him, holding up her hand. "Don't try to turn this back on me!"

His eyes widened. She'd never talked to him like that. "I'm not blaming you," he said in a cajoling tone.

When he reached for her hand, she drew it back. "Don't touch me! I won't let you hurt me again."

"I've never hurt you!" He took on an injured air.

"You know you have." She met his eyes. "You've manipulated me and intimidated me and been rough enough with me to hurt me. I've had the bruises on my arms to prove it."

He stared at her. "Where is all this coming from? Has Nick been feeding you some *Englisch* nonsense that you're being abused? Are you sure he doesn't want you for himself?"

"He's a family friend. He's our driver," she repeated.

She hoped she sounded convincing. She hadn't been so sure that was all Nick was since they'd visited Florida. But it didn't matter.

It was time to speak up for herself. She took a deep breath.

14

Nick felt his heart stop then start again when he pulled up outside the restaurant and saw a police officer talking with Naomi, who was sitting on a bench.

He slammed the car into park and killed the engine, then sprinted across the road.

"Naomi!" he called.

A horn honked and a car screeched to a stop just a few feet from him.

"What're you, an idiot?" the driver called. "Get outta the road!"

The officer turned, but before she could speak the driver was speeding off.

Now Nick's heart was pounding as he ran toward the sidewalk. "Is she all right?" he asked the officer. "Did that jerk hurt her?"

"She's fine," the woman said. "What's with you trying to get yourself killed? Maybe I need to write you a jaywalking ticket for not using the crosswalk."

"Please, don't," Naomi said tiredly. "Enough people have gotten into trouble over me today."

"You arrested John?" Nick asked the officer. "Can I shake your hand?"

Kate looked at him. "I didn't trust him. And you are?"

"Nick Talbot. You're not really going to give me a ticket for jaywalking, are you?"

"I'm thinking about it." Her stare was unblinking, her tone stern.

She turned back to Naomi. "Can I give you a ride home?"

"That's why Nick's here," Naomi said, standing. "He drives my grandmother and cousin and me to and from work. He came to get me after I met with John."

"I see."

"May I ask a question?"

"Sure." Kate put her hands on her equipment belt.

"Is there some reason you were here tonight?"

"I can't take a dinner break like everyone else?" Kate asked. "Food's really good here."

Nick watched tears well up in Naomi's eyes. "*Ya*, right," she said, surprising the officer with a hug. "I could tell John wanted to give me a hard time, but just after I told him I wouldn't be seeing him anymore he looked over and saw you a few tables away and changed his mind."

Kate's smile faded. "The first week or so is the most dangerous if an ex-boyfriend or husband is going to give you trouble," she told Naomi.

She pulled out a business card and pressed it into her hand. "You call 911 if there's any problem and give them my name. Now get out of here before I give your friend a ticket. I've had a long day. I didn't need to almost have someone splattered on the road right in front of me."

"Well, that was an image I didn't need to think about," Nick muttered.

"She was right."

"I know." He carefully guided Naomi across the street—using the crosswalk a few feet away, aware of the officer watching him, without him glancing back.

"She drew a gun on Chris."

He gave her a shocked look and would have stopped in the middle of the road, but she pulled him along. "You must really want to get on her bad side."

"I want the full story," he told her as they approached his vehicle. "Get in the front seat. Your hands are like ice. Why don't you have a warmer jacket on?"

"I wasn't expecting a cold snap," she told him. As soon as she buckled her seat belt she rubbed her hands together.

Nick got into the driver's side, started the car, and then turned on the heat. "It'll start warming up in a few minutes." Frowning, he put the car back into park. "I think I have a spare blanket in the trunk."

"No, no, let's get going," she said, glancing around. "I'll be fine."

He caught on to her nervousness and immediately clicked on the door locks and got the vehicle moving. "Are you afraid John is hanging around?"

"I doubt it," she said. "Guess I'm just overreacting to the officer's warning."

"I think it's wise to be careful," he told her.

Then, to get her mind off her tension, he began talking about the weather, comparing it to Florida. Soon he could see her visibly relax.

"So what's the story about Chris?"

She told him in as few words as possible and lapsed into silence after that. He started to ask her about how Leah was doing, but when they traveled under a streetlight and he looked over he saw a tear gleaming diamond bright on her cheek and he changed his mind.

When he pulled into the drive, a kerosene lamp glowed like a beacon of warmth in the front window of Leah's house. The door opened and light spilled out as Leah waited for Naomi to walk inside.

Naomi opened her purse to reach inside, but Nick put his hand over hers. "No charge. It's on the house."

"I can't—"

"A friend can't help a friend?"

She bit her lip. "You did so much on the trip and wouldn't take enough money."

"I don't want to hear about it," he said gruffly.

What he wanted was to reach over and stroke away the tear, to touch her shoulder and reassure her that everything was going to be all right, to tell her that you could survive not getting what you wanted.

But he didn't think he could convince her when he didn't believe those words himself.

"Bake me some of those rolls we had the first morning of the trip and we'll consider it even," he said lightly. "Now go on. Your grandmother's probably worried about you."

He waited while she got out and walked up to the front door, where he saw Leah embrace her. Leah waved to him, and placing her arm around Naomi, she closed the door. The lamp moved from the front window and he traced its path as one of them carried it to light the dark stairs and set it in a bedroom.

He pulled out of the driveway and drove home as darkness fell.

Life went back to normal—at least the kind of normal you had when you worked in a shop, thought Naomi as she straightened a display.

You never knew who would walk into the shop—local or tourist, new or longtime customer, buyer or browser.

Jamie, one of Mary Katherine's *Englisch* friends, breezed in with her hair in braids, wearing a short flowered skirt and a jean jacket covered with dozens of multicolored buttons and bows.

"Oh, a bird dropped a feather in your hair," Anna exclaimed, and started to pluck it out.

Jamie laughed and held up her hand. "No, I put it there! It's the latest fashion."

Anna raised her eyebrows. "Latest fashion?" She shook her head. "Imagine."

"You didn't notice my hair's brown now, not an unusual color."

Anna shrugged. "But I liked your hair when you colored it. I always thought it made you . . . you."

"Well, how about that."

"Glad to have you back."

"I'm glad to be back."

Jamie flopped down in a chair next to Naomi and studied the quilt she was sewing.

"What's that pattern?"

"Crazy quilt," Naomi muttered.

"Really?" Jamie looked at the random-sized pieces. "You feeling a little crazy? Maybe it's time for a Girl's Night In this week."

"Sounds like fun," said Anna. "We'll have to see if old married ladies can get away."

"Who are you calling 'old married lady'?" Mary Katherine asked, looking over from where she sat at her loom.

"You," Anna told her, giving her an impudent grin.

"How are you doing?" Jamie asked quietly. "I know Plain people are very private and don't make engagements public, but I knew. And I could tell something was wrong pretty quickly."

Naomi smiled slightly and leaned back in her chair. "And so now you know I'm not getting married, right?"

"I didn't tell her," Anna spoke up as she seated herself and pulled out her knitting.

"It's okay. Jamie's a friend." Naomi leaned back in her chair.

"So, you feeling a little discombobulated?" Jamie asked her, gesturing at the quilt.

"I thought I knew where I was going," Naomi told her slowly. "I thought he was the man God set aside for me and we'd get married and have children and—"

"Live happily ever after, like a fairy tale?"

She colored. "Well, we don't talk like that. That's just fanciful *Englisch* talk."

"Besides, there's no such thing as a happy ending," Anna blurted out, then looked startled at what she'd said. She pressed her fingers against her mouth, then jerked her head around and stared at Mary Katherine. "Sorry."

Mary Katherine stared at her, her expression sad. "No, I'm sorry, Anna. I'm sorry for what happened to you. I—"

"I don't want to talk about it."

"Anna—"

"I mean it, I don't want to talk about it." Anna shoved her knitting into the basket next to her chair and stood. "I'm going to see if *Grossmudder* needs help with the deposit."

As a group, they watched her leave the room.

"You're not going to go after her, try to talk to her?" Jamie asked.

Naomi shook head. "Not now. Anna would be very upset with us. She wants to be left alone when she's like that."

"But maybe that's not the best thing for her," Jamie persisted. "I remember when I took Psych—"

"Uh-oh, here comes the psychology class," Mary Katherine warned. "Look out, Naomi, here comes Dr. Freud."

Jamie grinned. "Okay, I know I talked a lot about the class when you and I discussed our fathers. But the class really helped me understand him."

"It's just we talk a lot about how God has this man set aside for us," Naomi said. "So why did Anna's husband die so young and leave her? Why did John—" she stopped.

"Why did John what?" Jamie pounced. "What did he do?"

Naomi shook her head. It wasn't right to talk bad about him.

"I can guess," Jamie finally said. "Abuse isn't a stranger to any community—*Englisch* or Amish."

"I'm not blaming John for anything."

"No. You think you did something wrong, don't you? Abusers are good at making their victims feel they're at fault, that they did something to make someone lose temper with them."

Naomi's fingers clutched at the quilt. "That psychology class taught you all that?"

"That and having friends who have gone through it. It's a bigger problem than you know." She checked her watch. "Gotta get to class."

She walked over and looked at the pattern Mary Katherine was weaving. "You talking to a class on weaving again this semester?"

"I am. And I'm enjoying the class your instructor is letting me audit."

No sooner had Jamie left than Elam Miller, an older Amish friend of their grandmother's, strolled in. Naomi had always liked Elam. He always had a smile for others and came around to help her grandmother with things that needed fixing.

Elam had lost his wife a little more than a year ago and she and her cousins had wondered if the two friends would marry after his time of mourning was over. But it hadn't happened.

"Is Leah here?" he asked, looking around.

"Elam?" she called from the back room. "Come on back."

He did as she asked and a few minutes later Anna came out and rejoined them in the shop.

"I was just told to get ready to close." She looked at the back room door, shut now, and seemed baffled. "I got the distinct feeling that they wanted to talk privately."

"Really? What about?" Mary Katherine asked.

"I don't know."

"He used to stop by and talk to *Grossmudder* when I stayed with her. I think he's sweet on her."

Naomi and Anna stared at her. "Really?"

"Really."

"You never said anything."

Mary Katherine shrugged. "He stopped coming for a while. I didn't think anything about it."

Anna smirked. "Then you and Jacob started seeing each other and all you could see was him."

It was so good to be back with them, Naomi reflected. They were closer to one another—closer than siblings. The day wasn't normal if they didn't say a loving word to one another—or bicker.

Days passed and people came and went in the shop. In between customers, Naomi quilted, Anna knitted, and Mary Katherine did her weaving. Life returned to the routine.

Except Nick didn't talk to her as often as he had before the trip—and definitely not as much as when they'd been in Pinecraft. She missed him.

The weather started warming up. Naomi didn't know if it was the signs of spring that made her heart feel a little lighter each day or the fact that she heard John had gone back to his own Amish community in another county.

She finished the crazy quilt and pulled out the material she'd bought at a store in Sarasota. Her cousins loved the tropical patterns and colors she'd found. Anna thought a quilt using the material with dolphins and seahorses would be perfect for a summer window display.

When Nick had wanted to buy one of her quilts John had carelessly told him that he didn't need to buy one at the auction-inflated price—that Naomi would make him one if he wanted.

She pulled out her sketchpad. Two patterns caught her eye. The first was one that was simple and used several coordinating materials. Her favorite was the one called Marine Life with a print of dolphins, sea turtles, and shells. It could be a reminder of the time they'd spent in Florida.

But then after she finished it, it just didn't seem like him. As he drove them home that night, he turned on the headlights and she remembered the quotation from the writer that he'd used on the way home from Florida.

It seemed to her that he'd been tuned in to her, hearing the bit of anxiety in her voice about finding a path home in the dark. He was like that, picking up on her emotions. He'd reassured her with it and shown her that he could be relied on to see her safely home.

A few days later, Naomi went looking for a pattern book in the back room of the shop. There, that was it, she thought as she found the one she wanted and brushed the dust from it. Her heart beat faster as she flipped through the pages and stopped to study the Mariner's Compass quilt pattern.

She walked out into the shop and began pulling bolts of materials: a rich navy blue, a turquoise, a light aquamarine, a cerulean. Some greens too, for when the sunlight hit the water a certain way.

She cut big spears of fabric, assembled them on a table to look like the pattern, and grew excited. The colors, the design—yes, this reflected Nick's personality, the way he'd grown up traveling, learning, seeking new adventures. His wasn't a life of staying on the tried-and-true path but of asking questions the way he did of Leah, of studying the people and places around him. Of his voracious reading.

He seemed on an inner quest for some meaning in his life, and while he didn't go around spouting some biblical phrase or trying to impress, he lived his spiritual beliefs by helping others and valuing the same kind of things she did.

This could be the quilt to give to a man like him. He'd understand that . . . well, that she understood him the way he seemed to understand her.

Sometimes, when she got into his van for the ride to and from work she caught him staring at her and she'd blush, remembering that kiss they'd shared on the beach. Remembering the way he'd seemed to care that night outside the restaurant when he'd seen her with the police officer and thought John had hurt her.

The image of him rushing across the street and nearly being hit by a car had seared itself into her brain. He'd been so worried about her that he'd been careless with his own safety.

In a way, he'd been a little responsible for her breaking things off with John. It hadn't just been that she'd realized she had feelings for Nick when they'd kissed.

No, if Nick hadn't been the man that he was—kind, caring, considerate, generous and not just to impress her—she might have believed that John was the measure of a good man and she'd have accepted that she should be with him. And she'd have accepted the manipulation and the slaps to her self-esteem.

Naomi smiled as she stitched. She had Jamie to thank for learning about that from her.

The gray clouds overhead—when sunshine had been predicted—reminded Nick of that saying "You don't like the weather? Just wait five minutes and it'll change."

He had mixed feelings about picking Naomi and Leah up this morning to drive them to a quilting show a couple of towns over. Maybe he should think about asking one of his drivers to switch routes with him, he mused as he drove to Leah's house. It might be better if he didn't have to have contact with Naomi for a while.

Maybe then he'd stop thinking about her so often. Maybe then he wouldn't be acting like a lovesick teenager over a girl he couldn't have.

He was glad that she'd started looking happier, more herself again. She'd obviously made peace with her decision and was moving past it.

So why couldn't he?

Leah opened the door when he knocked and invited him in. Naomi had gone to check on Mary, their elderly neighbor who lived next door.

"No more crutches?" he asked, gesturing at the footed cane she used. "No more ankle boot?"

"It's doing much better," she told him. "I promised my doctor I'd use the cane until my next visit."

She sat down in the living room and invited him to do so as well. He declined her offer of coffee and waited for Naomi.

"I'm not going with Naomi today," she told him. "I'm concerned about Mary. I'm going to stay with her until her daughter can come to be with her this afternoon. Naomi just went over there for a minute and then we're trading places."

Nick felt a mixture of elation and dread at the news.

"I see."

Leah smiled slightly. "I'm sure you know by now that Naomi is no longer going to marry John. And that he's moved away."

He nodded, not sure where she was going with this.

"I know that you have . . ." Leah hesitated, staring down at her hands in her lap as she tried to find the right words.

Then she lifted her chin. "I know that you have feelings for Naomi. We started to talk about it in Florida but we got interrupted."

"I haven't forgotten."

Suddenly restless, he stood and paced. "I know what you're asking. You want to know if I'm going to act on those feelings now that John's no longer in the picture."

He stopped in front of her. "The answer is no, Leah. And if it makes you feel any better I'll get you another driver for your work schedule. It's too late for today, but I promise I'll be on my best behavior."

"I'm not trying to hurt you, Nick."

"I know. You're just trying to protect Naomi." He sighed. "If you don't mind, I'll wait in the van."

"Nick! Come back!"

Just as he reached the door it swung open.

"Oh, Nick! I almost hit you with the door!" Naomi pressed her fingers to her lips. "Are you okay?"

"I'm fine. Are you ready to go?"

"Yes. Let me get my things."

"Nick, if I could talk to you for a minute," Leah began.

"Sorry, Leah, it'll have to be later. We have to go." He moved past Naomi. "I'll be in the van."

"But we have time if *Grossmudder* needs to talk to you," Naomi protested.

"We really need to get on the road," he said. "Traffic's always bad around these shows."

She joined him in the van a few minutes later, carrying a package wrapped in paper and a tote bag. He didn't have to wonder what was in the tote when the van filled with the delicious scents of cinnamon and coffee a few minutes later.

When he glanced over at her she gave him a cool look. "Since you rushed us out of the house I'm sure you don't have time to stop for coffee and a cinnamon roll."

"You're not that cruel."

"You'd be surprised." She stared ahead, her arms folded across her chest.

He subsided. The Naomi he knew had too generous a heart to make him suffer.

Sure enough, a few minutes later she turned in her seat. "You can pull over in that little park ahead."

Grinning, he did as she directed and offered to carry the tote. She handed it to him. "Might as well. You're going to eat most of what's inside anyway."

When they got nearer, they saw that the two wooden tables were occupied by others who had the same idea to have breakfast outdoors. Nick couldn't blame them. The sun had come out and a gentle spring breeze was chasing the clouds away.

She took the tote from him and handed him the package. "Here, open this. I made it for you."

Curious, he pulled the twine from the package and tore the paper off. "You made me a quilt! It's gorgeous."

"It's called a Mariner's Compass quilt. I thought you might like it."

"I love it." He stroked his hand over it.

"Go ahead, spread it on the grass."

He stared at her. "Are you kidding? It'll get dirty!"

"Then you can wash it," she said, smiling. "It's made to be used, Nick. You can throw it in the washer and hang it on the clothesline."

"I have a dryer."

"Then you can throw it in the dryer."

He watched as she lowered herself to the quilt, and when the wind lifted her hem she tucked her skirt under each leg, disappointing him.

"Aren't you sitting down?" she asked as she pulled a foil-wrapped package from the tote bag.

He sat.

She opened the foil and set the rolls near him. He chose one and bit in, letting the sticky roll melt on his tongue.

He accepted a napkin from her, but when she turned to unscrew the thermos of coffee he couldn't resist licking a couple of fingers before he used it.

"So good," he mumbled. "Thanks."

"They're not such a big deal, you know," she told him. "I'm sure there are fancier things I could have made for you."

"It's the simple things," he said, wiping his lips and taking a sip of coffee. "Like this," he said, gesturing with the hand that held the roll.

One of the couples that had occupied a nearby table walked to their car.

"Want to move to a table?" he asked Naomi.

"I'd rather stay here if you don't mind," she said. "Feels more like a picnic." She chose a smaller roll than Nick and took a bite. "I always loved picnics. No matter what the weather."

"Remember the one we had on the beach?"

She laughed. "We got sand in the sandwiches."

He made the mistake of looking at her then and their gazes met.

"I had a wonderful time there," he said slowly.

"Me too."

"I felt that—" he stopped. "I felt something changed between us. Was I wrong?"

Naomi looked away. "Nick, it doesn't do any good to talk about it."

"I'm right, aren't I?"

"Just because I'm not going to marry John doesn't mean—"

"What? Doesn't mean you're interested in me?" he persisted.

There was a flurry of movement to their side and the other people walked to their vehicle.

Naomi screwed the cap back on the thermos and shoved it into the tote, then began folding the foil around the uneaten rolls.

Nick's stomach churned. He threw the roll he'd been eating to the squirrel who'd been sitting by a nearby tree, watching them with avid eyes. The animal grabbed it and scampered off to eat it.

Getting up, Nick reached down to grasp Naomi's hand and help her to her feet just as she apparently started to rise. Her forward movement caught him off-guard and he steadied her, his hands grasping her forearms. She looked up at him, her lips parted in surprise, and then she raised up on her toes and kissed him.

His head reeled with the taste of her and his arms slipped around her waist and held her close, kissing her, kissing her.

He held her when they came up for air, his eyes sweeping her face, seeing the rosy flush on her cheeks. She looked stunned, the image of innocent passion, as she touched her fingers to her lips.

"I'm sorry, I shouldn't have done that," she whispered, staring up at him.

"Yes, well, I hardly fought you off," he told her, trying to lighten the mood because he was as shaken as she appeared to be.

"It can't happen again. It can't," she repeated.

He frowned at her. "Who are you trying to convince? You—or me?"

Naomi bent to gather up the quilt, shaking the few leaves and pieces of grass that clung to it. Just like he had in Florida, Nick picked up two corners and shook it with her, then they folded it, but this time, he moved closer and closer as they matched corner to corner, until they were standing less than a foot apart.

She bit her lip. "You said what happened in Florida stays in Florida."

"I know. I did. But I can't forget." He took the quilt and tucked it under his arm. "Can you?"

15

It was like being a kid in a candy store.

Quilts had been a passion for Naomi for years and years. She attended quiltings and quilt shows with her mother and grandmother, read quilting magazines, and quilted in slow periods during the day at the shop.

She couldn't get enough of quilting.

But today her mind just wasn't on it. Her mind was on Nick and how they'd kissed.

Even if she'd been able to forget the kiss, she couldn't forget him.

"Since when did you develop an interest in quilts?" she asked him.

"I'm a collector," he told her as they walked the crowded aisles of the building that housed the show.

"Collector? How many do you own?"

"One."

She stopped to admire a log cabin quilt. "One and the one I just gave you?"

"Nope. Just one." He smiled at her. "A perfect one. Custom order. Perfect."

Naomi blushed. "You don't have to say that."

"Well, it is. I love it, and it'll remind me of Florida every time I look at it."

Don't bring up Florida, she silently begged him.

"Naomi!" a woman called.

A friend hailed her and they chatted for a few minutes. The woman, Lillian, knew Nick and nodded at him before Nick excused himself so they could talk.

"I thought Leah was coming."

"She stayed home to be with Mary. She's not feeling well."

"I didn't know Nick liked quilt shows," the woman, who was her grandmother's age, remarked with an upraised brow.

"He drove me. He said he was bored waiting in the van and asked if I minded him walking around with me." She said it matter-of-factly, hoping that nothing seemed untoward.

"My Eli sure wouldn't want to be here with me," Lillian said. "Well, I think I'll be going now. Tell Leah I'll be by the shop later this week. I hear my order's in."

Naomi nodded. She turned to go down another aisle and Nick reappeared at her side.

"Lillian said Eli wouldn't have any part of the show."

"Yeah? He doesn't know what he's missing," Nick said. "The show's cool. And there's even a museum exhibit with Civil War quilts in the building next door. Did you know that?"

She nodded. "They often have a museum exhibit at this show. You know, you didn't have to walk away while I talked to Lillian."

"I know." He handed her a bag. "Bought you something. And I don't want to hear that I didn't need to do it. Not after giving me that quilt this morning."

Naomi lifted her shoulders and then let them fall. "And that was a thank you for all you did for my grandmother and me, taking us to Florida." She smiled at him. "She's like a different person since we came back."

She paused, thinking about it. Well, part of that could be because an old friend of hers had been stopping by to see her a lot. A male friend. But that was private, not something she'd be sharing with Nick.

She pulled out of the bag a pair of scissors that had a long ribbon to carry them around your neck. "Oh, perfect! I'm always putting my scissors down and then looking for them." She looked up at him. "Thank you."

As they walked around some more Naomi became aware that Nick's hand would occasionally brush against hers. At first she thought she was imagining it, but when she paid attention she found that he was, indeed; it wasn't her imagination.

They walked over to the Civil War quilt exhibit. The quilts displayed were worn and delicate, their colors faded. But the intricate stitching and the complicated patterns told a story of women who created something useful and beautiful from mere scraps of material after they'd worked hard all day.

Women had used scraps of fabric to fashion quilts to warm members of their family from birth to death—soldiers were often even buried in their quilts, she read on a placard.

Quilts had been used to finance the war at first, then, toward the end, medical treatment for the soldiers who were wounded or sick. The time period, the scarcity of them when textiles became hard to get, and the fact that women kept finding scraps and sewing in spite of the hardships and the tragedy made the quilts fascinating to Naomi.

It was there, reading the stories of each quilt, that Nick moved a little closer and took her hand in his. Startled, her initial thought was to withdraw it and glance around to see if anyone noticed. The Amish were very private, and couples didn't often engage in public displays of affection—PDAs, Jamie called them.

And they weren't a couple, she and Nick.

His hand felt so good in hers, large and warm and comforting. But this was dangerous, this . . . flirting with the attraction they felt for each other.

No one else seemed to notice as they stood surrounded by a group of *Englisch* and Amish studying the quilt.

"You okay?" he whispered. But she understood that his question was more, "Is this okay?" when he glanced at their joined hands, then at her.

She looked up at him and frowned, uncertain of what to say. Part of her wanted the contact. Part of her was scared to death to encourage his attention. It was like a war was going on inside her—a war of emotions.

He started to withdraw his hand but hers curled around it almost without volition. His was a comfort she craved. A secret temptation. A dangerous thrill.

Nothing could come of it. Her feelings for Nick were just a temporary infatuation. They were friends who had become a little more than they should have while in another place that was a paradise.

Now they were back in reality, where the Amish and *Englisch* were occasionally friends but seldom more than that. Certainly, only rarely were they more. She'd thought about this a number of times since she and Nick went to Florida with Leah. These were dangerous thoughts, and she had to stop thinking them.

Nick opened Naomi's door and helped her inside before rounding the hood and climbing inside.

He sat there, staring ahead, trying to figure out what to say to her.

"I think you have to put the key in."

Turning, he saw that she was smiling at him.

"Yeah, I know."

"So are you going to do it?"

He inserted the key and the engine roared to life. He started to put the van in gear but then stopped and turned it off.

"It's not all one-sided, is it? This attraction I have for you."

Naomi closed her eyes and then opened them. "I wish it was."

"Well, thanks." He drew back.

She touched his arm. "How can it not be? You're *Englisch*; I'm Amish."

"So that's it?"

She avoided his eyes and looked out her window. "It can't be anything else." Turning back, she met his gaze. "I don't know what I was thinking when I kissed you." She bent her head, feeling herself color. "I sure couldn't think afterward."

"Well, thanks." He liked knowing that he affected her. Then he realized that she was really upset. "I'm sorry."

"For kissing me? I was the one who started it today."

"I'm not complaining." He shot her a grin.

"No, you wouldn't, would you?" she asked seriously. "It's not as big a thing as it is in my community."

"Look at me." When he saw he had her attention, he said, "It was a big deal to me."

Her eyes widened. "Really?"

"Really." He hesitated, then found the words tumbling from his lips. "Naomi, I want to start courting you."

"Courting me?"

She stared at him, stunned as if he'd just turned into an alien.

"That's what you call it, right?"

"Well, that's what the older people call it. We call it dating."

He shrugged. "Dating sounds *Englisch*. Casual. Courting's what it's called when you're seeing a woman and you think you want to marry her."

"M—marry?"

"Did you think I'd offer anything less to a woman like you?"

"Nick, I never thought anything about it." She pressed her fingers to her temples. "I can't blame you for being confused. I haven't been myself, kissing you such a short time after I broke off my engagement with John. I don't know why any man—Amish or *Englisch*—would be interested in me."

She dropped her hands into her lap. "It's too soon. It's just too soon to think about it, Nick. It's just too . . . *big* to think about. It's not like we're both Amish or both *Englisch*. There are such . . . complications."

Suddenly he felt like the biggest jerk that had ever lived. He'd been so focused on how attracted he was to her, how much he wanted her, that he hadn't thought about what she was going through breaking up with John. He hadn't thought about what was good for her right now.

Determined to start thinking about her instead of himself, he touched one of her hands.

"What's the matter?"

"Nothing. I'm fine."

He was so used being around the Amish, felt so comfortable with them, that he hadn't thought enough about how Naomi would react to this attraction they had to each other. She hadn't been raised like the girls he'd been around all his life—*Englisch* girls.

A kiss was serious. A big commitment. She'd just been engaged and that was as close to being married as it could get in her community. He'd taken her response to mean that she was attracted to him as much as he was to her, but the truth seemed to be that she was feeling overwhelmed by everything.

So he wanted more from her. And for a little while there he thought she wanted it too. It didn't mean it was going to happen—at least right away.

Was he ready for marriage? Because that was the only step they could take.

A car passed them, sending a harsh beam of light slicing through the car. "I'm sorry if I'm pressuring you," he said, starting the car again. "Look, I don't want to lose you as a friend."

"Friends don't kiss," she pointed out with a wobbly smile.

"Sure they do."

"On the cheek," she said primly. "Not like the way we did today."

"Well, really good friends do," he teased, trying to lighten the mood.

"Nick!"

"Well, okay, you're right." He pulled out and got the van on the road. "But you have to admit it was a really good kiss."

"Stop making me blush."

"I love to see you blush." The interior of the van was dim so he couldn't see the delicate rose tint that always suffused her cheeks when she blushed. But he had a good memory.

He sighed, knowing what was coming next. "Are you leading up to telling me we shouldn't be kissing?"

"That's right."

"No kissing," he muttered. "Aw." Then it was as if there were a light that went on over his head. "That's fine with me."

"It is?"

He pressed his lips together, determined not to smile at how surprised—and maybe a little disappointed?—she sounded.

"Yes." He gave her a surreptitious glance and saw the uncertainty on her face. "Remember, you were the one who kissed me today. I'm sure that I can restrain myself from kissing you."

"Really?" She turned in her seat and he could feel her studying him. "I think you're teasing me."

"No, I wouldn't do that," he said in as serious a tone as he could.

"Nick, this isn't funny."

"No, it's not," he agreed.

He stopped for a traffic light and looked over at her. "But I don't think I thought enough about what it meant to fall in love with someone like you. People from different religions get married all the time in my world. But it's different in yours."

The light changed to green. "I'm going to let you decide what's next."

"You mean if I kiss you again?" Naomi asked.

He pulled up in front of Leah's house and shut off the engine. Turning in his seat, he took her hand.

"No," he said slowly. "I'm willing to be friends. I hope you want more at some point, but I'm not going to pressure you."

"Friends?"

Nick nodded.

He kissed her wrist and then got out and walked around to open her door. She sat there, not moving, looking stunned.

Finally, she moved, getting out and stumbling a little so that he had to reach out and steady her. Just as quickly—as if he had burned them at the contact—he snatched his hands back from her waist.

Dusk had fallen but Leah hadn't left a light burning at the front door so the path leading to it looked dim.

"Wait," Nick said, rummaging in the glove box. He found a flashlight and flicked it on, lighting the way to the door as he walked beside her.

She turned to say good-bye as she reached the door.

"Go make sure Leah's okay," he told her. "She's usually at the front door when we pull in."

She did as he asked, but just as she went inside Nick caught a glimpse of something moving out of the corner of his eye. Using a flashlight of her own, Leah was lighting her way from the neighbor's house to her own.

"Naomi's inside looking for you," he said quickly. "I need to talk to you before she comes out."

"*Ya*?" She looked at him with what could only be described as a wary expression.

"I'm sorry if I wasn't polite earlier—when I didn't want to talk," he rushed to say. "Naomi and I talked. She knows how I feel about her. She told me she's not ready for a relationship with anyone right now. We're staying friends for now."

"Really?" She peered at him. "Naomi agrees with that?"

"She's good with it."

Leah lifted her eyebrows. "Really?"

"Yes."

"I see. Well, *danki*. I appreciate you telling me." She studied his face. "I'm proud of you doing the right thing, Nick."

"Oh, that's me," he muttered. "Good old noble Nick."

Naomi reappeared in the doorway. "There you are, *Grossmudder*. I was looking for you."

"I was next door visiting with Mary and her daughter," she told Naomi. "Nick, want to come in?"

"No, thanks, I should be heading home. See the two of you Monday."

They said good-bye and he walked back to the van.

Bandit, his ragtag cat, greeted him when he walked in the door. He fed him, threw himself on the sofa, and turned on the television. Using the remote, he scanned the stations without interest. Anything would do. Just so he didn't have to listen to the sound of silence in the apartment.

16

Spring had sprung.

From the bench where she sat, Naomi couldn't help smiling. If her teacher from years ago could hear her thoughts, she'd be wincing.

Everywhere she looked, flowers had burst into bloom. Birds built nests and squirrels squabbled in a mating ritual before one chased another up a tree. She walked into the shop, took one look at Mary Katherine, who fairly glowed, and immediately started a baby quilt—without telling her, of course. If she was right, Mary Katherine would tell them soon enough.

Even her grandmother had a distinct spring to her step and it wasn't just because her ankle had healed nicely.

"I'll be back in an hour. You three have a nice lunch," Leah said as she turned the sign to "Out to Lunch" and locked the door behind her.

The three cousins looked at one another. "Well, that's the third time Elam's come to take her to lunch this week."

"I guess it goes to show you that it's never too late for love," Mary Katherine said with a dreamy smile.

Anna tossed her knitting into the basket next to her chair and left the room without a backward glance.

"What'd I say?" Mary Katherine asked Naomi.

"Don't worry about it," Naomi told her. "She's just a little moody."

Getting to her feet, she placed the quilt on a nearby table and brushed little bits of thread from her skirt. "Let's go eat."

"I'm starved," Mary Katherine said as she stepped away from her loom. She glanced at the quilt Naomi had set aside and her eyebrows went up.

"Is that for a customer or is somebody we know having a baby?" Then, when her question wasn't answered, she looked at Naomi. "Oh, are you still on that?"

"I'm not saying a word," Naomi said innocently. "But you know spring and the birds and the bees . . ." she trailed off meaningfully.

Mary Katherine rolled her eyes, but as they walked into the back room, Naomi saw her glance at the calendar on the wall and frown.

Naomi had no sooner pulled out the plastic container of sandwiches that Anna had brought than they heard a knock on the shop door.

"Can't people read?" Anna complained, but she got up to see who it was. When she returned, she looked disconcerted.

"Well, what a surprise," she began.

"Is it John Zook?" Naomi asked her, feeling a cold chill wash over her. "He was told not to come here."

Anna held up her hand and shook her head. "No, no. It's someone for Mary Katherine."

"Is it Jacob?"

"No." She stepped aside so Mary Katherine could see her surprise visitor.

"*Daed*!"

He held his hat in his hands and wore an expectant expression.

Mary Katherine jumped to her feet. "Is something wrong with *Mamm*? Is she ill?"

"She's fine, just fine," he hurried to reassure her. "I'm just in town for some supplies and thought I'd see if I could take you out to lunch."

Naomi watched the play of emotions rush over her cousin's face: surprise, uncertainty, joy. Mary Katherine had told them how her father had been trying to become a better father and husband since her mother's heart attack.

Just looking at him now, Naomi could see that he was not the stern and overly critical *onkel* she remembered from her childhood—that he'd been just a short year ago.

"Well, that leaves the two of us," Naomi said brightly after Mary Katherine left with her father.

"Are you really afraid John will bother you again?"

In the act of putting a sandwich on her plate, Naomi paused and frowned. "I wasn't until you said someone was here." She held out the container so Anna could choose a sandwich, then set it down on the table.

Anna got a bag of potato chips from the cupboard and opened them. "Mmm, nothing like a fresh bag of chips."

"You're addicted."

"True. But look at you," she said, pointing at the jar of bread and butter pickles Naomi brought to the table. "You can't eat a sandwich without a pickle."

"Guilty."

"You're not eating," Anna observed a few minutes later. "Something wrong with the sandwich?"

"No, I like your egg salad." She picked it up and put it down.

Anna set her sandwich down and reached for Naomi's hand. "It's going to take a while to get over him."

"I know. That's what I told—" she stopped but Anna had already gone on full alert.

"Told who?"

"Doesn't matter."

"Is someone already interested in you?" Anna leaned closer. "Who is it? Tell me."

"You'll drive me crazy."

"I'll drive you crazy if you don't tell me."

Naomi sighed. "True. But it wouldn't be fair to . . . "

"To?"

Shaking her head, Naomi pushed her plate away. "To the man. I can't see him."

"You mean you can't see him until you feel you're over John." Anna leaned her elbows on the table, staring at Naomi with bright, inquisitive eyes.

Naomi hesitated. She could almost see the wheels turning in Anna's head.

Anna clapped a hand over her mouth. "Naomi! He's not married?"

"Of course not!" She looked heavenward. "What on earth do you think of me?"

"Well, you said you couldn't see him and it's not because you need more time." She popped a potato chip into her mouth and frowned in concentration as she crunched. "What else could it be . . ." she trailed off. Then her eyes widened and she nearly choked.

Naomi pushed Anna's soda closer and watched her cousin take a drink.

"Nick," Anna gasped after she swallowed. "Oh, Naomi, you and Nick?!"

"What's going on?" Leah asked as she walked into the room.

Anna glanced up, her eyes wide, then back at Naomi.

"Lunch," she said brightly. Then, as Anna took in their grandmother's pink cheeks and smile, she pulled out a chair. "Sit down and tell us about your lunch," she told her slyly.

"Said the spider to the fly," Naomi murmured, grinning as she watched Anna in action.

She knew.

Nick had felt that prickling feeling at the back of his neck ever since he'd picked up Naomi, Leah, and Anna, and now he felt it even more.

He glanced over at Leah but she was looking over some receipts from the shop. Naomi sat in the backseat but she was looking out her window. That was her usual behavior lately—anything to keep from making eye contact.

But Anna. Every time he checked his rearview mirror, she was staring at him. No, her eyes were boring into him.

She knew.

Ever since they'd come back from Florida Nick had waited to see if one of the cousins would say something, but they hadn't. He'd finally assumed that Naomi hadn't said anything to them.

But that had changed.

He wondered why Naomi had said something to Anna but kept his eyes trained ahead. A fine mist and wet roads made his attention vital this afternoon. A buggy rolled down the road just ahead. This was a passing lane but he didn't want to risk an accident. Only when the buggy driver pulled to the right and gestured him on did he go ahead and pass.

"So, Nick, you and Naomi are losing your tans," Anna remarked casually. But her expression in the rearview was anything but casual.

"You're right," he said, and he felt a flush stealing up his neck.

"*Grossmudder*, why didn't you get a tan while you were in Florida?" she asked.

Leah turned in her seat and looked over her reading glasses. "I don't see the value of sitting under the sun and baking."

"So Nick—"

"Anna," Naomi said in a warning tone.

"But—"

"Anna, for goodness sakes, stop it!" Naomi hissed.

She cast Nick a helpless look.

He heard whispering in the backseat—or rather Naomi chiding Anna in a lowered tone. Just bits and pieces of words could be heard, but he thought he could hear Naomi accusing Anna of conducting an inquisition.

Then it became quiet, and when he glanced in the rearview mirror, Anna wore a stormy expression and her arms were crossed over her chest. Naomi was gazing heavenward as if asking her Maker a question.

Unfortunately, his route dropped Leah and Naomi off first.

"Sorry," Naomi mimed to him as she got out.

He nodded and shrugged. Obviously, he didn't know Anna as well as she did, but she wouldn't ruffle him. Sometimes family pushed each other's buttons far worse than they did outsiders.

"Wait!" Anna cried, after Naomi and Leah left the vehicle.

She slid into the front seat and smiled at him as she shut the door.

Her smile reminded him of something. . . . Oh, yeah, that big-toothed fish that had terrorized Naomi in the creek in Florida.

"So, tell me about you and Naomi," Anna invited as she fastened her seat belt.

"Anna!" Naomi peered into the open window and frowned at her. "*Grossmudder*, she's just going to give Nick a hard time on the way home."

Leah had stepped away, but now she walked over and gave Anna a stern look.

"It's okay," Nick assured them. "Anna doesn't bother me."

Naomi threw up her hands. "Come on, *Grossmudder*. He's a man. He doesn't think he needs our help."

Nick grinned as he pulled back onto the road.

"So, what about you and Naomi?" Anna asked again. "And don't tell me 'What happens in Florida stays in Florida.'"

"Where did you hear that?"

She shrugged. "Daniel said it once."

"Well, if there was something between us it would be private." He used his most authoritative, quelling tone. It had served him well when he'd had to get summer camp kids in line as a counselor.

"Save that tone for the camp kids," she said. "Yes, I remember you telling us once about how you did that during summers to earn college money." She continued to stare at him. "Come on, she's my cousin."

He made a turn onto the road that led to her house and pushed the speed up just a little bit.

She noticed. "Better watch out. Remember, there's a speed trap along this road."

He glanced at her. "Have you always been Amish?"

"You know I have." She leaned closer, alert. "Are you thinking of becoming Amish?"

"No." Regardless of what he'd been thinking—and what he hadn't—it was none of her business.

"Really? You don't think my cousin's worth it?"

He pulled up in front of her house. "You'd make a great *Englisch* detective, you know that?"

"I'm just interested in what your intentions are toward my cousin."

Getting out, he rounded the hood and opened her door. "Have a good evening, Anna. I'll see you bright and early tomorrow."

She stayed where she was. "Naomi's been through a lot. If you hurt her—" she broke off, struggling for words. "If you hurt her—"

"I don't intend to hurt her," he said quickly. "I love Naomi and I think she loves me. But I told her we had to be friends."

"You love her? Then why—"

He'd said too much. He'd been right about her interrogation techniques.

"*Gut nacht*," he said, and held her door open wider.

She blinked and he realized he'd slipped into Pennsylvania *Dietsch*.

"I'm not done talking to you."

"Yes, you are," he said quietly. "I know that you love Naomi and I know that your concern comes out of a very deep place. You don't want her to hurt the way you do."

She unsnapped her seat belt and practically threw it aside. "You don't know anything about me."

"I do," he said, leaning on the door and watching her. "You're stuck in your pain and you think it could happen to Naomi."

"Don't be telling me what I am," she snapped, grabbing her purse from the seat.

"I'm not saying it to hurt you," he told her quietly, as gently as he could. "I've watched you and I think you're so busy hiding your pain over losing your husband so young that you can't see that you need to take care of yourself first."

The color leeched out of her face as she stood, frozen, staring at him with wide eyes.

Nick reached for her arm but she backed away and fled, rushing up the steps of the little house. Once she had the door open, she stepped inside, spun around and opened her mouth as if she were about to say something, and then slammed the door shut.

He hadn't meant to upset her. Closing her van door, he walked up the steps and rapped on her front door, but she wouldn't answer.

Resigned, he walked back to the van and started the engine.

Everything was such a mess. And unlike Naomi, he didn't have anyone to talk about it with.

Bandit wasn't at the door when he got home—not that he often greeted him there. Nick went from room to room calling him and even used the electric can opener to signal a tasty fish dinner awaited. Still no Bandit.

A half hour later as Nick sat eating his microwaved frozen meal, Bandit appeared. He reached down to scratch the cat's ear and got his hand scratched for the trouble.

"Maybe I should have gotten a dog," he muttered.

Bandit stalked away, swishing his tail, as if he understood the threat.

It was a small shop but Anna managed to avoid Naomi for most of the morning the next day.

Naomi watched her wait on customers, perform several tasks their grandmother requested of her, and spend time in the storage room whenever Naomi was too occupied to confront her.

"What do you suppose she said to Nick after he dropped us off?" she asked her grandmother when they took a break.

Leah shook her head. "She's like a dog with a bone. But Nick's not a pushover. I'm sure he told her to mind her own business. Politely, though. Nick's always polite."

Naomi thought about that. Nick had so many good qualities. Kind, patient, thoughtful. Generous with his time and with his money. She knew that the arrangement he'd made with her grandmother for driving them to Florida had been very generous.

Stories had come to her, too, about how often he took some of his clients to doctor's appointments and grocery stores and so on and, knowing their financial situation, would refuse payment or accept baked goods or produce or something else they had to offer in return.

"It's not that I don't think Nick's a nice young man," her grandmother broke into her thoughts. "However, you have to understand that I'm concerned. Where could a relationship go between the two of you?"

She put a cup of tea before Naomi. "Nick understood that."

Naomi roused herself. "What?"

Leah colored, then she lifted her chin. "Nick and I talked about it when we were in Florida."

"I don't understand. What do you mean you talked about it?"

Sighing, Leah took a seat and stirred her tea. "Nick came to me worried about you being with John. He was afraid that John would hurt you even worse the next time. He told me that he knew what he felt for you—well, that he knew it couldn't go anywhere because you were baptized and you'd be shunned if you got married."

"But only if she left the church to marry him," Anna said.

Startled, Naomi turned. "How long have you been there?"

Anna walked into the room and got her own tea. "Long enough. I didn't mean to eavesdrop. It's just when I heard

Nick's name I stopped. He's not exactly my favorite person right now."

Leah smiled slightly. "Did he tell you to mind your own business?"

"In his own way. He had a few other things to say as well that I didn't want to hear."

She wrapped her arms around herself. "But after I thought about it for a long time, I realized that they needed to be said. He thinks that I—"

She stopped. "Never mind what he said. This is about you."

"No, I want to know what he said to you!" Naomi insisted.

"Me too!" Leah said.

"Too bad." She traced a finger on the tablecloth. "The thing is, if there's one thing I know, it's that life's short. We don't know what's going to happen. One day you're married and your whole life is ahead of you and the next—"

She stopped and bit her lip. "Well, anyway, the point is how do we know that Nick isn't the man God set aside for Naomi? Does he have to be Amish to be perfect for her?"

Naomi's head spun.

"Radical thought, huh?" Anna grinned at her. "Actually, sometimes I think Nick's more Amish than some Amish men I know."

Then her grin faded. "I've seen the way you look at him, Naomi. You love him, don't you?"

"Even if Nick's the man God intended, it's too soon," Naomi said slowly, sidestepping Anna's question. "I'm still so mixed up."

Anna shoved to her feet. "Oh, take your time. Maybe you'll have it. Maybe he'll wait for you."

She paused at the doorway. "Maybe God won't take him early. You'd know about that as well as I do, wouldn't you, *Grossmudder*?" She left the room.

Naomi let out the breath she found she'd been holding. "Well." She looked at her grandmother.

Leah sat there looking stunned. "*Ya*. That was a surprise. Even for Anna."

"I'm sure she didn't mean to hurt you." Naomi reached for her grandmother's hand. "She—"

"No, it's *allrecht*. She's right."

"She is? About what part of it?"

"Most of it." Leah sighed. "All of it. Of course I know about being a young widow. But just because God might take a loved one home sooner than we'd wish, it doesn't mean we rush headlong into something we shouldn't. God has a plan for us and we have to be patient."

Naomi considered her grandmother's words as they went back to work.

Mary Katherine walked in a little while later. "I was just at the doctor's office and you'll never guess!"

"You're pregnant!" Anna cried. She rushed at Mary Katherine but her cousin held up her hands.

"Will you stop that! No, I'm not pregnant. While I was there, Hannah walked in with Chris. She was in labor! She kept telling Chris that she wasn't, but he insisted on her getting checked out. They were calling for an ambulance to take her to the hospital when I left."

"I don't blame him for being concerned," Leah said. "Not after she had complications and went into early labor last time. That officer who comes in for quilt lessons delivered her first baby, didn't she?"

Naomi clapped a hand over her mouth. "Oh, Hannah won't be coming in to teach class this afternoon."

She turned to her grandmother. "Guess I'll be doing it."

"I'll go start the coffee," Anna said.

"Danki."

Naomi didn't mind taking over Hannah's class. The group of women had started out as strangers but had quickly become friends as they learned about quilting. Kate, the police officer, was new to the class.

"So I don't get to deliver another baby?" Kate asked. "Oh well, it was mostly Malcolm who did it the last time. He was a corpsman in the military. What did Hannah have?"

"We don't know yet. The hospital won't tell us."

Kate pulled out her cell phone and punched in a number. Within a few minutes, she got off the phone with the news that Hannah had just given birth to a girl.

"I know a few people at the hospital," she said, shrugging as Naomi thanked her before rushing off to tell her grandmother and her cousins.

"I just think it's so nice that you're doing such work," she'd overheard one older woman saying to Kate. "You're a role model. Why, in my generation we only got to be teachers and nurses. Not that those aren't noble professions, but a woman should get to do the job she wants."

The other ladies had nodded in agreement as they stitched.

Kate lingered after the class ended. She indicated the back room with a jerk of her head and Naomi followed her.

"How are things? Is the ex-boyfriend staying away?" she asked, her eyes intent on Naomi.

"I haven't seen him in ages. We heard he moved back to Franklin County."

Kate pulled a small notebook from a shirt pocket and jotted a few lines in it. "Do you remember a street address?"

Naomi could only remember a road, not a house number.

"That's fine. This'll be enough." She studied Naomi for a moment, then handed her a card. "Friend of mine's a counselor; has a group for women who've been involved with guys like Zook. Might be something you'd be interested in. No pressure."

Naomi fingered the card and considered the idea. "I'll think about it. Thanks."

"Here comes the jaywalker," Kate murmured.

She couldn't help grinning as Nick walked in and stopped in his tracks as he saw the officer. Then he strolled over and nodded at her. "Hello, Officer."

"Been using the crosswalks?" she asked with a smirk.

"Absolutely." He looked at Naomi. "How are you?"

"Good."

Nodding, he turned to an elderly woman nearby. "Ready to go?"

She handed him her big, stuffed tote bag. "Ready. See you next week, Naomi. I expect Hannah won't be back for a few weeks."

Nick turned back to Naomi. "Back at the usual time."

"Nice guy," Kate said quietly as Nick moved out of hearing range. "Is he the new guy?"

Her face flaming, Naomi shook her head.

"Really? Could have fooled me."

She gathered up her tote and shot Naomi a look. "Actually, you can't fool me. Thought I was going to have to arrest the two of you for spontaneous combustion that night outside the restaurant."

She sighed. "Well, this has been fun. Now I have to be getting home and look at what else I have to do for the wedding."

Naomi started to say something, then stopped.

"What?"

"It's nothing."

"You have a question. Ask it." She glanced around when Naomi hesitated. "Want to go in the back for some privacy?"

Naomi nodded and they went into the back room and shut the door. She twisted her hands in front of her. "I—this isn't really my business—"

"If I don't want to answer, I don't have to."

She tried to smile. "True." This woman appeared so different from others she knew: so confident, so strong. Yet so approachable and eager to help.

"You're getting married. To Malcolm."

Kate nodded.

"I know he's different now—" she stopped, not knowing how to go on.

"You wonder how I can marry him after he did bad things."

Naomi nodded. "We're—the Amish—supposed to forgive. But you're a police officer and you're going to marry him."

Kate poured herself a cup of coffee, held up the pot, and then set it down when Naomi shook her head.

"Malcolm had a lot of problems with alcohol and drugs during his military service overseas," she said seriously. "You know Chris Matlock testified against him. Then even after he was acquitted, he went after Chris. Hannah got hurt when she came between them."

Her eyes took on a faraway look. "I think Hannah saved Malcolm's life. Well, there's no 'think' about it. Malcolm says so. She forgave him and wouldn't press charges and convinced Chris not to do so either. And now you wonder how I can marry someone who has that history."

She looked directly at Naomi. "You wonder how he'll be with me."

Naomi nodded.

"The difference is that Malcolm got himself into rehab and he turned his life around. He's a different man, one who realizes he got more than one chance to change. He works two jobs and volunteers at the veteran's center. And he has never, ever hurt me."

"John refused to go to counseling."

"I thought there was less resistance to it in the community."

Naomi lifted her shoulders and let them fall. "Maybe there is. But not in John."

"Then you have to move on." She leaned forward. "You have to move on."

She nodded. "I know. I have."

"Good. If you need to talk, call me. You still have my card?"

"I carry it with me every day."

Naomi watched how Kate's smile transformed her face. "Good. Now, I'm going home to see if I can talk Malcolm into helping with a little wedding planning."

With that, she strolled out of the shop.

17

Nick pulled into the space in front of the hospital that was designated for picking up patients, shut off the engine, and got out.

He was here to pick up a very special passenger.

Chris pushed Hannah's wheelchair up to the van door. A nurse followed carrying a pink blanket-wrapped bundle. She handed it to Nick, who had to take a quick peek at the sweet little face inside.

"She's beautiful," he told her happy parents. They beamed at him.

He leaned into the backseat of the van, tucked her into the car seat he'd brought, and fastened her harness. Only when he was satisfied that the safety belt was secure did he back out of the van and let Chris help Hannah inside.

Chris looked over at him as the two men fastened their own belts and Nick started the engine.

"I really appreciate this."

"It's my pleasure," Nick said. "It's my new baby special. She gets her first car ride free and you two get to come along with her. It's a three-for-one deal."

He glanced in the rearview mirror before he pulled out. "Hannah, you okay back there? Anything you need?"

"I'm great," Hannah told him. She leaned over and smiled at the baby, who'd slept through the whole transfer from hospital to van.

"So, you decided to have the baby in the hospital instead of the backseat of a car." He grinned at her in the rearview mirror.

Hannah shot a glare at Nick, but then she grinned. "I thought Chris was going to make me spend the last month of my pregnancy there. It wasn't my fault that I had complications and went into labor so quickly."

"Then whose fault was it?" Chris teased, leaning around his seat to look at his wife.

They seemed so happy. Nick couldn't help thinking . . . Chris had been *Englisch* when he'd come here several years ago suffering from post-traumatic stress syndrome—and looking for spiritual answers and a sense of where he belonged.

He and Jenny Bontrager had met at a veterans' hospital and corresponded for a time after she came here to recuperate at her grandmother's house. They'd connected, Chris and Jenny, because both had been injured in roadside bombings overseas. Jenny had been a television network correspondent covering what war was doing to children. Chris had been a soldier. So it was an odd pairing—this disillusioned, weary warrior and Hannah, who'd been raised Amish.

Nick reflected on how Jenny—whose father had been born into an Amish family but hadn't joined the church—had been *Englisch* but joined the Amish church to marry the man who lived next to her grandmother. Chris had joined the church to marry Hannah as well.

Would he—could he—do the same in order to marry Naomi?

In a heartbeat.

"Can we stop at the pharmacy to pick up a prescription for Hannah?"

"Of course."

He drove them there and waited while Chris hurried inside.

"That's one happy man," he said to Hannah while they waited.

Rain began falling. It slid down the windows and the van seemed like its own little world. When he heard a strange noise he glanced in the rearview mirror. Hannah had apparently gotten the baby from the car seat and was holding her up to her. He started to say something, then his eyes widened as he took in the scene and realized what she was doing.

He jerked his head back and stared straight ahead through his windshield, feeling heat rise up in his face.

She was nursing the baby.

"Sorry!" he stammered. "I didn't realize what you were doing! I'll get out—"

"Stop!" she cried. "Don't be silly! We're all covered up!"

If a blush could register a temperature, a thermometer would show two hundred degrees, he thought.

"I just remembered I need something. I'll be right back."

"Shut the door quietly," she whispered.

He did as she asked and went inside the store to find Chris.

"Is something wrong?" he asked when he saw Nick.

"Just remembered I needed something." He looked into the cart. "Wow. Does a baby use that many diapers?"

"I figure this isn't something you want to run out of," Chris said, "so I thought I'd pick up some more since I was here anyway. If Hannah wants to switch to cloth diapers later, she can. But I want things to be easy at first."

Chris thought about that. "Easier."

When he added some little prefilled bottles of formula, Nick raised his eyebrows.

"What, you don't think the baby needs formula, either?"

Nick found himself going into the blushing and stammering routine again.

"Oh," said Chris, and he laughed. "Let me guess. The baby wanted to eat while I was in here."

"I didn't see anything!" Nick rushed to say.

"I'm sure you didn't," Chris said calmly. "Amish women are very modest."

"She seemed to think it was funny that I was embarrassed."

"That's my Hannah. She's not some quiet little mouse."

"I don't actually know many quiet little Amish mice. That's a stereotype."

"Exactly. What do you think? Don't you think the baby needs this?" Chris asked, holding up a bib that said "I love my Daddy!"

"Sure. When does she start wearing Amish dress?"

Chris laughed. "Soon enough."

Nick saw a display of children's toys and books and walked over to it. He picked up a book and a little plastic car and added them to the cart. "That's for me. Well, it's for me to give to your son."

"You don't have to do that. You've done enough."

"Not true."

"Guess we should be going," Chris said, pushing his cart toward the front of the store.

Nick watched Chris pile the things he'd picked up onto the counter, and the cashier began to ring them up.

"Can I ask you something?" he asked Chris as they gathered up the bags and began walking to the car. "It's confidential."

When Chris nodded, he took a deep breath. "How hard is it to become Amish?"

Naomi rushed to open the door for Mary Katherine when she saw her cousin struggling because her arms were filled with packages.

The skies opened up just after she got inside.

"Good timing," Naomi said, taking some of the packages from Mary Katherine's arms.

"There's a letter in here for you," her cousin said, handing her a tote stuffed full.

"Did you see who it's from?"

"No name or return address on it." She carried the packages to the back room and Naomi followed her.

Digging into the tote, Mary Katherine retrieved the letter and handed it to her.

Naomi grimaced when she saw the postmark from the town where John was living. She ripped the letter open and sank into a chair when she recognized the familiar scrawl. "John. It's from John."

"What's he say?"

She scanned the letter. "He's apologizing. Says he's sorry for upsetting me."

"And?"

Naomi looked up. "What?"

"What else does he say?"

"Oh. Says he wishes me well and knows I'll do the same for him. He's seeing someone."

Mary Katherine reached for the cookie jar and sat down at the table. She opened the jar and held it out to Naomi. When

Naomi shook her head, Mary Katherine pulled out a big cookie and began munching it.

"I'm not surprised. Are you?"

"No." She sighed.

"How do you feel about him moving on?"

"Relieved for myself. Concerned for the other woman. What if he treats her the same way he did me?"

Mary Katherine frowned. "I know. But you have to trust. You got away from him."

"Who got away from whom?" Leah asked as she walked into the room.

"Naomi got a letter from John."

Leah stopped and looked at Naomi. "I thought he hadn't contacted you."

She shrugged. "He hadn't." She glanced at the letter and then handed it to her grandmother.

The room was silent for a few minutes as Leah read the letter. "So you're worried about this other woman he's interested in."

Naomi nodded.

"God knows what He's doing, *liebschen*. I always liked what my friend Phoebe says. You know, Jenny Bontrager's grandmother. She says that worrying is arrogant. God knows what He's doing."

She sighed. "I know."

Her grandmother waved a hand at the letter. "So what are you going to do about the letter?"

"I wasn't planning on doing anything."

Leah's eyebrows went up. "Really?"

"I guess that's not polite."

"You might think about forgiving him."

Naomi jumped to her feet. "Forgive him? Have you forgotten that he's the one who hurt *me*?"

"No. But can you? Can you forgive him?"

She folded her arms across her chest, then realized she was being defensive.

"Forgiveness isn't about John. It's about who you are."

Leah pulled her purse out of a cabinet. "I'm going to run an errand. I'll be back in a little while."

She patted Naomi's cheek. "Think about it. Holding on to hurt feelings or resentment hurts us more than the other person."

"Wow."

Naomi looked at Mary Katherine. "Yeah." She sat and put her chin in her hand and propped her elbow on the table. "She's right."

"So what are you going to do?"

"I'm going to write him." She stood and began pawing through a drawer. "We must have some stationery around here."

"We have some in the front desk. I'll get it for you."

Mary Katherine took another cookie from the jar, closed it, then put it back on the counter.

"You okay?"

"Yes, why?"

"You don't usually eat between meals."

"Don't start," Mary Katherine said, giving her a sharp look. "My wanting some of your oatmeal cookies doesn't mean I'm pregnant." She opened the refrigerator and pulled out a carton of milk.

"Whatever you say," Naomi told her.

"Keep it up and you'll be the last person I tell when—" she stopped herself. "*If* and when I get pregnant."

She left the room with what could only be described as a flounce.

Naomi laughed. Mary Katherine couldn't keep a grudge. And neither could she. When her cousin returned with the stationery, she sat down to pen the letter.

It took a few minutes to figure out what she wanted to say. She reflected on how John had always tried to make her feel that his mistreatment was her fault. The leader of the group Kate had recommended worked hard to dispel that for her and the other women who attended the meetings.

But she had emphasized that the women needed to work on their self-esteem—that they had to value themselves or no one would. They could find a new man but, in the words of the counselor, they'd just find someone with a different head. Naomi smiled wryly at that image.

Her thoughts drifted to Nick. She didn't believe he'd treat her badly even if she thought she wasn't worthy of his love.

She smiled as she thought about him.

"What's going on?"

Snapped out of her reverie, Naomi blinked.

"Bet I know who you're thinking about."

Anna reached into the refrigerator for sandwiches for lunch. She set the plastic box on the table and leaned over to see what Naomi was doing.

"Oh, no! You're sitting there looking dreamy over *John?*"

Naomi folded up the paper and stuffed it into the envelope with his letter. "Of course not. I'm writing him to accept his apology, but I wasn't just thinking of him."

Before Anna could tease her more, Mary Katherine walked in. "I turned the sign around and locked the door. What's to eat?"

She'd just sat here and eaten three cookies, Naomi couldn't help thinking. But she wasn't going to point that out, especially when Mary Katherine began chattering about how thoughtful Nick had been earlier that day. Anna tried to tease her again but Mary Katherine was talking nonstop and she couldn't get a word in edgewise.

Naomi smiled at a frustrated-looking Anna and began setting plates on the table.

"I made sandwiches from last night's leftover ham."

"And Swiss cheese?" Anna asked as she plucked one from the box.

Naomi tried not to grin. Anna would be too busy eating for the next few minutes to continue trying to ask Naomi questions.

As they sat there, tucked into the kitchen chatting and eating, a gentle rain beginning to drip against the back room window, Naomi felt a peace settle over her.

She didn't know what path her life would lead her down next, but it was okay not to know. God was in charge. His will would be done.

"So I've heard Amish men are really old-fashioned and controlling."

Naomi looked at the group leader, then at the woman who'd made the statement.

"We have traditional marriages, but most of our men aren't like that."

"But this guy was?"

She sighed and nodded.

"Not a good sign when you were only engaged," another woman said.

"I started dating at fifteen. The guy was sixteen and he was already that way." Joan, a woman Naomi had seen chain-smoking before she came inside, spoke up. "Nearly every guy I've dated since then has been the same way."

"That's why it's important to learn how to spot them early on," Ivy, the counselor, said.

Naomi had called Ivy, who'd invited her to attend a meeting of the group. She was in her fifties and had kind eyes, but Naomi had noticed that she could be blunt and didn't let the group members make excuses for their behavior.

"No one has the right to beat up on you," Ivy said. "But are you valuing yourself enough? Are you making excuses for him? Just how long are you going to tell yourself he'll change?"

"I don't think he'll change," Naomi blurted out. "I broke off the engagement."

"Do I hear a 'but' here?" one of the women asked.

"What do you mean?"

"If you broke off the engagement and you're not going to see him again, why are you here?"

Naomi bit her lip and stared at her hands.

"That's a good question," Ivy said. "Is your new boyfriend acting the same way?"

"I don't have a new boyfriend."

"Afraid to let another guy close?" another woman, named Joy, asked sympathetically.

"There's someone I care for but he's not Amish." *Care for,* she thought. *That's a pretty mealymouth way to describe what I feel for Nick.* "We can't marry."

"Ever?" Melissa wanted to know.

"Well, I joined the church, so I'd be shunned. And few *Englisch* join our church."

Just as she said that, she thought of Jenny Bontrager and Chris Marlowe. But that didn't happen often.

"I couldn't live without electricity," Joy stated emphatically. "And no television? Forget it."

"They have really strict rules about stuff," Melissa said. "I wouldn't want some man in the church—what's he called, a bishop?—telling me what to do."

"Most of them aren't like that." Although the current one wasn't one of her favorites.

She wondered if Nick would ever consider becoming Amish. Best not to even think about it. Amish life wasn't just about the things they'd mentioned.

"But it doesn't sound like you've discussed it," Ivy pointed out.

Naomi blinked. "Well, no, because I hadn't even broken off the engagement with John until recently."

"Then you don't know if he'd do it—the new guy, I mean."

Turning to stare at Melissa, Naomi didn't know what to say.

"No," she said finally. "I guess I don't. But he's backed off since we came back from a trip with my grandmother and me."

Ivy looked at the clock on the nearby wall. "Why don't you think about that and let's talk about it some more next week, Naomi?"

She began handing out some papers they were to do for "homework" for the next week. Naomi glanced at it and saw it was some kind of score sheet to fill out about how much they were worth.

"Too many women don't value themselves," Ivy was saying. "I want you to think about if someone isn't valuing you as a person, maybe you've let them think you don't value yourself."

Naomi didn't think she had that problem, but then again, John had seemed to treat her more like a commodity, like a person who existed solely for his needs.

"Ready to go?" Ivy asked her.

"Oh, sorry, I was just thinking."

"Good," Ivy said cheerfully, slinging a huge purse over her shoulder as they walked to the door. "I like a woman thinking about her choices." She waved to the security guard by the door as she unlocked her car.

"I appreciate you giving me a ride."

"No problem at all. I wonder sometimes if that's why I don't see more Amish women at our meetings. If you hear of anyone who needs to attend, let me know and we'll arrange a ride for her."

"I don't know of anyone at the moment," Naomi said honestly.

"Good. We have a full house these days what with how the economy is affecting couples."

Before she knew it, Ivy was pulling into the driveway of her grandmother's house. "I hope you found the group helpful enough to want to come back again next week."

Naomi nodded. "I'd like that."

18

They were only a few miles from Leah's house when Nick heard and felt a small explosion at the rear of the van.

"Nick? What's the matter?" Leah spoke up from the back seat.

"A flat," he decided, as he took his foot off the accelerator and gently tapped the brake.

He glanced in the rearview mirror to check for traffic before he flicked on the turn signal and pulled off onto the shoulder. "Don't worry. I'll have it changed in no time."

"I wasn't worried," she said calmly.

Nick activated the emergency flashers and shut off the engine. The light drizzle that had started when he picked up his passengers at the shop dripped cold and wet on his head and shoulders.

"Need some help?"

He jumped. "Naomi! Get out of the rain!"

"I'm fine. I won't melt."

He grinned. "I know. You're sweet but you're not made of sugar."

"Exactly," she said. "I'm made of sterner stuff. I can help."

" 'I am woman; hear me roar,'" he murmured.

"What?"

"Just lyrics to a song," he said. "An anthem to women. I'll explain sometime. Get inside and stay dry."

"I'm already wet," she pointed out.

He froze. *Don't look. Keep your eyes straight ahead*, he warned himself. The rain had plastered her dress so closely to her body.

He pulled the jack from the storage compartment, then walked to the rear left-side tire. If you were going to have a flat, it was always good to have it on a rear tire.

Naomi's skirt brushed his arm. He looked up. "It's too dangerous out here," he said, glancing back at the road. "Get back in the van."

"If it's dangerous, then I'm going to stay out here and keep an eye out for you."

"Stubborn," he muttered.

"Careful." She watched him and felt a lightness she hadn't experienced in a long time. "Caring."

He jerked his head up to stare at her.

"You don't have to thank me."

There was a clip-clopping sound. Nick straightened as a buggy approached. Jacob was waving with one hand as he held the reins in the other. He guided the buggy over to the shoulder of the road behind Nick's van.

"Need some help?"

"I got it," Nick said. "Just a flat. But if you could give Naomi and Leah a ride home I'd appreciate it."

"Where's Anna?" Mary Katherine asked.

"She was staying the night at Jamie's."

A rumble of thunder made them look up. The storm was getting worse.

"Go get your grandmother," Nick told her.

He watched as she returned with Leah, helped her inside, then nodded at Jacob.

"Wait! Naomi!"

She waved at her grandmother. "I'll be home soon. I'm helping Nick."

He looked at her. "How much do you know about changing a tire?"

"About as much as you know about driving a buggy," she said with a grin.

He pulled her closer to the van when a car whizzed by too fast.

"Come on, let's get this tire changed. I see what you mean about it being dangerous."

One look at her told him it would do no good to argue with her. Resigned, he warned her to keep an eye on traffic to protect herself, and then set to work changing the tire as quickly as possible.

He frowned when he realized that the ground was still damp from the previous night's rain. Getting up, he located the two pieces of wood he kept to use under the jack to provide a better base.

He was turning to return to the flat tire when a flash of color and sound caught his eye. A car was traveling too close to the emergency lane and Naomi wasn't paying attention. She was looking at him, not at the traffic. .

"Move!" he said urgently.

She glanced back and he realized that she'd registered the danger but was too shocked to move.

Dropping the wood, he threw himself toward her, knocking her out of the path of the car.

There was a whoosh of air at one side as the car missed them, then he felt himself free-falling with her. He wrapped his arms around her, hoping to cushion her fall, but they fell and rolled down the grassy slope, coming to rest in a ditch filled with muddy water.

"Naomi? Are you all right?"

Her eyes were open and her mouth was moving. "Can't breathe."

He raised up and levered himself off of her. "You probably got the breath knocked out of you."

Leaning forward, he pressed his lips against hers, breathing in.

"Mmmph." She thumped her hands against his chest.

When he moved away, she struggled to sit. "You're kissing me at a time like this?"

"I was doing mouth-to-mouth."

She drew in a deep breath and let it out. "I don't need mouth-to-mouth."

Incredibly relieved, he wiped mud from her cheek. "Maybe you need a kiss?"

She stared down at her torn and mud-splattered dress and then up into his eyes. "Yeah, just what I need—" she began in a sarcastic tone.

He ignored the tone and went with her words, kissing her until both of them were breathless.

Then he wrapped his arms around her and felt hers encircle him, and they just sat there with the rain falling on them, washing away the mud.

"You folks okay down there?"

Nick looked up to see Kate standing up on the hill, staring down at them with concern.

"Never better!" he called, turning back to Naomi, his eyes taking in everything about her. The rain, the police officer up the hill . . . everything faded away but Naomi.

"It's just like Anna said," she told him. Her voice was a little dreamy and it frightened him, making him wonder if she'd struck her head on a rock on the way down. "Everything can change in a moment."

"Are you okay?" the officer asked as she crouched near Naomi.

"Never better," Naomi told her, smiling at her. "I'm going to marry this man."

Kate turned to Nick and her eyes narrowed. "Are you telling me you're down here proposing to her?"

He shook his head. "No. Do you think she has a concussion?"

"I don't know. Maybe you shouldn't try to get up, Naomi," Kate said, pressing Naomi's shoulder with her hand to keep her seated.

"Don't be silly. I'm fine." She struggled to get to her feet.

Kate tried to help her up but they both slipped on the wet grass and landed on their fannies.

Nick got to his feet and assisted them in standing.

"Don't go trying to get out of it," Naomi warned as Nick wrapped his arm around her waist and they made it up the slope.

"Can we hold off on making plans for a wedding until we get you safely home?" Kate groused as she pulled a blanket from the trunk of her car and got Naomi settled in the backseat.

But Nick saw her hiding her smile.

"Just happy we had a good ending here," she told them, casting a steely glance at cars passing them. "People aren't careful about passing cars on the side of the road. Too busy gawking or not realizing that the force of the air from their vehicle can cause problems."

Nick located the boards and the lug wrench and set about changing the tire.

Once he climbed into the van and Naomi was in the passenger seat, Kate leaned in the open window on Nick's side.

"Sometimes adrenaline carries people through but they wake up the next day and realize they're hurt. If that happens, you get yourself to a doctor, hear?"

"Yes, ma'am." Nick thrust out his hand. "Thanks so much."

A car sped by going considerably faster than the speed limit. Nick watched Kate brighten.

"Gotta go," she said, sounding almost gleeful. "Gonna go catch me a speeder."

"You're sure you didn't hit your head against a rock?"

"You've asked me that twice," Naomi complained.

She looked into the mirror and winced. One cheek was bruised, her *kapp* had gone missing, and her dress looked so tattered she was certain it would end up as cleaning rags.

Nick hadn't fared much better. His tie had been ripped as well as his shirt and pants. Some green, slimy substance matted his hair. She didn't have the heart to tell him to look in his own mirror. It didn't matter. He had never looked dearer to her and she didn't want to let him go.

"I need my hands to drive," he said, but he didn't pull them away. "If we're not out of here soon, Kate is going to come back and give us a ticket for loitering."

"She's not going to do that."

"Well, let's not take any chances. Besides, we've already seen it's not safe to be on the side of the road."

She looked at the green goo in his hair. "You're safe from my advances."

"You're not from mine," he warned.

With a sigh, she let go of his hands with some reluctance and gathered her blanket around her.

"We need to talk," she said as he started the engine.

"*Ich liebe dich.*"

She stared at him. "I love you too."

He laughed. "Why are you so surprised? I've been studying German and Pennsylvania *Dietsch* for the past few years. Your grandmother and a few of my clients have helped me."

He checked for traffic and accelerated out onto the road. They rode in silence. Pulling into Leah's driveway, he stopped the van and shut off the engine.

"Let's get you inside and cleaned up, then I'll run home and do the same. Then we'll talk to Leah."

Naomi bit her lip, tasted mud, and made a face.

"I know. She's not going to be happy—"

"She's very fond of you," Naomi rushed to say. "She—"

"But she wasn't encouraging about my having a relationship with you. I don't blame her. Becoming Amish and marrying someone—well, it's not done very often. We're going to have some opposition, if not from her, then from the bishop."

He tilted his head and studied her. "What? Did you think I'd ask you to give up your church? Your family and your friends?"

She pressed her fingers against her temples. "Be sure this is what you want," she whispered. "It's a big decision."

He took her hands and started to press them to his lips but she wouldn't let him. "Who knows what you'll catch if you do that!" she laughed.

Then, as he continued to gaze intently at her, she sobered.

"It's the easiest decision ever, loving you," he told her slowly. "The easiest decision ever."

"Watching the clock never made time move faster."

Naomi tried to smile at her grandmother. "I know."

"Maybe Nick got called out for an emergency."

"He'd have phoned. I just checked the machine in the shanty."

"Yes, he would have," Leah agreed.

"Maybe he had an accident—"

"I'm sure he didn't," Leah soothed. "Don't go jumping to conclusions. Something probably just happened. Not anything bad," she said quickly. "Just something that held him up. He'll be here. You know how much Nick likes my cooking."

Naomi went to peer out the front window again. She'd wanted Nick with her when she told her grandmother they were getting married, so she hadn't told her yet—just said that Nick was coming back for supper after he cleaned up.

Her grandmother had been upset when Naomi walked in bedraggled and filthy. She'd run a hot bath and helped her shed her clothes and then carried them out with two fingers, tsk-tsking and saying they were going straight to the trash—forget washing them and using them as cleaning rags.

So Naomi had soaked and scrubbed and showered to make sure she was squeaky clean, then scrubbed the tub before she dressed. Then she went downstairs and set the table and even made a pan of biscuits to go along with the stew her grandmother had made. Nick always complimented her biscuits.

And still he wasn't here.

Maybe he'd changed his mind.

Her heart raced and her hands became clammy. He'd said the decision was easy because he loved her, but maybe he'd started thinking how much his life would change.

A lot of outsiders were intrigued by the idea of becoming Amish. In the last few years people had started looking to the Amish as if they had a solution to the problem of being over-stressed and consumed by materialism—like they had a magic answer.

But when those outsiders came here they saw that the life was simple but very hard and full of sacrifice, that it meant obeying the *Ordnung*—the rules that guided the life—which were strict and so different from their unstructured life, and that there was a closeness and interdependence they weren't always comfortable with.

But Nick wasn't like that, she reminded herself. He'd lived here for years and years and he knew the life, knew the hardships as well as the joys. He'd even revealed recently that he was studying German, and he already knew much Pennsylvania *Dietsch* from driving his clients around. She'd never seen his home—a small apartment, he'd said once—but he dressed simply and didn't seem the type to think about material things much. He was known for quietly helping out those who had to stretch their pennies each month.

He'd been kind and generous and thoughtful to her—so concerned when he found that John had been hurting her. Her thoughts skidded to a stop. That was it. Once he'd thought it over, maybe he'd decided she was flawed, that she had made John hurt her. Or that she would be too needy.

His van pulled into the drive, shattering all the crazy thoughts.

She schooled her features. No need to let him know that she'd worried—obsessed, really—and imagined he didn't want her anymore. She remembered how she'd attended that meeting of women who worked to overcome abuse. Allowing herself to feel unworthy, to be guided by someone else's opinion—that had to stop. She'd been given a second chance with Nick.

Taking a deep breath, she opened the door, but he wasn't standing on the porch. He was sitting in his van, looking deep in thought. Then he looked up, and when he saw her, he shook his head slightly as if he suddenly realized where he was. He got out and strode up the walk.

"I'm so sorry I'm late," he said quickly as he climbed the front steps.

"I thought you'd changed your mind," she blurted out in spite of herself.

He'd been bending to kiss her cheek but jerked back and stared at her.

When he didn't immediately deny it, her heart sank.

"It's not like that!"

"Naomi? Is that Nick?" Leah called.

"Tell her we need a minute," he said tersely. "Please?"

Miserable, she shook her head. "It's all right. You can just go. I'll—"

"Tell her, Naomi. Then let me explain."

Torn, she turned back to her grandmother. "We'll be there in just a minute!"

She shut the door and stepped out onto the porch, wrapping her arms around herself. She'd forgotten how cool the weather had turned.

Nick pulled off his jacket and wrapped it around her, then guided her to a rocking chair and gently pushed her into it. He drew up one next to it and reached for her hands.

"So cold," he murmured, chafing them with his own strong, warm hands.

"I'm sorry I worried you," he began, searching her eyes as he spoke. "I was standing in the shower and washing off all the mud—and green slimy stuff you didn't tell me was in my hair—and suddenly, it hit me."

"Reality," she said in a leaden tone.

"Sort of," he told her. "I thought I had figured it all out, but I was wrong."

"Our differences—"

"Ssh, you don't know where I'm going with this."

Of course she did, she wanted to say. But she stayed silent and let him continue.

"Anyway, I was standing there and it suddenly hit me—I'd forgotten all about something very, very important. It's big, Naomi. Really big. No, don't look like that. Wait."

He took a deep breath. "I hadn't thought about how I was going to support us, *lieb*."

She opened her mouth, but he waved a hand to silence her. "No, listen. I thought, the only thing I know how to do is drive for a living. I was panicked. I don't want to be a farmer and even if I did, farmland is too dear in Lancaster County."

"You don't have to be a farmer to—"

"Let me finish," he said. "I almost flunked shop class in high school. Handyman work? I tried changing out the toilet seat in my bathroom last year and when I couldn't budge the hinge screw, I tapped it with a hammer to loosen it."

He stopped and laughed as he shook his head. "A metal hammer. Just as I tapped it I realized what I was doing, but it was too late. Dumb, dumb, dumb. Cracked the porcelain base and had to get a plumber to put in a new toilet."

"I can support us until you find something," she said quickly. "And I have some money saved."

He raised her hands to his lips and kissed them. "Sweetheart, you don't have to. I realized I was trying to work everything out and then it struck me that I don't have to."

He stopped. "I don't want to," he corrected himself. "One of the things that I've been trying to do is believe in God's will. That He has a plan and purpose for us. So I sat down and prayed like I've never prayed, Naomi. And I gave it to God. I told Him that I needed His help, that I didn't know what to do."

"Funny thing," he said as he stared at his van. "Sometimes I've prayed and waited a very long time for an answer from God. Sometimes I haven't gotten what I thought was an answer at all and just had to trust. But today? I nearly got run over by the answer."

"I don't understand."

"I had to wait at a light for a buggy and everything fell into place. Naomi, I'm going to buy Abe Harshberger's business. I heard last week that he wants to sell it and move to Ohio where he used to live."

Naomi frowned and tried to take it all in. "He takes tourists for buggy rides."

"I'll still be in the transportation business."

"But you've never even ridden in a buggy, let alone driven one, have you?"

"I think you should take me for a ride in one after supper." His eyes gleamed with mischief. "A long, long buggy ride."

She laughed and put her hand on his chest to stop him from leaning forward to kiss her. Someone had to keep a level head. "Sounds perfect."

"Buying Abe's business or the buggy ride?"

"Both," she said shyly.

He stood and pulled her to her feet. "I think it's time to go inside and tell Leah, don't you?"

Naomi saw the curtain move at the front window. She smiled. "I think she might have guessed," she told him, gesturing at the window.

He squared his shoulders. "I prayed for her approval too," he admitted as he opened the door and escorted her inside.

She remembered the talk she'd had with her grandmother about Nick and squeezed his hand. "Me too."

Maybe it was wishful thinking, but she suspected that her grandmother wasn't going to have the objections to their marrying that Nick felt she had. Her grandmother had always acted fond of Nick, almost as if he was the son she hadn't had.

Raising herself on her tiptoes, she kissed his cheek.

"One step at a time," she told him. "You remember when we were driving back home from Florida and I said it was so dark beyond the headlights? You quoted that writer. I forget his name."

He smiled. "E. L. Doctorow. He said, 'Writing a novel is like driving a car at night. You can only see as far as your headlights, but you can make the whole trip that way.'"

She touched his cheek. "We don't have to figure everything out right now. We'll take it one step at a time."

"Starting now."

Nodding, she leaned forward and embraced him. "Starting now."

The End

Glossary

allrecht—all right

boppli—baby

bruder—*brother*

daed—dad

danki—thank you

dat—father

Der Hochmut kummt vor dem Fall.—"Pride goeth before the fall."

Englisch, Englischer—non-Amish person

fraa—wife

grossdochder—granddaughter

grossmudder—grandmother

guder mariye—good morning

gut—good

gut nacht—good night

gut-n-owed—good evening

Ich liebe dich—I love you

kaffe—coffee

kapp—prayer covering or cap worn by girls and women

kich—kitchen

kind, kinner—child, children

kumm—come

lieb—love

liebschen—dearest or dear one

maedel—young woman (maid)

mamm—mother

mann—husband

nee—no

onkel—uncle

Ordnung—The rules of the Amish, both written and unwritten. Certain behavior has been expected within the Amish community for many, many years. These rules vary from community to community, but the most common are to not have electricity in the home, to not own or drive an automobile, and to dress a certain way.

Pennsylvania *Deitsch*—Pennsylvania German

rotrieb—red beet

rumschpringe—time period when teenagers are allowed to experience the *Englisch* world while deciding if they should join the church. According to Amish sources, it is not the wild period so many *Englisch* imagine.

schul—school

schur—sure

schweschder—sister

sohn—son

wilkumm—welcome

wunderbaar—wonderful

ya—yes

Discussion Questions

Caution: Please don't read before completing the book, as the questions contain spoilers!

1. At the beginning of the book, Naomi begins to realize that the love her fiancé, John, claims to have for her may not be healthy. More young women than ever before are finding that their boyfriends, fiancés, or husbands are too controlling—sometimes even violent. Could you identify with her? How?
2. How do you recognize the danger signs in someone who may be a potential problem?
3. Do you believe that only women who suffer from poor self-esteem fall into this trap?
4. How can you help someone break free from an abusive relationship?
5. Sometimes it's not easy to think that a man who looks like a rescuer will in fact be a problem himself. How can someone avoid this?
6. Nick wants to help Naomi but in a way complicates things for her. How does he do this?
7. Do you believe that people from different religions can forge a successful marriage? Do you know someone who has done this?
8. How long do you think someone should avoid getting into a new relationship after breaking off the old? How do you think people can avoid getting into a "rebound" relationship?

9. What would you give up to be with the person you love?
10. Naomi reads *Gift from the Sea*, a book by Anne Morrow Lindbergh, in which the author maintains that a woman must have a time and place to herself in order to have something to give to her loved ones. What do you do to have a well of strength and love for your family?
11. The Amish—and many other people—believe that God has "set aside" a person for them. Do you believe that there is just one person for you, or do you think that there is more than one person for you to love?
12. How important is it for the person you love (as a husband, boyfriend, or significant other) to love God?

Yoder's Amish Restaurant Famous Peanut Butter Pie

Pudding:

1 cup cold milk
½ cup cornstarch
1 teaspoon salt
1 teaspoon vanilla
3 egg yolks
3 cups milk
3 tablespoons butter or margarine
⅔ cup sugar

Crumb mixture:

1 cup powdered (confectioners') sugar
½ cup crunchy peanut butter
baked 9- or 10-inch deep pie shell
whipped topping (sweetened)

To make pudding:

Mix cornstarch, salt, 1 cup milk, egg yolks, and vanilla with a wire whisk and set aside.

Heat 3 cups milk, butter, and sugar until scalding, stirring constantly. Add cornstarch mixture to hot milk while stirring with whisk. Cool until thickened. Remove from heat before boiling. Chill.

To make crumbs:

Mix powdered sugar and peanut butter until small crumbs form.

Place half of the crumbs into pie shell. Spoon pudding onto crumbs. Place remaining crumbs on top of pudding, reserving a little for the topping. Top with whipped topping. Serves 6 at Yoder's (or 2 small pieces).

Grateful acknowledgment is given for permission to share this recipe by Yoder's Amish Restaurant, Sarasota, Florida

Shrimp and Grits

1 cup stone-ground grits
2 cups water
2 cups milk
1 teaspoon Old Bay seasoning
2 cloves garlic, finely minced
6 tablespoons butter
4 slices bacon, finely diced
4 cloves garlic, finely diced or minced
1 large onion, chopped
1 tablespoon all-purpose flour
1 pound pink Gulf shrimp
¾ cup water, divided
½ teaspoon Old Bay seasoning
2 tablespoons seafood or vegetable bouillion granules

Heat 2 cups water, milk, 1 teaspoon Old Bay, garlic, and 3 tablespoons butter to almost boiling in a medium saucepan. Add grits and cook for 6-8 minutes, stirring occasionally. Meanwhile, in a separate skillet, melt the other three tablespoons of butter and sauté bacon, garlic, and onion. When lightly browned, add flour and make a basic roux. Stir until fully blended. Add shrimp and ¼ cup water, ½ teaspoon Old Bay, and bouillion. Simmer until gravy thickens. Serve grits with shrimp and gravy. This makes a delicious dish for brunch or supper.

Recipe by Sherry Gore, Pinecraft, Florida

—From *Taste of Pinecraft: Glimpses of Sarasota, Florida's Amish Culture and Kitchens* by Sherry Gore

Fruity Florida Coleslaw

2 Florida oranges (or canned mandarin oranges)
2 apples, chopped
1 head shredded cabbage
1 cup red grapes
¼ cup coconut flakes
½ cup chopped walnuts
1 whole banana, sliced
1 (16 oz.) can pineapple chunks, drained
Dash of salt
½ cup mayonnaise
¾ cup whipped topping
1 tablespoon sugar
1 tablespoon lemon juice

Place cabbage, fruits, and nuts in large bowl. In small bowl, mix remaining ingredients well. Pour over cabbage mixture and serve in your prettiest glass dish.

Recipe by Shannon Gore, Pinecraft, Florida

—From *Taste of Pinecraft: Glimpses of Sarasota, Florida's Amish Culture and Kitchens* by Sherry Gore

Key Lime Pie

1 8-inch baked pie crust
½ cup fresh lime juice
1 14-ounce can sweetened condensed milk
1½ to 2 cups Cool Whip
Green food coloring (optional)
Additional Cool Whip

Beat lime juice and condensed milk together. Add Cool Whip and food coloring and pour into pie crust. Top with additional Cool Whip. Fresh lemon juice will work same as lime.

Recipe by Laura Yoder, Sarasota, Florida

—From *Taste of Pinecraft: Glimpses of Sarasota, Florida's Amish Culture and Kitchens* by Sherry Gore

Stitches in Time is a very special shop run by three cousins and their grandmother. Each young woman is devoted to her Amish faith and lifestyle, each is talented in the traditional Amish crafts and in new ways of doing business—yet each is unsure of her path in life and love. It will take a loving, insightful grandmother to guide them gently to see they can weave together their traditions and their desire to create, and forge loving marriages and families of their own.

And now for a sneak peek into the first chapter of *Heart in Hand*, Book 3 of **Stitches in Time**, Anna's story.

1

It felt like dawn would never come.

When Anna first realized that it was going to be one of those nights—one of those awful nights that felt like it would never end—she reached for the book she'd been reading and read for a while with the help of the battery lamp on the bedside table.

Reading didn't help. Knitting didn't either, and knitting always relaxed her. Reaching for her robe, Anna pushed her feet into her slippers and padded downstairs to the kitchen. There was no need for a light for she knew her way from all the dozens—no, hundreds—of nights she'd gone downstairs in the dark.

Even before the first time she stepped inside this house, she knew it like the back of her hand. She and Samuel had drawn the plans, spent hours talking about how he and his brothers were going to build it. As soon as the house was finished, he'd started crafting furniture for it. The final piece he'd made was a cradle for the baby he hoped they'd have soon.

His sudden illness stopped him in his tracks. "Leukemia," said the doctor. One day it seemed he was an agile monkey climbing up the frame of a barn he and other men were raising, then just a few days later he could barely get out of bed and she'd joked he'd turned into an old man. She'd insisted that he see a doctor and reluctantly he'd done so.

Six months later, he was gone, and she'd shut the door to the room with the tiny crib. She buried her dreams the day she buried Samuel.

She filled the teakettle and set it on the stove to heat. How many cups of tea had she drunk in the middle of the night? She wondered as she reached for a cup and the box of chamomile tea bags.

Before Samuel had died, she'd heard about the seven stages of grief. She'd been naive. You didn't go through them one by one in order. Sometimes you walked—faltered—through them in no certain order. Sometimes they ganged up on you when you least expected them.

And sometimes—it felt like too many times—no one seemed to understand.

She couldn't blame them. The only way she got through the first month, the first year, was to put on a brave face and pretend she was getting through it. There was no way she could get through it otherwise—she'd shatter into a thousand pieces that no one would be able to put back together again.

Humpty Dumpty, she thought wryly. Then she frowned, wishing that she hadn't thought of the childhood story. A closed door didn't keep out the memory of the tiny crib that lay behind it.

The teakettle's piercing whistle broke into her musing, its sound so sharp and shrill that she put her hands over her ears to block it while she got up to take it off the flame. She poured the hot water over the tea bag, then took the mug back to the kitchen table and sat there, dipping the bag in and out of the water.

Finally, she pulled the bag out and set it on the saucer. Sighing, she massaged her scalp and wondered if she should take an aspirin to stop the pain. Then she flicked her hair behind her shoulders and hunched over the cup. In a minute, she'd get up and get the aspirin. Her mind might be awake, but her body felt tired and full of lead.

As she trudged back up the stairs a few minutes later, she heard something—it sounded like a laugh, a high, excited one that went rushing past her up the stairs. She watched, tired, leaning against the wall as she saw herself—lifting the hem of her nightgown so she wouldn't trip, Samuel reaching for her as she flew up the stairs to their room.

She blinked, not sure if she was dreaming or seeing ghosts of the two of them, so young and in love, so unaware that anything bad could touch them.

When she reached her room, there was no one there. Climbing back into bed, she pulled the bed quilt around her shoulders and lay on her side facing the uncurtained window. The wedding quilt that her cousins Naomi and Mary Katherine and her grandmother had sewn for her and Samuel lay wrapped in muslin and tucked in a box in the closet of the same room as the cradle. She hadn't been able to bear lying under it after Samuel died.

She'd thought she wouldn't be able to bear living without him in this house they had built, but her grandmother had brought her here after the funeral to pack and she'd found she couldn't leave it. Somehow, it felt like she'd be abandoning everything they'd worked so hard for.

Her grandmother had understood. She'd done the same thing—continued to live in the house she'd shared with her husband, who'd also died too young. She'd continued to stay there for nearly two decades. Only in the last couple of years had Mary Katherine and then Naomi come to stay with her.

Hours passed. Anna remembered reading that it was always darkest before dawn. She could vouch for that.

Finally, the sky began lightening. She got up and made the bed before she went to shower. The reflection in the mirror made her wince. She looked tired, with faint lavender shadows under her eyes.

Funny, everyone said that she and her two cousins—Mary Katherine and Naomi—who worked with her at Stitches in Time all looked so much alike with their oval faces and brown eyes and brown hair, although Mary Katherine's was a bit more auburn. But she felt like she just looked like a dull version of them lately. She was the youngest, yet she looked older and more subdued.

With a sigh she center-parted her hair and began arranging it in a bun, then she placed a starched *kapp* on her head. She chose her favorite dark blue dress and hoped the color would flatter and not make her look pale.

Her first cup of coffee helped her get moving. The knock on the door startled her as she sat eating her breakfast.

She opened her door to find Nick standing there.

"Sorry, I had to come a little early," he apologized as she invited him inside.

"It's okay, I'm ready."

He touched her shoulder. "You look tired."

"I sure hope you don't ever say that to Naomi," she responded testily. "No woman wants to hear that kind of thing."

"I'll remember that."

She regarded this man who was engaged to marry Naomi. He had dark hair, angular features, and sharp green eyes. Not as handsome as Samuel had been.

Nick was quiet and serious and had a heart just as big as Samuel's. She could trust him with someone as dear as Naomi.

"Want some coffee before we go?"

He shook his head. "I have a thermos in the car."

She took a plastic box filled with sandwiches from the refrigerator and tucked it into a tote bag. A bag of cookies was next.

Catching Nick's interest, she pulled another plastic bag from a nearby cupboard, filled it with half a dozen, and handed it to him.

"Oatmeal raisin," he said with a satisfied sigh. "Will you marry me?"

"Sorry, the Amish don't believe in plural marriage."

Gathering up her sweater and her purse, she walked to the door with him and locked it behind her.

After they climbed into the van, Nick set the cookies on the seat between them.

"You know you're going to eat them now."

"They're oatmeal," he reasoned. "Just because it's not hot and in a bowl . . . "

"So very logical," she agreed, trying not to smile.

"That's me, logical."

She opened the bag so he could slide his hand inside to pull one out and take a bite. "Please give Naomi the recipe."

"Are you sure you want to tell your intended that you like my oatmeal raisin cookies better than hers?"

He considered that. "Maybe not. She wasn't happy when I complimented Leah's rolls."

"Exactly."

"Maybe you'll sneak me some of these now and then?"

"Maybe," she agreed with a grin.

Nick glanced at his watch and turned the radio on. "I want to check out the weather forecast."

"Partly sunny and hot in Paradise, Pennsylvania," she said as the jingle that announced the news broadcast filled the interior of the van. "Chance of afternoon showers. Tell me how it can be partly sunny. It's either sunny or it's not."

"I agree."

They listened to the quick news report and then the weather before Nick turned the station off.

A yawn overtook her. She covered her mouth and shook her head. "Sorry."

"S'okay. Rough night?"

"Yeah."

"Why don't you close your eyes and try to get a little shut-eye?"

"Don't want to be rude," she said, stifling another yawn.

"I don't mind. I might fall asleep in front of you someday."

She blinked at him. "Don't do that when you're driving!"

He laughed as he reached for another cookie. "I saw Abe Miller asleep at the wheel the other day."

"Abe was driving his buggy," she pointed out. "I heard the horse got him home okay." She studied him. "How are the lessons going?"

"The last time I remember being around a horse, my mother was putting me up on it for a kiddie ride," he said with a grin. "I was five. I didn't really like it very much and never wanted to be around a horse again. Now here I am buying a business where I'll have to work with a horse for hours every day. Feed it, water it, care for it. Hitch it to a buggy, persuade it to walk along a route for me."

He glanced at her. "Deal with manure." He made a face, then patted his steering wheel with one hand. "Big change from this horseless carriage."

"It sure is."

"Thank goodness I made training me a condition of the sale," he said.

"How's the other instruction going?"

Nick reached for a third cookie. "Just as hard. I thought I knew what was involved, but there are so many more rules than I thought."

He began telling her about the lessons he was taking to become Amish. It hadn't been all that long ago that she'd taken them. She found her attention drifting off even as she frowned and wondered why she'd never noticed how Nick spoke in a monotone. Snuggling her cheek against the upholstery of the back of the seat, she heard him chuckle.

"Am I boring you?" he asked. "I never bore Naomi."

"She has to put up with you." Anna felt her eyelids growing heavy and she jerked awake once, then twice.

"You're chicken-pecking," he told her. "Relax and shut your eyes. Don't worry, your cousins will wake you up."

"Let her sleep," Nick was whispering. "I don't have to be anywhere for another half an hour."

"I'm awake," Anna said, yawning and straightening in her seat. "There's no need to babysit me while I nap."

She saw that they were parked in front of the shop. Turning, she saw Naomi and her grandmother sitting in the backseat, staring at her, concerned.

"Rough night?" her grandmother asked, her eyes kind and a little sad.

"Had trouble sleeping." She unsnapped her seat belt. "I'm fine."

Anna stepped out and looked at the shop while her grandmother unlocked the door. The name of the shop, Stitches in Time, was emblazoned on a sign with needles and thread and little quilt squares dancing around the letters. She'd just changed the window display the night before, so she stopped to examine it before going inside.

Everything about the display was designed to say "summer." Naomi had sewn the cutest red and white quilt with ants marching across it. It just said "picnic quilt" to Anna, so she'd arranged it on a bed of artificial grass and set a picnic basket stuffed with goodies atop it.

Mary Katherine had made big floor pillows to sit on and woven tote bags to carry and they were part of a vignette atop sand in another part of the window. Their grandmother's cute little Amish dolls sat under a grape arbor enjoying books.

And Anna had knitted a lacy ivory-colored shawl so delicate it might have been a spider web. It draped across a chair with a flowered dress, ready for an *Englisch* girl to wear on a summer evening.

The delicate shawl was quite a departure from the plain, warm woolen ones Anna and other Amish women knitted. For the most part, the things she knitted were more for the fall and winter seasons—cute sweaters and vests and her personal favorite: the whimsical hats for babies that kept their precious little heads warm.

She started to go inside and then realized that Naomi still hadn't gotten out of Nick's van. There was nothing she liked better than teasing—not just the two of them, but particularly them. Marching back to the van, she knocked on the window.

"Hey you two, no PDAs!" she called.

Naomi rolled down the window. "You are so obnoxious! All we're doing is exchanging a good-bye kiss!"

"You're steaming up the windows," Anna said with a grin. "Get inside before you get arrested."

Nick leaned over and gave Naomi one last kiss. "Have a great day."

"You've been cheating on me!" she exclaimed, licking her lips. "Whose oatmeal cookies have you been eating?"

"I don't know what you're talking about," he told her as he brushed crumbs from his tie.

"You!" Naomi said, pointing a finger at Anna. "You've been tempting him with your oatmeal cookies."

"Guilty," Anna agreed, grinning. "Maybe if you help me with a design idea, I'll share the recipe."

Naomi climbed out of the van. "Maybe I should rethink this wedding if my future *mann* can be so easily tempted."

Nick got out and rounded the hood. "You know you don't want to do that," he told her, his eyes alight with mischief.

He swept Naomi up into a kiss that had some tourists laughing and clapping as they stood observing on the sidewalk.

She beat her hands on his chest. "Stop that! You know you can't behave like that!"

"I'm not Amish yet," he told her, unrepentant.

Backing away, Naomi tried to look stern. "And at that rate, you're not likely to be." She glanced around her. "What if the bishop had seen you?"

He winked at her before strolling back to his side of the vehicle and getting in.

"Men!" Naomi huffed as she walked inside the shop.

"*Ya*, men," said Anna, suddenly feeling like a balloon that was deflating. She sighed and went inside.

The interior of the shop, crammed with colorful fabrics, yarns, and supplies, raised her spirits. What would she have done if her grandmother hadn't asked her and her two cousins to join her in opening it? she wondered as she walked to the back room to store the sandwiches in the refrigerator.

She'd needed the creative work, the company, the daily routine so much after Samuel died. What did people who were grieving do when they didn't have the support of their loving family and community, the people they worked with in a job that fulfilled them?

Chiding herself for the way she'd vacillated between self-pity and sadness during the sleepless night, she stopped, closed her eyes, and thanked Him for reminding her that she should be grateful for all she had and not to focus on what she didn't.

Determined to live with a grateful heart—even if it meant moment by moment today—she walked back into the shop to ask her grandmother what she should do first.

If you enjoyed *The Heart's Journey* and haven't picked up the first book in the Stitches in Time series, here's a glimpse of *Her Restless Heart*.

Come meet Mary Katherine, her cousins Naomi and Anna, and their beloved grandmother, Leah, who run a very special shop in Paradise, Pennsylvania. Each young woman is devoted to her Amish faith and lifestyle, each is talented in the traditional Amish crafts and in new ways of doing business—yet each is unsure of her path in life and love. It will take a loving, insightful grandmother to guide them gently to see they can weave together their traditions and their desire to create, and forge loving marriages and families of their own.

And now for a sneak peek into the first chapter of *Her Restless Heart*, Book 1 of **Stitches in Time**, Mary Katherine's story.

1

A year ago, Mary Katherine wouldn't have imagined she'd be here. Back then, she'd been helping her parents on the family farm and hating every minute of it.

Now, she stood at the front window of Stitches in Time, her grandmother's shop, watching the *Englischers* moving about on the sidewalks outside the shop in Paradise. Even on vacation, they rushed about with purpose. She imagined them checking off the places they'd visited: Drive by an Amish farmhouse. Check. Buy a quilt and maybe some knitting supplies to try making a sweater when I get back home. Check.

She liked the last item. The shop had been busy all morning, but now, as people started getting hungry, they were patronizing the restaurants that advertised authentic Amish food and ticking off another item on their vacation checklist. Shoofly pie. Amish pretzels. Chow chow. Check.

"Don't you worry, they'll be back," Leah, her grandmother, called out.

Smiling, Mary Katherine turned. "I know."

She wandered back to the center of the shop, set up like the comfortable parlor of an Amish farmhouse. Chairs were arranged in a circle around a quilting frame. Bolts of fabric of every color and print imaginable were stacked on shelves on several walls, spools of matching threads on another.

And yarn. There were skeins and skeins of the stuff. Mary Katherine loved running her hands over the fluffy fibers, feeling the textures of cotton and wool and silk—even some of the new yarns made of things like soybean and corn that didn't feel the same when you knitted them or wove them into patterns but some people made such a fuss over them because they were made of something natural, plant-based, or more sustainable.

Mary Katherine thought it was a little strange to be using vegetables you ate to make clothes but once she got her hands on the yarns, she was impressed. Tourists were, too. They used terms like "green" and "ecological" and didn't mind spending a lot of money to buy them. And was it so much different to use vegetables when people had been taking oily, smelly wool from sheep and turning it into garments for people—silk from silkworms—that sort of thing?

"You have that look on your face again," her grandmother said.

Mary Katherine smiled. "What look?"

"That serious, thoughtful look of yours. Tell me what you're thinking of."

"Working on my loom this afternoon."

"I figured you had itchy fingers." Her grandmother smiled.

She sighed. "I'm so glad you rescued me from working at the farm. And *Dat* not understanding about my weaving."

Leah nodded and sighed. "Some people need time to adjust."

Taking one of the chairs that was arranged in a circle around the quilt her grandmother and Naomi worked on, Mary Katherine propped her chin in her hand, her elbow on the arm of the chair. "It'd be a lot easier if I knitted or quilted."

Leah looked at her, obviously suppressing a smile. "You have never liked 'easy,' Mary Katherine."

Laughing, she nodded. "You're right."

Looking at Naomi and Anna, her cousins aged twenty and twenty-three, was like looking into a mirror, thought Mary Katherine. The three of them could have been sisters, not cousins. They had a similar appearance—oval faces, their hair center-parted and tucked back under snowy white *kapps*, and slim figures. Naomi and Anna had even chosen dresses of a similar color, one that reminded Mary Katherine of morning glories. In her rush out the door, Mary Katherine had grabbed the first available dress and now felt drab and dowdy in the brown dress she'd chosen.

Yes, they looked much alike, the three of them.

Until Mary Katherine stood. She'd continued growing after it seemed like everyone else had stopped. Now, at 5'8", she felt like a skinny beanpole next to her cousins. She felt awkward next to the young men she'd gone to school with. Although she knew it was wrong, there had been times when she'd secretly wished that God had made her petite and pretty like her cousins. And why had he chosen to give her red hair and freckles? Didn't she have enough she didn't like about her looks without that?

And Naomi and Anna always looked calm and serene, as they did now. Mary Katherine had always had a problem with that—oh, not with Naomi and Anna. Who could have a problem with them?

No, Mary Katherine had always almost bubbled with energy, and lately it seemed her moods were going up and down like the road on a rolling hill.

"Feeling restless?" Naomi asked, looking at her with concern. Nimbly, she made a knot, snipped the thread with her scissors, then slid her needle in a pincushion.

Anna looked up from her knitting needles. "Mary Katherine was born restless."

"I think I'll take a quick walk."

"No," Leah said quickly, holding up a hand. "Let's eat first, then you can take a walk. Otherwise you'll come back and customers will be here for the afternoon rush and you'll start helping and go hungry."

Mary Katherine was already mentally out the door but she nodded her agreement. "You're right, of course."

Leah was a tall, spare woman who didn't appear old enough to be anyone's grandmother. Her face was smooth and unlined and there wasn't a trace of gray in her hair, worn like her granddaughters.

"I made your favorite," Leah told Mary Katherine.

"Fried chicken? You made fried chicken? When did you have time to do that?"

Nodding, Leah tucked away her sewing supplies and stood. "Before we came to work this morning. It didn't take long." She turned to Naomi. "And I made your favorite."

Naomi had been picking up stray strands of yarn from the wood floor. She looked up, her eyes bright. "Macaroni and cheese?"

"Oatmeal and raisin cookies?" Anna wanted to know. When her grandmother nodded, she set down her knitting needles and stood. "Just how early did you get up? Are you having trouble sleeping?"

"No earlier than usual," Leah replied cheerfully. "I made the macaroni and cheese and the cookies last night. But I don't need as much sleep as some other people I know."

"Can you blame me for sleeping in a little later?" Mary Katherine asked. "After all of those years of helping with farm chores? Besides, I was working on a design last night."

"Tell us all about it while we eat," Naomi said, glancing at the clock. "We won't have long before customers start coming in again."

"I worry about Grandmother," Anna whispered to Mary Katherine as they walked to the back room. "She does too much."

"She's always been like this."

"Yes, but she's getting older."

"Ssh, don't be saying that around her!"

Leah turned. "Did somebody say something?"

"Anna said she's hungry," Mary Katherine said quickly. "And she's wondering what favorite of hers you made. After all, everything you make is Anna's favorite."

Anna poked Mary Katherine in the ribs but everyone laughed because it was true. What was amazing was that no matter how much Anna ate, she never gained weight.

Nodding, Leah continued toward the back room. "We'll have it on the table in no time."

Anna grabbed Mary Katherine's arm, stopping her. "Shame on you," she hissed. "You know it's wrong to lie." Then she shook her head. "What am I saying? You've done so much worse!"

"Me? I have not! I can't imagine what you're talking about."

Turning so that her grandmother wouldn't see, Anna lifted her fingers to her lips and mimed smoking a cigarette.

Mary Katherine blushed. "You've been spying on me."

"Food's ready!" Leah called.

"Don't you dare tell her!" Mary Katherine whispered.

Anna's eyes danced. "What will you give me if I don't?"

She stared at her cousin. "I don't have anything—"

"Your afternoon off," Anna said suddenly. "That's what I'll take in trade."

Before she could respond, Anna hurried into the back room.

Exasperated, Mary Katherine could do nothing but follow her.

The minute they finished eating, Mary Katherine jumped up and hurried over to wash her dishes. "I'll be right back," she promised, tying her bonnet on the run as she left the store.

Fall was in the air. She shivered a little but didn't want to go back for her shawl. She shrugged. Once she got moving, she'd be warm enough.

She felt the curious stares as if she were touched.

But that was okay. Mary Katherine was doing a lot of staring of her own. She had a great deal of curiosity about the *Englisch* and didn't mind admitting it.

She just hoped that her grandmother didn't know how much she'd thought about becoming one of them, of not being baptized into the Amish church.

As one of the tourists walked past, a pretty woman about her own age, Mary Katherine wondered what it felt like being covered in so little clothing. She suspected she'd feel half-naked in that dress she'd heard called a sundress. Although some of the tourists looked surprised when she and her cousins wore bright colors, the fact was that the *Ordnung* certainly didn't mandate black dresses.

Color had always been part of Mary Katherine's world. She'd loved all the shades of blue because they reminded her of the big blue bowl of the sky. Her father had complained that she didn't get her chores done in a timely manner because she was always walking around . . . noticing. She noticed everything around her and absorbed the colors and textures and spent hours using them in her designs, which didn't look like the quilts and crafts other Amish women created.

She paused at the display window of Stitches in Time. A wedding ring quilt that Naomi had sewn was draped over a quilt rack. Anna had knitted several darling little cupcake hats for babies, to protect their heads and ears from the cold. And there was her own woven throw made of many different fibers and textures and colors of burnt orange, gold, brown, and green. All echoed the theme of fall, of the weddings that would come with the cooling weather after summer harvests.

And all were silent testament to Leah's belief in the creativity of her granddaughters, thought Mary Katherine with a smile. The shop featured the traditional crafts tourists might expect, but also the new directions the cousins came up with.

It was the best of both worlds, thought Mary Katherine as she ventured out into the throng of tourists lining the sidewalks.

Jacob saw Mary Katherine exit her grandmother's shop. His timing was perfect because he'd heard from a secret source what time they took a break to eat at the shop during the day.

He watched her stop to gaze at the display window and she smiled. It was that smile that had attracted her to him. Oh, she was pretty with those big blue eyes and soft skin with a blush of rose over her cheekbones. But her smile.

She hadn't always smiled like that. He started noticing it just a few months ago, after the shop had opened. It was like she came to life. He'd passed by the shop one day a couple of weeks ago and stopped to glance inside. He'd seen her working at her loom, a look of absorption on her face, a quiet smile on her lips.

Something had moved in his chest then, a feeling he hadn't had before. He'd resolved to figure this out.

He hadn't been in a rush to marry. It had been enough to take over the family farm, to make sure that he didn't undo all the hard work that his *daed* had done to make it thrive. He didn't feel pride that he'd continued its success. After all, Plain people felt *hochmut* was wrong. In school they had often practiced writing the proverb *Der Hochmut kummt vor dem Fall*. Pride goeth before the fall.

But the farm, its continuity, its legacy for the family he wanted one day—that was important to him. To have that family, he knew he'd have to find a *fraa*. It was important to find the right one. After all, Plain people married for life. So he'd looked around, but he had taken his time. He likened the process to a crop—you prepared the ground, planted the right seed, nurtured it, asked God's blessing, and then harvested at the right moment.

Such things took time.

Sometimes they even took perseverance. She'd turned him down when he approached her and asked her out.

He decided not to let that discourage him.

She turned from the window and began walking down the sidewalk toward him. *Look at her*, he thought, *walking with that bounce to her step*. He looked at the way she glanced around, so animated, taking in everything with such animation, such curiosity.

He waited for some sign of recognition but she hadn't seen him yet. When they'd attended school, their teacher had often gently chided her for staring out the classroom window or doodling designs on a scrap of paper for the weaving she loved.

Mary Katherine moved through the sea of *Englisch* tourists on the sidewalk, who parted for her like the waters had for Moses. He watched how they glanced at her the way she did them.

It was mutual curiosity at its best.

He walked toward her, and when she stopped and blinked, he grinned.

"Jacob! What are you doing here?"

"You make it sound like I never come to town."

"I don't remember ever seeing you do it."

"I needed some supplies and things are slower now with the harvest in. Have you eaten?" He'd casually asked Anna what time they took their break, but he figured it was a good conversational device.

"Yes. We ate a little early at the shop."

He thought about that. Maybe he should have planned better. "I see. Well, how about having supper with me tonight?"

"Did you come all the way into town to ask me out?"

Jacob drew himself up. "Yes."

"But I've told you before—"

"That you're not interested in going out."

"Yes."

"But I haven't heard of you going out with anyone else."

She stared at him, oblivious of the people who streamed around them on the sidewalk. "Who did you ask?"

Her direct stare was unnerving. His collar felt tight but he knew if he pulled it away from his neck he'd just appear guilty. "I'd have heard."

"I'm not interested in dating, Jacob."

When she started past him, he put out his hand to stop her. She looked down at his hand on her arm and then met his gaze. "Is it you're not interested in dating or you're not interested in dating me?"

Her lips quirked. "I'm not interested in dating. It's not you."

"I see."

She began walking again.

"Do you mind if I walk with you?"

"*Schur.* She glanced at him. "Can you keep up?"

He found himself grinning. She was different from other young women he knew, more spirited and independent.

"Where are we going?"

She shrugged. "Nowhere in particular. I just needed to get out and get some fresh air."

Stopping at a shop window, she studied its display of tourist souvenirs. "Did you ever think about not staying here? In Paradise?"

"Not stay here? Where would you go?"

She turned to look at him and shrugged. "I don't know. It's a big world out there."

Jacob felt a chill race up his spine. "You can't mean it," he said slowly. "You belong here."

"Do I?" she asked. Pensive, she stared at the people passing. "Sometimes I'm not sure where I belong."

He took her shoulders and turned her to face the shop window. "This is where you belong," he told her.

She looked at the image of herself reflected in the glass as he had directed. He liked the way they looked together in the reflection. She was a fine Amish woman with a quiet beauty he'd admired for some time. He'd known her in school and of course they'd attended Sunday services and singings and such through the years. He hadn't been in a rush to get married and he'd noticed she hadn't been, either. Both of them had been working hard, he at his farm, she in the shop she and her grandmother and cousins had opened.

He began noticing her shortly after the shop opened. There was a different air about her. She seemed more confident, happier than she'd been before.

He reminded himself that she'd said she didn't date.

So why, he asked himself, was he trying again? Taking a deep breath, he turned to her. "Mary Katherine—"

"Jacob!" a man called.

He turned and saw a man striding toward him, a newcomer to the Plain community.

Though the man hailed him, his attention was clearly on Mary Katherine. He held out his hand. "Daniel Kurtz," he said. "Remember me?"

Out of the corner of his eye, Jacob saw Mary Katherine turn to the man and eye him with interest.

"You live in Florida now."

"I do." He eyed the shop. "So, this is yours?"

"My grandmother's. My cousins and I help her."

Daniel nodded. "Very enterprising." He glanced around. "Is this the size of crowd you get this time of year?"

Mary Katherine nodded. "After-Christmas sales bring them out. But business slows down while people eat this time of day."

"I came into town to pick up a few things and I'm hungry. Have you two eaten?"

"I asked Mary Katherine but—"

"We'll join you," she said quickly.

Jacob stared at her. But the two of them were already walking away. With an unexplained feeling of dread washing over him, he followed them.

Want to learn more about author
Barbara Cameron and check out other great
fiction by Abingdon Press?

Sign up for our fiction newsletter at
www.AbingdonPress.com
to read interviews with your favorite authors, find tips
for starting a reading group, and stay posted on what's
new on the horizon. It's a place to connect
with other fiction readers or post a
comment about this book.

Be sure to visit Barbara Cameron online!

www.BarbaraCameron.com
www.AmishHearts.com
www.AmishLiving.com
and on Facebook

What They're Saying About...

The Glory of Green, by Judy Christie
"Once again, Christie draws her readers into the town, the life, the humor and the drama in Green. *The Glory of Green* is a wonderful narrative of small-town America, pulling together in tragedy. A great read!"
—Ane Mulligan, editor of *Novel Journey*

Always the Baker, Never the Bride, by Sandra Bricker
"[It] had just the right touch of humor, and I loved the characters. Emma Rae is a character who will stay with me. Highly recommended!"
—Colleen Coble, author of *The Lightkeeper's Daughter* and the *Rock Harbor* series

Diagnosis Death, by Richard Mabry
"Realistic medical flavor graces a story rich with characters I loved and with enough twists and turns to keep the sleuth in me off-center. Keep 'em coming!"**—Dr. Harry Krauss, author of *Salty Like Blood* and *The Six-Liter Club***

Sweet Baklava, by Debby Mayne
"A sweet romance, a feel-good ending, and a surprise cache of yummy Greek recipes at the book's end? I'm sold!"**—Trish Perry, author of *Unforgettable* and *Tea for Two***

The Dead Saint, by Marilyn Brown Oden
"An intriguing story of international espionage with just the right amount of inspirational seasoning."**—*Fresh Fiction***

Shrouded in Silence, by Robert L. Wise
"It's a story fraught with death, danger, and deception—of never knowing whom to trust, and with a twist of an ending I didn't see coming. Great read!"**—Sharon Sala, author of *The Searcher's Trilogy: Blood Stains, Blood Ties,* and *Blood Trails*.**

Delivered with Love, by Sherry Kyle
"Sherry Kyle has created an engaging story of forgiveness, sweet romance, and faith reawakened—and I looked forward to every page. A fun and charming debut!"**—Julie Carobini, author of *A Shore Thing* and *Fade to Blue*.**